Fletcher E. Marine

Sketch of Rev. John Hersey, Minister of the Gospel, of the M.E. Church

Fletcher E. Marine

Sketch of Rev. John Hersey, Minister of the Gospel, of the M.E. Church

ISBN/EAN: 9783337097387

Printed in Europe, USA, Canada, Australia, Japan

Cover: Foto ©Raphael Reischuk / pixelio.de

More available books at **www.hansebooks.com**

OF

Rev. John Hersey,

Minister of the Gospel,

OF THE

M. E. CHURCH.

By Rev. F. E. MARINE.

———◄●►———

.

"Earth Exchanged for Heaven."

Behold! God is my SALVATION; I will trust and not be afraid; for JEHOVAH is my strength and my song; He also is become my salvation. ISAIAH xii: 2.

Epitaph of J. H.

———◄●►———

BALTIMORE, Md.

HOFFMAN & CO., PRINTERS

No. 293 W. Baltimore Street.

1879

INTRODUCTION

—BY—

REV. ISAAC P. COOK, OF BALTIMORE.

Rev. Fletcher E. Marine, author of the Life of the late Rev. John Hersey, has modestly styled his valuable publication, a "*Sketch*," of that remarkable and well known, itinerant local preacher, plain and unpretentious, of the Methodist Episcopal Church.

The accompanying pages have been examined with thrilling interest, and pleasant memories of that holy, self-denying, charitable man of God.

All who ever knew him, will recognize the unique portraiture of the man, whose single object was to glorify God, and promote the salvation of his fellow-men.

To all other christian people, the volume may prove to be a pleasing, useful contribution to religious biography.

The advent of Mr. Hersey, as missionary and street preacher in Baltimore City, occurred in 1836. At that period, the "Wesleyan Home Missionary Society" was formed and which still exists. The now departed Samuel M. Barry, was President; John Nelson McJilton, Secretary, and the writer, Treasurer.

The objects of the Society were to improve the religious condition of the poor and neglected, and to relieve their temporal necessities as far as possible.

On the presentation of a proper Church certificate of character, Mr. Hersey was employed as missionary for two years, at a salary of three hundred dollars per annum, which was paid by the Society.

Permission was obtained from the then Mayor of Baltimore, for Mr. Hersey to preach the Gospel in the streets and market places.

His first sermon was delivered near the centre of the city, in a neighborhood of more than doubtful character. The hearers formed a motley crowd, from well dressed ladies and gentlemen, down to the old timed sweep boy, with his sooty blanket; the order was excellent and the sermon impressive. That was the commencement of almost daily preaching in private houses and public places, by that tireless, faithful christian missionary.

The public were assured, that money donated to charity, would not be expended for any other purpose, than the relief of the worthy poor, with fuel and bread. Contributions large and small, were generously made by all religious denominations.

The late excellent Henry Patterson, of the Baptist Church and the late worthy Charles Howard, of the Protestant Episcopal Church, on more than one occasion, quietly threw into the door of the house of the treasurer, fifty dollars each, with the simple endorsement "*Feed the poor.*"

These were evidences of the stronghold which Mr. Hersey's piety and faithfulness had on the public mind.

The same work of religious charity was continued for a number of years, by his indefatigable successors in missionary work.

The formation and admirable management of the City "Association for the relief of the poor," rendered smaller sources of aid, however useful, comparatively unnecessary.

From the above date, the name of John Hersey, became almost a household word in Baltimore city.

Mr. Marine's "Sketch" of that devoted missionary, furnishes far more important and interesting facts.

All who knew Mr. Hersey, are aware that he was a peculiar man in dress, articles of food, places and hours for rest, in fasting and prayer. His manner of life, sometimes rendered him caustic and severe, towards those who did not fully measure up to his standard of morals.

At a certain camp meeting, Mr. Hersey had preached at night from the narrative, which includes the words: "Jesus I know, and Paul I know; but who are ye?" The preachers at the proper time, had nearly all retired to their tents for repose. A belated minister, found his usual bed occupied by some other person; full of wit and humor, the minister exclaimed "*Paul I know, and these brethren I know; but who art thou in my bed?"* That was too much for Mr. Hersey, who was never known to laugh. He instantly arose from his pallet and administered a seathing rebuke for trifling with the Scriptures. He was reminded that the words only partly quoted, were uttered by an evil spirit, and not by the blessed Jesus, or His Apostle Paul.

On another occasion, long before day-break, Mr. Hersey had arisen from his hard bed, and began earnest prayer to God, which he uttered aloud, to the discomfort of the sleeping ministers in the same tent. The late Rev. John Davis, remarkable for piety and good sense, arose from his bed and addressed Mr. Hersey at a proper time: "Before I retire to rest, I pray to Almighty God for the pardon of all my sins, and for my protection during the night. Not expecting to sin in my sleep, I can safely trust my soul and body to His protection, until the night be past. You seem to be afraid to trust God, and are disturbing your brethren with your prayers before day-break."

The cheerful sun light of christian pleasure, would have been a great relief to Mr. Hersey, in his pilgrimage to heaven.

No man, however religious, can be a perfect model for his fellow men. The good should be imitated, the doubtful avoided. In the most important respect, Mr. Hersey may be followed safely by all.

Holy, ardent, constant devotion to God.

"Pure religion and undefiled before God and the Father is this.—To visit the fatherless and widows in their affliction, and to keep himself unspotted from the world." That pure religion he possessed and practiced.

Such a life had a glorious consummation. His last hours on earth, were scenes of glorious triumph, through the Lord Jesus Christ. "Well done, thou good and faithful servant, enter thou into the joy of thy Lord."

December, 1879.

CONTENTS.

--PREFACE.--

Biography of one who is no more, is the taking that individual from the dust, that he may live over again his past history, and impress afresh upon his friends his various traits —lovely or otherwise, to a prosterity who knew him not. Another reason for it is, the subject of it was connected with enterprises, the distant outlines of which, will ever be held dear into whatever section of country that enterprise may be carried. As long as the civilization of America and Africa, and their religious redemption shall be dear to the Philanthropist, so long every memoir will be valued that may give the history of an individual that has connected with him a single important incident in the commencement of so great a work.

John Hersey who was extensively known for his plainness, simplicity and zealous preaching of pure christianity, in Africa and in the United States—North and South; tales of his courage, of his valor, his deeds of daring, worthy of the days of Martyrs, hath awakened in me an ardent desire to know more concerning him.

I have been trying to learn his history, and rescue from oblivion, facts that would soon be lost forever.

The history of many of the noble pioneers of Methodism is unwritten, except in the records of eternity; many of them died and were buried, and no monument, or tombstone, to tell where their dust is sleeping. There is an unwritten history, which, if it could be recovered, would be invaluable to the church; but it is now too late. How few of the men who were acquainted with Methodism in its heroic age, remain to tell the story; this shows the importance of early gathering up historical facts and incidents, and recording them; for the fathers will not be with us long to repeat the story. The fathers, where are they? and the prophets, do they live forever?

In order to obtain light in regard to Father Hersey, I have conversed with those who were personally acquainted with him, and with others I have corresponded.

The author takes pleasure in referring to the assistance which he received in the preparation of the work, from Rev J. F. Chaplain, D.D., G. W. Lybrand, J. Pasterfield, M. C. Johnson, S. W. Thomas, of the Philadelphia Conference; Rev. B. F. Price, Joseph Dare, J. A. Brindle, J. T. Vanberkalow, Rev. E. J. Way, of the Wilmington Conference; Rev. J. H. Brown, D. D., George W. Cooper, of the Baltimore Conference, the Maryland Historical Society, the Peabody Institute, the History of Methodism, by Revs. N. Bangs and J. Lednum; also, the Annual Reports of Local Preachers' National Conventions. He also returns thanks to many of his brethren in the ministry, and membership, for important facts furnished, as to this servant of the most High; particularly Rev. Charles Reese, at whose house Father Hersey exchanged mortality for immortality, shouting with his expiring breath, "Salvation;" who kindly placed in my possession, letters and what information he was in possession of, in reference to his old friend, with the hope and *prayer* that I would be able to furnish to the church and world, the life and character of Father Hersey. I have done the best I could, under, I believe the guidance of Divine Providence; how far I have succeeded, shall leave others to judge; but after all, there is an unwritten history of the wonderful man, whose fame is in all the churches, and will long be remembered. The fragmentary leaves we have been able to gather only make us desire a more complete history; we have only the outlines, we would have a full and perfect portrait; we have only the preface, we wish for the volume.

This little book has cost me more time and labor, than I shall ever receive credit for; but if it has rescued one of the noble heroes of Methodism from oblivion, that otherwise would have perished and been forgotten, and if it inspires any with a hatred to sin, and a love for righteousness; if the publication of this memoir shall be the means of reviving the earlier spirit of Methodism, and contributing to the return to its former purity, spirituality and simplicity, I shall not regret my labor of love.

F. E. M.

—SKETCH.—

CHAPTER I.

Seventeen years, Nov. 17th, 1879, will have passed away, since that unyielding champion of the Cross—JOHN HERSEY, fell, sword in hand, shouting, "victory! victory!! victory!!! salvation;" loaded with honors, covered with glory, and went up to receive his crown

JOHN HERSEY was one of the most remarkable men of an age, that developed many striking characters in the Methodist Episcopal Ministry, as a self-sacrificing christian minister of the New Testament; teaching by precept and example, the way to the Kingdom of Heaven—few his equals—none his superiors.

To *Delaware*, we are indebted for this remarkable man of God.

Wilmington was among the earliest settlements in the country; Fort Christianna, near where the city now stands, fell before the fire of the artillery of the Danes, and the surrounding country passed from under the dominion of Sweden in 1665. In the suburbs of the city, still remains the quaint old church of those distant times, and around it are the graves of pastors and members who died in the early part of the seventeenth century, whose bodies there await the final resurrection. Near the church mingles the waters of the Christianna and the romantic Brandywine; eight miles above, on the 11th of September, 1777, the waters of the last named stream, ran crimson from Chad's ford, where the battle of Brandywine was fought and lost.

Methodism was introduced into Delaware, by Capt. Thos. Webb, in 1769; the first Methodist Society in the State was formed in *New Castle County*, 1770.

Just four miles beyond, or west of Christianna, there lived *Isaac* and *Jane Hersey*, where it is written in history, that as early as 1771, they opened their house to *Methodist Preachers* and *Methodist Preaching*; here a society was raised up, and afterwards a church called Salem, was built

about 1809. This is one of the oldest appointments in
the State of Delaware. The house of his brother, Solomon
Hersey, was the first place at which Mr. Asbury preached
on the Manor, Cecil County, Maryland. He had the preaching at his house for a number of years ; and though the first
Methodist preaching on the Eastern shore of Maryland was
in Kent County, yet the evidence in the case leads to the belief, that the first society on this shore was formed at Solomon
Hersey's house, in 1772.

This society is still represented at the Manor Chapel.
Another brother of his, Benjamin Hersey, was the leading
spirit, if not the father of the union appointment on Smyrna
Circuit; Rev. Benjamin Abbot preached at another brother's,
named J. Hersey, in 1780.

JOHN HERSEY, son of Isaac and Jane Hersey, was
born *August 2nd*, 1786. His family being identified with
the early history of Methodism, the subject of this Memoir,
enjoyed from these connections, marked religious advantages.
He often referred to the influence of mothers, and spoke in his
last illness of his own precious mother, and that in answer
to her prayers, he was brought to Christ. She in early life
was a *Friend*, and when she became a Methodist, she retained
the simplicity of manner and plainness of dress, which characterizes that people. Highly favored as he was, he spent
the earlier years of his manhood, as a man of the world.

In early life he was convinced that the Lord had a work for
him to do. As he grew up to riper years, his convictions were,
that at some period of his life, he would be a Methodist
Preacher. In more mature years he threw off those convictions, by conforming to the gayety, fashions, and sinful
pleasures of the world ; his venerable parents died before he
reached his majority ; the date of their demise we are not in
possession of. Bishop Asbury who paid them his annual
visits from the year 1772, writes, August 1st, 1801 : "I
could not pass my old friend, Isaac Hersey, without calling;
we could with gratitude review the past, and dwell upon the
present dealings of the Lord with us as a people, and say—
What hath God wrought ?" The last entry which he makes
in his journal of his old friend I H., is, Aug. 3rd, 1802 :
"Came as far as Isaac Hersey's, dined with him" ; the probability, before his next annual round, his old friend was away
in the Glory-land.

The boyhood and youth of John Hersey passed swiftly away—no more eventful, than may be inferred from the humble quietness of his situation. It was an important period to him ; for he was laying the foundation of his usefulness, in the hardihood, industry, energy and intelligence of his character.

At an early period of his eventful life we hear of him operating salt works in the lower county, on the Eastern shore of Maryland. It is related that Father Hersey, when a young man of 23, was much *overcome* by listening to a sermon preached by Rev. Freeborn Garrettson, at Georgetown, D. C., at the house of Bro. Elliason, who was a relative of Father Hersey ; he was at this time a visitor, and meeting here this aged servant of God, and former pastor and friend of his father's house, no wonder he should be overcome.

How painfully pleasing the fond recollection
    Of youthful emotions and innocent joy,   -
When blessed with parental advice and affection,
    Surrounded with mercies, with peace from on high,
I still view the chair of my father and mother,
    The seats of their offspring as ranged on each hand,
And that richest book which excels every other,
    The family Bible which lay on the stand,

The old-fashioned Bible, the dear blessed Bible,
    The family Bible that lay on the stand.

That Bible, the volume of God's inspiration,
    At morn and at evening could yield us delight,
The prayer of our sire was a sweet invocation,
    For mercy by day, and safety through night ;
Our hymns of thanksgiving with harmony swelling,
    All warm from the heart of a family band,
Half raised us from earth to that rapturous dwelling,
    Described in the Bible that lay on the stand,

The old-fashioned Bible, the dear blessed Bible,
    The family Bible that lay on the stand.

Ye scenes of tranquility, long have we parted,
    My hopes almost gone, and my parents no more,
In sorrow and sadness, I live broken hearted,
    And wonder unknown on a far distant shore :
Yet how can I doubt my Redeemer's protection,
    Forgetful of gifts from His bountiful hand ?
Oh, let me with patience receive His correction,
    And think of the Bible that lay on the stand.

The old-fashioned Bible, the dear blessed Bible,
    The family Bible that lay on the stand.

Bro. Garrettson was now paying his last visit to his spiritual children who had come from Delaware, and the Eastern shore of Maryland, and settled in Washington and Georgetown. In speaking of this visit, Bro. Garrettson in his journal (at Baltimore.) writes: June 26th, 1809, "I took the stage, and in the evening, arrived at Georgetown: I lodged at *Mr. Elliason's*, a very worthy family; they are some of my old Eastern shore friends. The 27th, I preached in the evening to many people, with a degree of freedom; 28th, in the afternoon, *Bro. Elliason* came for me; this evening I preached in Georgetown again; here we have a respectable society; and had I been an *Apostle*, they could not have treated me *much better*." Although Mr. Hersey was much affected on this occasion, all those impressions passed away in the life of gayety, which he led; he always declared that he would be a Methodist Preacher before his death, which was completely verified.

John Hersey, about this time, established himself in Mercantile business in Georgetown, D. C., and one writer informs us, he purchased in New York sixty thousand dollars worth of goods and paid for them, but a second adventure was not so successful The state of the country at this period was unsettled; war was declared with Great Britain, and "to arms" was the cry from Massachusetts to Georgia, on both land and sea. The British having entered Washington in 1814, burnt the Capitol and President's house, as well as destroying private property; soon after the war came to a close, a collapse in business circles caused him to fail.

Rev. Wm. C. Lipscomb, an aged minister of the M. P. Church, of Washington, D. C., writes March 19th, 1879: "Father Hersey 65 or 70 years ago, during his early manhood, was engaged in mercantile business in Georgetown, D. C.; during this period of Mr. Hersey's life, he was a gay and fashionable young man. What cause produced his failure, I never heard; soon after this occurred, he left Georgetown: where he went I never knew; he subsequently returned, but evidently, a very different man—think at that time he had commenced preaching. During his sojourn thenceforth, we became pretty well acquainted, and he passed a few months in my family. I esteemed him as a very pious, self-denying christian, though extremely eccentric in his dress." Bro. Thomas S. Clark, a venerable and highly esteemed member of the M. E. Church, in E. Balto. Station, informs the writer, that he heard of Father Hersey when a boy; he was in the milling business, in Mathews Co., Virginia.

C. B. Hudgins, an aged and esteemed Baptist brother, writes:

Mathews Co., Va., Aug. 4th, 1879.

DEAR SIR:

Received your letter of inquiry of Rev. John Hersey. There was such a man came to Mathews Co.; the date I do not know, but believe it was in the year of 1815 or 16; where he came from I do not know; he ran a saw and grist mill, which were burnt down; during the time he ran those mills, he was a wicked man. I was a mill boy, that used to go to his mills, but the Lord took his heart by taking his mills away. Hersey left Mathews County; when he returned, he was a changed man, altogether. I do believe he was a converted man. He then traveled to Richmond, Fredericksburg and elsewhere, preaching; he wore his beard and hair the same length, well down his back, he wore no shoes on his feet, would not sleep on a bed, but a pallet; he was a Methodist believer, and the churches in which his notices were given, would be filled; the great talk of Bro. Hersey, was like that of Spurgeon.

Bro. Lipscomb, lost sight of Hersey from Georgetown. He says he left; where he went he never knew; but as the rising and setting of the Sun, so with Father Hersey: he could not be hid. Bro. Lipscomb lost the sight, Bro. Hudgins gained it—the one knew not whither he went, the other from whence he came; so it was with John Hersey. He rolled around with the year, and never stood still, till the Master appeared; for a season he disappeared from both, *neither* knew whither he went, nor when he would return. One says he was a fashionable, gay young man, the other "the most wicked he ever saw."

Hark! Beloved brethren, hear the Master, "I will show John Hersey what great things he must suffer for my name's sake, and the Gospel's. for he is a chosen vessel unto the Lord; and must testify of me to the Africans, as well as the Red men of the forest; thus saith the Lord. John Hersey, your salt works of the Atlantic, to you, are a thing of the past; your merchandise, like the early dew of the morning, has passed away. You retired to the secluded swamps of the Rappahannock; thy mills are burned with fire. I have called and ye have refused, I have called again; set thy house in order, I have a work for thee to do, no other can perform; get ye up, go administer justice and judgment to my poor and down trodden people, the Africans and Indians, in the desert swamps of Alabama; thou shalt testify of me to them, and shall be as the voice of John, that crieth in the wilderness, 'prepare ye the way of the Lord; make straight in the desert a highway for our God.' I will be enquired of by this people, and thou shalt lift up a standard. Behold thou shall call a nation that thou knowest not, and nations that knew not thee, shall run unto thee, because of the Lord thy God and the Holy One of Israel, for he hath glorified thee; the wilderness and the solitary place shall be glad for them, and the desert shall rejoice, and blossom as the rose, they shall see the glory of the Lord, and the excellency of our God. Then shall thy light break forth as the morning, and thine health spring forth speedily, and thy righteousness shall go before thee: the glory of the Lord shall be thy reward. Fear thou not, for I am with thee; be not dismayed, for I am thy God, I will- strengthen thee; yea, I will help thee ; yea, I will uphold thee with the right hand of my righteousness, and will bring thee up again in peace."

Having obtained strength of the Lord, and his comfortable assurance that His presence should go with him. Father Hersey conferred not with flesh and blood, but obediently left all to follow Christ.

Bro. C. B. Hudgins informs us, that God took his heart, by taking his mills, which gives us a key to the *commencement* of the religious life of true devotion to his Lord and Master's divine call.

Father Hersey, writes, Greensboro, Green Co , Alabama, December 13th, 1859. "I *partly* began my christian and ministerial life in this State, nearly forty years since," which takes us back to the year, 1819 as the probable year his mill burnt, when he started for the kingdom of heaven,

CHAPTER II.

INDIAN AGENCY IN ALABAMA, 1819.

On the 4th of March, 1817, James Monroe, of Virginia, became President of the United States, and Daniel D. Tompkins, of New York, Vice-President. The new President followed the same general policy as his predecessor; he called John Quincy Adams to become Secretary of State, and Wm H. Crawford, of Georgia, was placed at the head of the Treasury Department. In December, John Calhoun, of South Carolina, was appointed Secretary of War, and Wm. Wirt, of Maryland, Attorney-General.

In the Summer of 1817, the Seminoles, a powerful tribe living within the Spanish Territory on the borders of Georgia and Alabama, joined by some runaway negroes and refugee Creeks, commenced a series of depredations on the frontier settlement.

Gen. Gains, who commanded a post on the Flint river, destroyed several of their villages, but he encountered so fierce a resistance, that Jackson was ordered into service with volunteers from Tennessee. In March, 1818, Jackson took the field with his brave Tennesseans; he burnt a number of Seminole towns; drove the enemy before him, and seized on their corn and cattle. During Monroe's administration, five new States were admitted into the Union: Mississippi, 1817; Illinois, 1818; Alabama, originally embraced in Mississippi Territory, 1819; Maine, 1820; Missouri. 1821. Florida was organized as a territory, and Andrew Jackson was appointed its first Governor; as before stated, Alabama was admitted into the Union, 1819, and her Constitution was adopted, Aug. 2nd, 1819; Wm. W. Bibb elected Governor, John Crowell, representative to Congress.

The plan of a United States Government trade with the Indians, dates as far back as the year 1796; the system was one of pure humanity; embracing a supply of the wants of the Indians, and receiving in exchange from them, furs and peltries at fair prices. The convenience of the Indians was consulted, in establishing factories along the borders; suitable and competent persons, as factors, clerks and interpreters, were appointed to carry on the trade.

President Madison, appointed on the 2d of April, 1816, Thomas L. McKenney, a merchant of the District of Columbia, Superintendent of the United States Indian Trade, with the Indian tribes; which office he held until the agency was abolished.

In the same year, Oct. 1819, Alabama was made a State.

John Hersey, a resident of Georgetown, D. C., recently a merchant there, received the appointment under James Monroe's administration, to the Agents' trading house in Alabama, as a suitable person to represent the United States Trade Agency, and to deal justly and mercifully with the Choctaw Indians, which position he held up to Oct. 1822, when the act, abolishing the United States Indian trade establishment, was passed, when John Hersey returned to Georgetown, D. C., his home. It will be seen that Father Hersey was identified with the fathers of his country at this early age, on May 6th, 1822. Provision was made for the appointment of an agent to wind up the affairs of the concern; when Thomas H. Benton made a speech in the Senate, in reference to abolishing the agency, which reflected upon the Superintendent of the Indian Bureau, and lead to a thorough examination of the affairs of the agency, as well as a vindication of its efficient management. John Hersey was an important witness, and we here give his testimony as published in the proceedings of the Congressional examination.

"I, John Hersey, resident of Georgetown, late factor at the Choctaw trading house, in the State of Alabama, testify and say, that in October, 1819, I was appointed *factor* at said trading house, and continued to act in that capacity to Oct. 1822; that on entering on the business at said house, as near as I can recollect, the amount of goods delivered over to me by my predecessor, was about $14,000; many of which goods were so much damaged, or so unsalable, as to render it impossible to sell more than $2,000 or $3,000 probably, of them. During the time I was factor, I received as near as I now recollect, about $12,000 by the year; all of which came to me through the medium of Mr. T. L. McKenney;

about one sixth of which came from New Orleans and Mobile, such as coffee, sugar, lead and salt; the residue were from Columbia District and New York. When we received the goods at said house, we generally received accompanying invoices. I then thought most of the articles were of a fair price, and certainly of a good quality, except in a few instances; some were damaged on their passage from Col. McKenney. I received instructions to add from 66⅔ to 100 per cent to the invoice prices; the sales, on an average for the whole three years, were about 80 per cent advance on the invoice prices. In payment of these things sold, I received deer-skins, furs, bees-wax, tallow and cash. The re: gain to the Government during the whole three years, was between $8,000 and $9,000, after paying freight on such articles as we received from Mobile, and besides a remuneration to myself, and all others employed. When I took charge of the house, I think, as near as I now can recollect, the amount of outstanding debts due the Government, was upwards of $13,000, not more than $1,000 of which was probably collected while I was there; and I now am of the opinion that one-third of the remaining $12,000 may be collected. I presume a majority of the debtors to the Government when I went there, afterwards traded with me; many of whom might deliver me peltry and other things to an amount as great as the debts, then due from them severally; each one however, took other goods, to an equal and sometimes greater amount, so that in most instances, the old debts remained on the books uncancelled and unliquidated."

JOHN HERSEY,

Late Factor, C. T. II.

Mr. Hersey's second examination by Col McKenney.

Question 1st.—Was there not in the Choctaw factory when you took charge of it, a large quantity of old and unsalable goods?

Answer.—There was.

2d.—Did I not, in my letters, direct that they should be disposed of at reduced prices, and on long credit, *provided*, you could get unexceptional security?

Answer.—I was requested by you to dispose of the old and damaged goods, I think, at reduced prices, and long credit, *provided*, such security could be obtained.

Question 3d.—Were not the goods which you received of me, in general, suitable and fairly charged ? And did you not do out of them your principal business?

Answer.—To the best of my knowledge, they were charged at fair prices ; they were of good quality, and out of them I did my principal business, while there.

The reader will see the same straightforward course persued in giving his testimony, as marked his conduct in after-life.

During Jackson's term as military Governor, a friend of Father Hersey, states that he said to him on one occasion, General Jackson had cursed him, and wrote to Washington to have him dismissed : that he was the first man that had ever done so ; another friend says, whilst he (Hersey) was in the Agency, and had saved up his money, being desirous to pay it to his creditors, he obtained a leave of absence for a short time, also, a draft for his money; when about to leave for Washington, Mr. H. K. R. said to him, Mr. Hersey I see you have provided all for your creditors, nothing for the expense of your journey. Father Hersey drew from his pocket a Spanish "quarter-dollar," saying, that will do for the journey; after being absent a few weeks, he returned, the same party said, well Mr. Hersey, how did you succeed? Mr. Hersey drew from his pocket the same piece of money, remarking, he always found kind friends wherever he went, and they usually supplied his wants, which were but few. After the Agency had been abolished, and closed up, Father Hersey returned home to greet his friends, and to engage in other pursuits.

The year 1819 is memorable as the year in which the State of Alabama was admitted into the Federal Union ; as the year she adopted her constitution, and elected her executive officers; as the year John Hersey was appointed Indian Trade Agent, and located at the town of Cahawba, the seat of Government of the State ; the year he began his Christian Ministerial life; the year the Methodist Episcopal Church organized her great Missionary Society; the year that *Alabama* was made a district in the Mississippi Conference and Thos. Griffin appointed P. E., with John Murron, William Ledbetter, John J. E. Byrd, preachers, at the Conference of 1820, they reported 968 white, 172 colored members ; for 1821, white 1,190, colored, 322.

During this year they held in the district four camp meetings, one for each of their four circuits. Presiding Elder Griffin says of Alabama District, "It appears the work of reformation is progressing in our country. It is certainly cause of exultation to witness the growing prosperity of the Redeemer's Kingdom in our newly settled States and Territories. While the hardy emigrants are felling trees of the forest, and opening the bosom of the earth for the reception of seed, the heralds of salvation are itinerating through their scattered settlements, breaking up the fallow ground of their hearts, and sowing the seed of eternal life. At a camp meeting held on the 6th of July, on Pearl river, a few miles from Montecello, the congregation was large and attentive, many were awakened to a sense of their need in Christ, and five or six gave evidence of a change of heart. On the 20th, we held another meeting on the river Chickasauhay, about fifty miles from the borders of the Mobile, where we have a flourishing society; there were two traveling and four local preachers present (Father Hersey was likely one of them); on Friday and Saturday, the Lord favored us with a solemn sense of His presence; sinners were struck with awe, and stood with solemn silence, whilst believers rejoiced in God, their Saviour. On Sabbath we administered the Lord's Supper; all were serious; and I believe much good was done; about ten professed justifying Grace. On the 27th July, we held another meeting, about thirty miles from St. Stephen's, near the Tombigbee and Alabama rivers; the principal part of the people were irreligious, yet they behaved with great order and decorum; five professed to be converted. On the 2nd of August we commenced a camp meeting on the banks of the Alabama river, thirty miles below the town of Cahawba, the seat of government of this State. From the paucity of the inhabitants, and the afflictions many were suffering from a prevailing fever, there were not many attending this meeting; some disorder was witnessed at this meeting, but He that commanded the boisterous winds to be still, appeared in our behalf; before the exercises closed. some were brought as we have reason to believe, to a knowledge of the truth. August 10th. another meeting began thirty miles above Cahawba; a numerous concourse of people attended, and much good was done; on Tuesday morning I requested all who had obtained an evidence of their conversion to God, to come forward to

the altar, when thirty seven presented themselves. The two
last meetings were held in the forest, and the Indians were
fishing in the river; while we were preaching and praying,
the bears were ravaging the cornfields, and the wolves and
tigers were howling and screaming in the very woods in the
neighborhood of our meeting. These accounts may seem unimportant to those accustomed to more numerous congregations
and who have the privilege of assembling in convenient
houses; but to us, who are struggling with many difficulties
in this newly settled country, it is highly gratifying, and
fills us with a pleasing hope of yet seeing the desert blossom
as the rose."

The reader will see a picture of a newly settled State, and
the condition of things when John Hersey was appointed
Trade Agent to Alabama, and took charge of that important
station, which he held for three years, during which time he
assisted in the establishment of the State Institutions, and
of the M E. Church. No wonder after forty years toil he
could and did stand on the same soil, and praise God that
his hopes had been realized; that the desert had blossomed
as the rose. We will insert his letter in another chapter,
written in 1859, on his last visit to Alabama. The reader
will see John Hersey lived and labored at an age that tried
men's souls. He was identified with the great men of the
country, as well as of the church, in laying the foundation
of both civil and religious liberty in highly favored America, as well as Africa. His ministry began the same year
that Bishop Paine joined the Tennessee Conference, and was
sent to Flint river Circuit; here is where they formed
their acquaintance, that Bishop Paine, speaks of in his letter,
when he says, "I became acquainted with Bro. Hersey about
40 years ago. In the Autumn of 1822, or Spring of 1823,
he returned to his home in Georgetown. D. C., to greet his
friends and to enter upon his life work." No wonder that
Bros. Lipscomb and Hudgins saw a change, and believed him
a converted man; for his whole after-life corresponded to his
profession.

We now greet him as Father Hersey, a minister of the
Gospel of the blessed God; and as such we introduce him to
the reader.

CHAPTER III.

ENTERING UPON HIS MINISTERIAL WORK.

The life to which Father Hersey had now devoted himself, and to which he believed God had called him by his Spirit and Providence, was one of the gravest consideration; humble though it might seem in the eyes of the world, to him the aspect assumed was one of untold interest; no other, with him, could compare with it. While he looked upon himself as an earthen vessel, and a frail one too, he felt that he was a messenger of Christ, and that with the faithful discharge of that sacred trust, was identified the future, the everlasting destiny of some, at least, of his fellow-beings. He knew by engaging in it—such was the state of Methodism, even apart from other considerations—that he entered upon a st..:e of se vere trial; it was a life of hardship, a life of exposure, and one that connected with it not a little suffering; he went forth trembling, weeping, we may say, "Bearing precious seed"—but a seed whose fruit was to blossom, and shed its fragrance, not only on this, but another world; and we think we are safe in saying—that it was the bearing that his calling had upon eternity alone that moved him to engage in the work; nay, it was this that kept him in it, and kept him from fainting by the way. The reader is not to suppose that Mr. Hersey had before him some sequestered, or even opulent parish, which could tempt him with that which pleased the eye and charmed the heart; where want, neglect, or pain of absence was not to be felt. He was now a Methodist preacher, a minister of the Gospel, without a settled pastorate, or regular contributing congregation, who at best, could only obtain a meagre support, and that by personal effort, or the benevolence of kind friends, unsolicited upon his part.

His first work in his new and important relation was under the direction of a Presiding Elder; in this capacity, he traveled the Culpepper Circuit in Virginia, on foot—a circuit of 240 miles, without missing an appointment. There is a striking resemblance, in one particular, of Father Hersey to the Apos-

tle Paul.   In the confession of Paul, he acknowledges that he
was a persecutor of the church, as well as the chief of sinners —of Father Hersey, it is said, he was a proud, gay, sinful young man, but in both, as soon as they were converted,
they began to preach Jesus and the resurrection, and straight-
way, "Conferred not with flesh and blood," but boldly, as far
as in them, set to work to counteract their previous wickedness,
by precept and example, and to the same persons and in the
same places, where they had reviled the name of the Lord.
They went and lifted up the standard of the Cross, and be-
seeched men to be reconciled to God.   As the early sinful days
of Father Hersey were in Virginia, he spent the earlier days of
his christian ministry with the same people, in trying to bring
them to God.

Rev. W. C. Lipscomb states, when Father Hersey returned to Georgetown, he was certainly a very different man—
he had commenced preaching ; Bro. Hudgins says, when
he returned to Mathews Co., he was changed altogether.
I do believe he was a converted man.   He traveled to Richmond, Fredericksburg, and elsewhere, preaching; and the
churches were filled ; (his fame went far and near,) the people
said he talked like Spurgeon.

Rev. J. W. Reeves writes: "I heard Father Hersey preach
in Alexandria, Va., 1824; he often preached at Sun rising,
and great crowds would be out to hear him ; his preaching was with demonstration and power, and many were converted to God.   I shall never forget, it was under his ministry,
I was awakened and converted, and, am happy to know such
a man as John Hersey ever lived. "

Rev. F. S. Evans writes: "My acquaintance with good
Bro. Hersey, began in 1825, and was renewed at intervals
up to near the time he went home to Heaven."

Bishop Paine of the M. E. Church, (South.) in a letter,
before me writes, February 11th, 1860 : "I became acquainted
with Brother Hersey, about 40 years ago : I never knew a
more consistent and devoted minister."

Bishop J. L. Keener of same church, writes, New Orleans,
April 7th, 1879 : "Your favor, asking for items of information
in reference to Rev. J. Hersey.   I knew him as a preacher,
calling at my father's home, when I was a young man and
just from school, and I afterwards entertained him in

New Orleans, for a week or two before the war, where he preached in our church. He was a delightful man; exemplifying the beauty of holiness for years, wherever he went; and an able minister of the New Testament."

Rev. Henry Slicer says: "Father Hersey I knew long and intimately; he has spent weeks at my house; I was his pastor in Fredericksburg, Va., in 1825. He was then a Commission Merchant; he however, failed in business, and this fact furnishes the reason, why he never entered the itinerant ministry. He feared there might be some taint or 'suspicion attached to him on account of his former indebtedness; he never considered himself released from obligations to his creditors, until he had paid them the last dollar. For upwards of forty years, he was an itinerant local preacher. As an evangelist, he traveled through nearly all the States. He was ordained deacon, by Bishop Soule, at Baltimore, April 10th, 1825; elder, by Bishop Roberts, in Lynchburg, Va., March 1st, 1829."

After these years, he spent much of his time in Baltimore, with his friends Armstrong & Plaskett, who were the publishers of his first works: "*Extracts of Wesley*," "*Importance of Small Things*," "*An Appeal to Christians on the Subject of Slavery*." With these, he went forth everywhere, scattering the seeds of eternal life. And eternity alone will reveal the good John Hersey did with word, work and pen, aided by the blessed Spirit of Almighty God, which we all need so much; without which, the word will return void, will not accomplish that whereunto it is sent. "O for the Spirit of the fathers to be poured out on all the churches; then will her ministers in deed and in truth, teach transgressors thy way, and sinners *shall* be converted to God."

CHAPTER IV.

His Christian and Ministerial Character.

FATHER HERSEY, as he was reverently called, was a cherished household name in many portions of our country for the larger portion of half a century. To numerous individuals and families of the generation passing away, his memory is endeared. If not a star of the first magnitude, John Hersey shone with no mean lustre; he was indeed a "living and shining light." His nativity it will be seen, marks an illustrious era. Three years after the achievement of American Independence, and two years after the organization of the Methodist Episcopal Church; and it may be noted that he died when the great Rebellion had assumed its fiercest proportions, and the North and South were engaged in deadly and uncertain strife; an event of which he seemed to have had prophetic foresight. But he was untouched by its terrors; and before the conflict ended, he was away in the land of everlasting peace. He was early in his ministry, we believe, a member of the Baltimore Conference; at least on trial in that body, but desiring a wider range than Conference-limits, and the privilege to chose his own field of labor, he was allowed this freedom. Yet he could not be called a local preacher, for all his time and talents were devoted to ministerial work, and he traveled as much and preached as often as most of his contemporaries. He itinerated at will over most of the Continent. We find him following the tract of the pioneer emigrant, proclaiming the glad tidings, and scattering the seed of truth that made the solitary places rejoice, and the wilderness blossom as the rose. It may be said he was erratic—he never could be called insubordinate. He yielded submission to our ecclesiastical economy and vindicated by precept and example, conformity to the discipline of the M. E. Church.

An esteemed friend, an honored and able minister of the Wilmington Conference, writes: "My acquaintance with Father Hersey commenced in the days of my youthful ministry. He was with me at my stopping places, and made himself on several occasions, every way a useful congenial companion. I was at that time—nor have I ever fully outgrown the habit—given to asking questions; he answered readily and usually to my satisfaction, all the questions I asked him. Nor is it a small matter to find one superior to yourself in years and in experience and intelligence, replying to your persistent and often perplexing inquiries. In this way for my part, I have had the luck in more than one case, to find "libraries in men." While I was a single man, Father Hersey in several instances visited my fields of labor, and was always welcome, and after I had a home of my own, if the itinerant's place of sojourn can be called his home—he was always a cherished guest; and on more than one occasion, he blessed our fireside with his presence

Father Hersey was an early riser. In the towns he visited, making appointments for preaching at five o'clock in the morning, he usually had a good attendance. In one of these morning discourses, in speaking of the Divine Will, he used language like the following: "The heart is deceitful," but if I know myself, were my Heavenly Father to send his angel to address me thus, "John I am commissioned from the THRONE to offer you any situation in life you may chose; only state your wishes and they shall be gratified. I think I would answer, go back Gabriel, and tell your Lord and Master, I have no choice to make, and am satisfied with with the lot he assigns me."

On one occasion Father Hersey was a guest at a friend's house to supper. In those days the cone shaped loaf sugar was popular. It was white and hard, and for table use was broken in small pieces and used for tea. He used the ordinary herb teas, rejecting coffee; yet he declined the loaf sugar and requested brown, which was intended for coffee. His host asked him the reason for his preference—supposing his choice was influenced by a motive of economy and self-denial, and remarked that there was little or no difference in the cost, whilst tea was spoiled by sugar. His answer was, "We are commanded to abstain from all evil," and added, "Blood is forbidden—loaf-sugar is clarified with blood, and I feel bound not to use it." The conversation ended on the subject, for the friend was silent for such delicate scruples of conscience. Father Hersey was particular in his diet. He abstained from luxurious, but ate heartily of ordinary wholesome food. He scrupulously avoided food cooked on Sunday when it came to his knowledge, or was self-evident.

He preferred a hard bed, that is, some couch without the luxury of feathers—even in winter. Mattresses were not then in general use.

Once while visiting a friend, it is related, that before retiring, he made private request, if convenient to have a hard bed; another clerical friend being a guest at the same time, who was not so self-denying, overhearing Father Hersey's request, remarked "Brother, you will have to put up with a feather bed to-night, you are to sleep with me, and I prefer feathers." He acquiesced and the brothers lodged together. Father Hersey objected to superfluities of all kinds; fine clothes, costly furniture, table luxuries.

He preached against them, and he practiced what he preached—a consistency not found in all reformers and evangelists. He held that it was contrary to the Spirit of the Gospel to indulge in these things, while so many of our Heavenly Father's children were destitute of proper clothing and the common necessaries of life. A friend remarking on one occasion, that self-denial on his part would not supply the destitution of the sufferers, he replied, that he felt it his duty to bear their burdens, to suffer with them in imitation of Him who was touched with the feelings of our infirmities, and who, though he was rich, for our sake became poor. The friend was constrained to acknowledge the magnanimity of his motives. Being reminded that the manufacture of various fabrics and the mechanical arts in general gave useful employment to many persons, and contributed greatly to the prosperity and peace of society; he seemed to admit the theory, but re-avowed the importance of self-denial. When told, "You are the only person known, who practices as well as preaches a life of such a rigid self-denial; certainly all other religious professors are not deceived" His answer was "I do not judge others, but so understand the Scriptures for my own faith and practice." In this connection, being asked if he had ever made a convert to his ideas and mode of living, he said he believed he had met with one lady who had adopted them.

This was undoubtedly a low estimate of the effect of his close preaching, and holy example. No doubt *many* through his doctrines and manner of life were led to a closer walk with God, and presented perfection in Christ Jesus. There was this excellence in Father Hersey, he never dogmatised his opinions, and did not make himself an oracle. He was, fond of visiting the South, and often spent the Winter there, where he found pleasant homes among people of wealth and refinement, but in the midst of such surroundings he adhered to his abstemious habit, and was respected and beloved; when he returned from these annual sojourns, like the birds of Spring with unaltered plumage and song, his mantle was unsoiled, and his zeal was unquenched.

On the slavery question he was once heard to say, "The Abolitionists are right in principle," implying as his hearers took it, that they were wrong and erred in the methods by which they sought to carry out the principle. It was at this point the issue came between the conservatists and the ultraists. There is no doubt, but that Father Hersey conducted himself fairly and squarely, both to master and slave, making the word of God, "the man of his counsel," and being all things to all men for their good.

But like all sincere and outspoken men, Father Hersey, was often misunderstood upon this subject. When the strife and controversy between the emancipationists and their opponents waxed warm, and the questions involved, pro and con, were discussed with vigor and order in the Legislature of Virginia, Father Hersey arranged, collated and published a small volume of these speeches, and offered them for sale in the State of Virginia.

A storm of indignation arose in the Old Dominion against the veteran divine, who was denounced without stint as an Abolitionist by all who had never seen his book; a box of the books were seized and publicly burnt in the streets of Richmond; whilst Father Hersey himself, who was attending a Camp Meeting near Fredericksburg, at the advice of his friends, had to fly to prevent the execution of an order emanating from Richmond, authorizing and directing his arrest and detention. Under the influence of returning reason, an examination of the book which before had not been thought of, resulted in a reconsideration by the tribunal and countermanding of its order. But ere this, the books were in flames and their compiler a fugitive, exclaiming as he left the Camp ground, with tears streaming from his eyes, "Never before have I been called an enemy of my country."

Father Hersey would often show that his mind was troubled as if some prophetic apprehension disturbed him. He would not unfrequently intimate, both in public discourse and private conversation, that we were on the eve of tumultuous times—a storm was brewing.

The terrible civil war through which the country passed, did transpire. As fearful as it was, it scarcely reached the horrors of his vision of dark events. This may have been the preliminary "woe," and others, it may be, are yet to come in the drama of Providence, when Church and State, nationalities, races and religions, will blend in the strife. If this shall ever come to pass, the spirit of our sainted friend may watch the scene from the celestial bastions.

Mr. Hersey spent some years of his early ministerial life among the Red men of the frontier. He was first an agent, afterwards a missionary among the the Choctaws, previous to their removal west of the Mississippi. In after years, he revisited the scenes of his early ministry, and was warmly welcomed by its dusty children—his first converts. About thirty years before his death, Father Hersey made a voyage to Liberia, to preach to the colonists and natives.

The missionary spirit prompted him to go to benighted Africa, so as to impart some gift through the ministrations of the gospel to these people, and to respond to the desire of relief expressed by the scripture words ''Ethiopia is stretching out her hands unto God.'' It is quite probable that he did not find a fruitful field for his talent there. His conviction was that the standard of morals was not high enough in the lives of those who represented christianity, to impress the heathen with elevated ideas of its excellence and divinity.

Father Hersey was an author, and published several works. His *Extracts from Wesley*, was probably, the first emanation from his pen. *Importance of Small Things*, which followed in 1830–33, is a very useful production, and can scarcely be read by any one without profit; it went through more than one edition. His work on *Christian Perfection*, says a Methodist Minister of great learning, and author of great merit, ''is technically if not theologically anti-Methodistic; that is anti-Wesleyan. He earnestly contends for holiness of heart and life as a present work and experience, and essential to the believers acceptance with God and his salvation. That every child of God is pure in heart, created anew in Christ Jesus, bearing the image of him that begat him.'' Father Hersey it would seem from the testimony of our religious literature, is not alone in these opinions; but their entire harmony with the law and testimony, it would be difficult I think, to maintain on the one hand, or disapprove on the other. The truth as it is in Jesus in this case as in others is rather a matter of faith and experience, than of analysis and interpretation.

In 1833, he published his 2nd edition on *Slavery;* which was followed by his views on *Baptism*, *Life of Prayer*, *Advice to Parents, The Two Witnesses,* and just before his death, with *Satan Unmasked, or Revelations Revealed.* Father Hersey was never married. As far as information could be elicited from him on this delicate subject, he was far from being insensible to the charms which invest this question, but he was so hemmed in by circumstances, that he could not allow it to enter into his life purposes. He was not situated to incur domestic responsibilities, and followed Paul's advice in the case. There had been a period when the question was fresh and serious in his thoughts; for did there ever live a man or woman exempt from its spells? Some shadow, no doubt, crossed his path, and the question, perhaps, at an early date became obsolete; its odor however, was exhaled in the romance of memory.

In early life he had been a man of the world, drifting with the tide on the stream of fashion. He was a merchant in the District of Columbia about the time of the war of 1812. He was then in the pride of his early manhood. On one occasion he purchased in New York a cargo of tea and salt on credit, to the amount of sixty thousand dollars, which he paid ; but afterwards a collapse in business circles coming at the close of the war, caused him to fail, largely in debt. Shortly after this, he became religious, and his life thenceforth, was destined to be the antithesis of his former one. Involved in debt, he applied all his savings from the sale of his books, and the gift of his friends, to its liquidation. The generosity of his creditors allowed him his own time, and a few years before his death, he visited New York, sought out the widow and child of his last creditor (he being long since dead), and astonished them by tendering several hundred dollars in liquidation of a debt, of whose existence they did not even dream.

On this occasion he writes to a friend—"I am again a freeman, for no one can say that John Hersey owes him a cent."

Changed by the logic of events from a merchant full of pride, to an itinerant, overflowing with piety, moving in a different sphere, and toiling with different aims, are we not safe in saying, that the self-denying itinerant achieved a grander work, than if he had pursued his mercantile calling, and become the wealthiest capitalist of the country,

To mortify his former pride, and by way of reparation for

his previous extravagance and vanity, Father Hersey resorted to plainness of dress, and of diet ; he did not indulge in eating; he was no epicure, but enjoyed his meals, eat what was set before him ; always finding something good and wholesome His friends were careful to accommodate his scruples.   Nor was there anything in him morbid, peevish and morose.   On the contrary, his cheerful contentment and gratitude, made him free from offensive moods, and an object of interest and even of admiration to all who knew him

He was social and genial in a high degree ; genuine religion does not destroy the human side of our nature, it is the *carnal* it seeks to uproot and destroy, but it enters into and runs through the channels of the human or the "earthly vessel," and brings out our individuality into nobler relief. Wearing the image of the heavenly, transforms and utilizes our natural characteristics.   Paul's mighty energy seen in persecuting the church, was, after his conversion, sanctified and directed in building up what he had sought to destroy. So Father Hersey's devotion to the world, and his "pride of life" were superseded after he became a christian, by a life of usefulness and of unflinching self-denial.

His visits to families were marked occasions ; parents and children, masters and servants, and guest, all came in for a share of his attention ; with true courtesy and in the spirit of love, he gave to each in turn, some appropriate advice. This was his invariable practice : nor were these salutatory or parting words soon forgotten.   In his personal habits, Father Hersey was cleanly to a fault.   Although dressed in "Lindsey-wolsey" which was his chief attire, he was always neat, and when his clothes became thread-bare, which was sometimes the case, no man in broad-cloth had more the bearing of a gentleman.   Although rigid in his habits of self-denial, and close in his preaching, he was never censorious, and although really (as all who met him were forced to admit) "Better than other men ;" he had nothing of the bearing, or the boast of the Pharisee.

If ever severe in reproof, it was when the misdemeanor partook of the nature of sacrilege.   In such case the offender might lookout for words of keenest rebuke.

A friend writes :   "On one occasion I was the unwitting instrument of disturbing his accustomed gravity.   As singular as he was in his modes of abstinence and self-denial, yet for everything he was prepared to give a sensible reason I said, Father Hersey I hold the same truths, the same theory of morals and religion you do, and I am trying to reduce them to practice, but my way differs from yours in carrying them out. I could imitate you mechanically, but wouldb e at a loss for so doing. The fact is, I hav'nt sense enough to adopt your habits of life. A blush, accompanied with a hearty laugh, was his only answer." He was regarded by some of his contemporaries as wild in his singularity. He was singular, eccentric, if you please, but this was the mark of a strong character. His eccentricities consisted in his abstemious, laborious life—in his holy walk and conversation, and in his tireless efforts to do good to his fellow-men. They subjected no one to inconvenience, but himself. He was a *living martyr*, but in that martyrdom he honored his Master and found a joy that the princes of this world would barter crowns to possess. Father Hersey was consistent and reliable. You always knew where to find him ; he did not vacillate. Numbers of young men on entering the christian ministry, who assume a plain attire, with other tokens of humlity, and after a short period lay it all aside as unbecoming the dignity of their positions, and as oppressive to the tastes of cultivated people. What is this but weakness and vanity ?

Father Hersey through "Evil report and good" continued and ended as he began. In youth and in age he was the same. He persued the even "Tenor of his ways," neither officiously presenting himself as a pattern, nor yet stooping to be an imitator. Father Hersey, when not acting in his independent style as a traveling missionary and itinerant, was employed by Presiding Elders to supply vacancies, chiefly in the old Baltimore and Philadelphia Conferences. He also performed ministerial work in most of the Middle, Southern and Western States. He visited from house to house and in private, and in public, preached the gospel, giving full proof of his ministry ; and until a few years of his death, traveling mostly on foot.

As a preacher, he had gifts sufficient to have taken high rank. His powers for swaying an audience as a speaker, were probably never fully exerted ; for some reason and by some influence, they were held under restraint, as if fearful

it might seem like parade to do his best. He was intelligent,
and comprehended the methods by which to illustrate and
enforce the truth. His emotional nature seemed to be aglow,
and his impulses were quick and generous. He had sublime
conceptions which he sometimes expressed in thrilling terms.
In preaching, he was textual; he brought before his audience
the strong points of a passage, and never failed to give the
gist of the subject. He knew by verbal construction to set
forth and apply the truth, so that every one felt that it con-
tained a message for him. The listener became convinced
that the speaker cared little for man's criticisms, so he could
please God. and save their souls. He was true to his own
conviction, and described religion as a solemn personal matter, which antagonized our depraved nature, and placed us
in responsible relations with a Holy God. He described the
way to heaven as intricate and narrow; and yet the preacher
was so gentle and pitiful, loving and happy, that while he
led you to feel unworthy and sinful, yet failed for the most
part to cause any alarm, for the reason that the thought
gained control of the hearer's mind, that if the preacher is so
gentle, surely our Heavenly Father cannot be severe.
Again, he was earnest and pathetic, he might be justly called
a weeping prophet ; not for the many tears he shed, but for
his dirge-like voice, the effect of which was to excite in the
hearer a sympathy for the speaker, rather than concern for
himself. The same state of mind seemed to control certain
persons in the Saviour's days, which led him to say, "Daughter of Jerusalem, weep not for me, but weep for yourself and
your children.". A lady once became greatly excited with
apparent alarm under his preaching, but he soon made the
discovery that her nerves more than her conscience was the
seat of her fears.

These facts with others, are furnished to form some analysis
of a remarkable character, and to make the portrait as life-
like as possible.

Father Hersey was more of a logician than a philosopher.
A man may reason well, when his premises are incorrect,
when in discourse they may be technically misplaced, or
misstated, which will involve mistaken deductions. In such
a case, philosophy might adjust the argument.

Mr. Wesley furnishes an example to this effect, where
philosophy was master of the logic. There were three prin-

ciples that met in Father Hersey, which in their combination moulded his character and controlled his life, namely : faith, conscience and common sense. In default of the adjusting force of these with the prevailing idiosyncracies of his nature, he would have been a fool or fanatic ; but he was farthest removed from either ; nor was he a bigot, nor an egotist, nor a sectarian. Religiously he was a *christian*, denomination-ally a *Methodist*, and in vocation a *preacher*. The phrase that would best state what he was, is "One who earnestly contended for the faith once declared to the saints," or, in the words of Jesus himself applied to another, "An Israelite indeed, in whom there is no guile."

Father Hersey evidently underestimated the fruits of his labors. He was not a revivalist, as the term is usually understood. He was far from being a sensationalist, but be-lievers were quickened, and communities were moved by his preaching. His ministry, like that of the Saviour's great fore-runner, attracted numerous hearers. He might, with the greatest emphasis, be called an evangelist, but for one thing, and yet it cannot be said that he was not an evange-list, for some of the marks of an evangelist he possessed in a very high degree. The exception in his case, was the lack of the *doctrinal* element. He did preach doctrine, and sound doctrine too. But he was a teacher, rather than a a theologian. The instructer of a Sabbath School class, the mother in the nursery, are teachers in their departments, and very important ones too, in the rudimental knowledge of re-ligious truth, but it would not be proper to call them evan-gelists. Such was Father Hersey compared as a teacher with the theologian; it being understood that every theologian is not a teacher. Father Hersey's tendency was more in the order of the true pietist, than that of the evangelist. Be-lieving in ethical instruction, and in preaching christian morality; still we must admit, that precept without doctrine, weakens a discourse. Possibly, there was not enough of theology in Father Hersey's preaching, to make him a thor-ough evangelist; but it may truly be said, that the work of an evangelist is more to enforce the teaching and practicing of the truth, than to present expositions of systematic divin-ity ; yet still, the basis of all successful evangelists, is the doctrinal truth as it is in Jesus.

Wesley was a theologian, and so was Luther. Like the

Apostles John and Paul. All of these were great evangelists. But after all, it must be conceded, that Father Hersey
was in his order, an able minister of the New Testament.
The trumpet he blew, gave no uncertain sound. His feet
were shod with the preparation of the Gospel of Peace. A
halo attended his steps. In him was seen the beauty of
holiness, and we cannot doubt that many souls were saved
through his labor, who will shine as stars in his crown of
rejoicing. Circulating as he did, so widely, and calling the
attention of the people to the subject of religion, with such
earnest words, and moving so rapidly from place to place,
the effect of his ministry was to cause those who heard him,
to go to the regular places of preaching, and here it, just as
the presence of a comet in the sky widens our view of the
extent of creation, and leads persons to observe the stars,
who would otherwise scarcely look heavenward. The mission of some men may seem erratic, but there is in it a God-
like philosophy.

In his later years, it is easy to recall the appearance of
dignified meekness, and the cheerful smile that played over
his countenance, which wore the blended tokens of benignity
and sorrow. There was always in him the attractive force
of sympathy. You could scarcely see him without a touch
of sadness. Yet it was of the kind that promises a virtue ;
for by it, the heart was made better, and it became at once a
source of strength and joy to the beholder ; and although the
weight of years was bending his form and causing his steps to
falter, there still remained in him a noble beam of his former days. It is refreshing to turn to these things in the
diary of memory, as all who have shared the acquaintance of
this venerable and holy man will testify that it was made to
them a blessing, which they would fain transmit as a price-
less heir-loom to their posterity.

About this time, he was greatly exercised on the question
of colonization, having spent three of his earlier years,
south. Learning much those years on the subject of American
slavery, he was in full sympathy with colonizing in Africa,
the colored race. He published in 1833, the same year he
sailed for Africa, his "Appeal to Christians on Slavery."

CHAPTER V.

AFRICAN MISSION AT CAPE PALMAS, 1833.

Slavery in the United States may have been considered the remote, and christian philanthrophy, the proximate cause of establishing the colony in Africa, known as LIBERIA, under the auspices of the American Colonization Society. This society was formed in 1816, by some benevolent individuals, with a view of transporting to Africa, such free people of color, from the United States as might consent to migrate, and establish themselves as a colony, with all the rights and privileges of freemen. The first experiment, however, proved unpropitious. In 1818, a number of emigrants sailed from the port of New York, in the ship *Elizabeth*, accompanied by that eminent philanthropist and christian minister, the Rev. MR. BACON, whose commendable zeal in the cause of African Colonization, led him to embark in this hazardous undertaking, as the principal Agent of the society; the place at the mouth of the Sherbro River proved to be an unfortunate selection for the site of this important colony.

In 1821, the society purchased of the native chiefs, a district of country on the western coast of Africa. Here a settlement was commenced under favorable circumstances, and the town was called MONROVIA, in honor of the popular chief magistrate who then occupied the Presidential chair, (President Monroe.) These emigrants were accompanied by the pious and lamented ASHMAN, who fell a victim to his zeal in striving to build up a colony in that place. Nor were the churches inattentive to these movements. The Missionary Society of the M. E. Church, had not been an indifferent spectator to the spiritual wants of these people who had gone from our shores; many of them were members of our churches, and some were local preachers of reputable standing, and they sent back a cry, "Come over into Africa and help us" Rev. Melville B. Cox, offered his services as a missionary to Africa, and was accepted by the Bishops.

After making the needful preparation, on the 16th of Nov. 1832, Mr. Cox set sail in the ship JUPITER, from Norfolk, Va; after a long and tedious voyage, he arrived in Liberia on the 8th of March, 1833, and was most cordially received by the acting Governor, Rev. Mr. Williams, a local preacher of the M. E. Church.

Mr. Cox in taking leave of a young friend at the Wesleyan University, said to him, "If I die in Africa, you must come and write my epitaph." "I will" said the youth "But what shall I write;" write, replied Mr. Cox, "Let a thousand fall before Africa be given up." He fell asleep, July 21st, 1833, but—

> Victorious his fall, for he rose as he fell,
> With Jesus, his Master, in glory to dwell:
> He has passed o'er the stream, and reached the bright coast,
> He fell like a martyr—he died at his post.

Father Hersey hearing the news of the demise of his friend and brother in Christ, determined to take the post vacated by his death; and in six months and six days thereafter, being the 27th day of January, he stood by the grave of the fallen hero. Who can tell what were his emotions on this eventful occasion? The memory of the sainted dead is ever a source of true inspiration; all the thoughts that a godly life can awaken, are reproduced from the cold, inanimate ashes of one who has served humanity; but in so doing, has been animated by paramount duty to God. There is an incense from 'the grave of a righteous man ever fragrant:

> "And can we the word of his exit forget,
> O no; they are fresh in our memory yet;
> An example so brilliant shall never be lost;
> We will fall in the work, we will die at our post.

Melville B. Cox planted the Methodist Church at Monrovia, Africa, April, 1833. His death prevented the successful prosecution of his christian benevolence Afterwards, John Hersey appeared upon the scene, and through his efforts, the first Methodist Episcopal Church was erected at Cape Palmas, April, 1834. (Thus far we have anticipated the narrative of the subject of this memoir; his connection with the Liberian scheme is full of interest.)

The Maryland Colonization Society was incorporated during the year 1832. On the 24th of March, of the same year, there was held in the chambers of Judge Brice, at the Court House in Baltimore city, a meeting of the persons named in the Act of Incorporation of the Maryland State Colonization Society, which Act of Incorporation was passed by the Legislative Assembly of 1831. Those who assembled on this occasion under a published call, were, George Hoffman, Nicholas Brice, John Gibson, Peter Hoffman, Charles Howard, Thomas Elliott, Luke Tiernan, Moses Sheppard, Soloman Ettinge and John H. B. Latrobe. No one who is familiar with the past history of the "Monumental City," can scan the above list of names without recognizing the fact, that it embraced worthy and eminent citizens, who in their day have creditably adorned the professional and other pursuits to which they devoted themselves. They were men of liberal ideas, and meant well in this particular work of charity. George Hoffman was the presiding officer of this meeting, with John H. B. Latrobe as secretary. At a subsequent meeting, Sept. 9th, 1833, Doctor James Hall was selected as an Agent of the society by the Board of Managers, to superintend the settlement and colonization of those colored people who were willing to establish their homes and abide by their fortunes at Cape Palmas, on the south-west coast of Africa; and John Hersey was selected to act as Agent in Maryland. with authority to retain $——— out of collections to be made by him, as compensation for the services he was to render in the hazardous undertaking to which he was now committed. But the aforegoing action of the Board of Managers does not appear as final, for on the 9th of October, 1833, on motion of Mr. Williams it was resolved, that the subject of the amount of compensation to be awarded Mr. Hersey, who was now selected as assistant Agent, be postponed; the mover of the resolution assigning as a reason therefor, that the assistant Agent does not desire to stipulate as to salary, but prefers to wait and see what will be the results of the enterprise, and the fruits of his labors expended in its behalf.

Here we have exemplified a trait of character always prominent in Father Hersey's life ; his was no sordid soul, cankered by the love of worldly gain. The noble impulse of his generous nature soared away heavenward ; and embarking in the service of the cause of colonization, he sought but one consummation, the redemption of his fallen fellow man, and the fastening of his allegiance to Christ.

All needed preparations having been made, Thursday morning, November 24th, 1833, at the hour of 9 o'clock, the brig ANN, under charge of Captain———, sailed from the port of Baltimore, laden with a cargo of supplies and merchandise. There were eighteen emigrants on board, accompanied by the Agent of the society, Dr. Hall, and his assistant, Father Hersey; also the Revs. Messrs. Williams and Wynkoop, of the American Board of Foreign Missions, who accompanied the expedition to represent that cause.

Those who sailed to make Liberia their clime and home, were Joshua Stewart, 24 years of age; and Louisa, his wife, 23 years old, and their infant son, Joseph, one year old; James Stewart, 19 years old; Pormaly Delworth, 15; William Conell, 25; Francis, his wife, 31; Charles, their son, two years old: all of whom were from the city of Baltimore. The remainder were from Frederick County, Md., viz.: Jacob Gross, 45, and Rosanna, his wife, 33, with their children, Clarsisa, 10 years old, Margaret, 8, Nancy, 5, Caroline, 3, and Roasnna, eight weeks old; Nicholas Thompson, 40 years old; Oden Nelson, 19 years old. A perusal of the aforegoing list of names and ages, will be attended with pregnant suggestions; what the fate that awaited them proved, no line of ours can tell; but they were the vanguard of a scheme which has not yet been totally effaced from recollection

The following notice of the sailing of the brig *Ann* is from the files of the *Baltimore American*, and appeared in that journal the day subsequent to her departure:

"The brig Ann, Captain———, cleared yesterday and dropped down the river, and will proceed with the first fair wind to the west coast of Africa. She is chartered, it will be recollected, by the Maryland Colonization Society, and carries out the emigrants and missionaries, who design to settle a new colony, which is to be established at Cape Palmas, under the auspices of our own State Society. They carry with them the prayers of many for a safe voyage and prosperous issue of their important undertaking."

Sea voyages are not always pleasant when surrounded by agreeable associates of a congenial nature: whether Father Hersey's was, can best be described in the following letter to Mr. McKenney, General Agent for the Society in Maryland, of dated at sea, the 14th of January, 1834:

"We have had thus far a boisterous, tedious and most unpleasant passage, nor can we form any correct idea, when it will end. For your own edification and the benefit of the Maryland Colonization Society, and not to murmur on my part, I will mention. Soon after we left the Capes, the Captain became enraged in the cabin and poured out a dreadful volley of oaths and blasphemies, expressed in the most vulgar and uncouth manner. As soon as the storm abated a degree, I observed that it was exceedingly unpleasant to some of us, who were his passengers and confined to his cabin, to hear such oaths and bitter imprecations; that we would esteem it a peculiar favor if he would refrain. He immediately flew into a most violent rage and cursed us all (myself in particular), in the most vulgar and outrageous manner."

During the voyage, circumstances seem to have taken place, that rendered it impossible for Father Hersey to continue in the service of the Society, he refers to the subject himself in a letter dated January 27th, 1834, wherein it is stated:

"After a passage of sixty one days, we reached Monrovia. I have concluded to sacrifice my own feelings and continue on with the expedition to Cape Palmas. To do otherwise would be a serious injury to the cause." * * * * * *

I calculate on remaining with the expedition until it is settled and secured on the continent at Cape Palmas. * *

To remain in my present situation, I cannot; if I am alive and in this country when your next expedition arrives, and the Board of Managers have no objection, I will thank them to provide a passage for me to the United States.

February 3rd, of the same year, writing to the Hon. John H. B. Latrobe, from Monrovia, he states the "The brig *Ann* with all who embarked on board in the harbor of Baltimore, arrived in health and safety at Monrovia, Jan. 27th., after a tedious passage of sixty-one days. I regret very much that I am compelled at this early period, respectfully to resign my situation as assistant Agent of the Maryland Colonization Society. If it should be deemed necessary for me to assign a reason for this step, perhaps it will be sufficient to impeach myself. It is from an honest conviction that I cannot be really serviceable to the colony or society, that I have been influenced to adopt this course. The complexion of a family is not generally, if at all, reviewed from a sub-

ordinate member thereof, but from the parent or master
who has supreme control of the household. In my present
situation, there is no definite duty assigned to me; consequently, I can have no actual authority, but must from
principle of righteousness and honor, obey the commands, and
wishes of —————— ——————, who does not regard the Bible as
the word of God. If my life is spared, I shall remain
with the expedition until the emigrants are settled, and after
that object is effected, I shall consider my connection with
the society and colony dissolved. I am pleased and agree-
ably disappointed at the prospect which Africa presents
as a comfortable, happy home for her degraded and oppres-
sed children now breathing in our christian land. I think
there cannot be a rational doubt, but that the country
generally, will be as healthful for our colored people after
they have become acclimated, as any part of our Southern
States; it is equally certain, that if the principles of righteousness and peace are sacredly observed on our part, the
natives will meet us in same friendly spirit. Africa must,
and will be located and become a christian country, and to
her alone can we rationally look for a place of refuge for her
unfortunate sons, whose present condition is a disgrace to
our own country. The cause is good and must prosper,
however unjustly it may at first be managed; therefore, I
would say to your philanthropic society, go on, let no difficulty discourage you in this noble enterprise. You shall
have my best wishes and feeble prayers for your prosperity
and entire success at home and in Africa. May the blessings
of Almighty God rest upon your society, individually and
collectively. May your efforts be crowned with most happy
and honorable consequences.''

On the 6th of February, 1834, the brig *Ann* reached
Cape Palmas. The natives had been apprised of her coming,
and on the 13th, a grand council was held, to debate in relation to the purchase of the territory; the negotiations
were successful; after which, the emigrants were landed, and
work was at once begun to establish the colony. The Board
had sent the frame and materials for the erection of an
Agency House. It was at once built; other buildings rapidly arose, and within a month after the first landing, the settlement began to wear the appearance of a compact and
comfortable village. In all the enterprises, Mr. Hersey was
a conspicuous worker; he was not only content to give

attention to the temporary concerns of the colonists, but through his efforts, there was built a meeting house of the Methodist denomination, the first temple dedicated to the worship of Almighty God that was reared upon the territory of the society.

Father Hersey, about the first of April, 1834, to the great sorrow and regret of the colonists, embarked on the schooner *Edgar*, and set sail from Cape Palmas, for the United States. After a passage of forty-three days, he landed in New York city, on the 27th of June, 1834. Here he was detained a few weeks; after which he proceeded to Baltimore, and on the 21st of July he made the following written report to the Board of Managers of the Maryland State Colonization Society:

"Having been informed by the Captain of the schooner *Edgar*, that Dr. Hall had visited his vessel in person, and gave him a letter for the society, I concluded certainly, that he had made a communication to your Board. I regret sincerely the circumstances, which constrained me to resign my situation in the colony. The reasons which led me to adopt that course were most painful to my feelings, but I forbear to say anything on that subject. It was not my own personal feeling, but a duty I owed to Almighty God and his church on earth, which influenced my conduct. After sending by the ship "Jupiter," my resignation, I continued with the expedition until the new colony was permanently settled at Cape Palmas. As my resignation was unexpected to myself, as well as to your Board, I shall present no claim for my expenses; the whole amount of which, from the time I left Baltimore, until I arrived in New York, did not exceed thirty dollars. I gave several poor colonists a little assistance. I believe, could you know the circumstances, you would esteem it a favor to pay; the whole amount, including several items since my arrival, will be not less than sixty dollars. I only mention for your information; I do not put it as a claim. May your laudable efforts to promote the cause of humanity be crowned with complete and honorable success."

The Board acted kindly and considerately towards Father Hersey. At its meeting on the 3rd of May, on motion of Mr. Latrobe, his resignation was accepted; the corresponding Secretary was directed to address him a letter of thanks for his interest in the cause of African Colonization, and ten-

dering such remuneration for his time and services as might
be acceptable to him. This was succeeded by the presentation of an amount greater than the unpretentious expendi-
tures, which was so modestly communicated to the Board.

CHAPTER VI.

Return From Liberia.

When Father Hersey left New York, he tarried a short
time in Philadelphia; in both of these cities, he was the
guest of numerous friends. When he reached Baltimore in
July, his health was much impaired. He retired to the
hospitable home of his old class-leader, and a local minister,
Rev. John L. Reese; here he was quite ill. Sister Reese was
constant and untiring in her ministrations towards his recov-
ery, and was rewarded, by his restoration to health, after
many weeks of painful illness. When his strength was sufficiently regained, he entered upon the active duties of a
missionary. He also attended to the publication and sale of
various books, of which he was the author; this was to him
a most inviting field of ministerial labor; he visited the sick
and needy, and administered comfort to the dying. He was
always ready to assist the city pastors in their works of
revival. During the summer months he visited very many
camp meetings, and as a herald of the cross, was its earnest
exponent.

He was an itinerant in the true construction of that word;
when he had performed his work at one place, he did not
longer remain, but hastened to some other post of duty; he
was often heard to say, "I must be about my Father's
business."

He frequently related his sufferings and triumphs, and
many an account did he give, of his missionary efforts in
Africa. At times he was despondent; the dark picture of
life would be placed before him. One such incident is
related as having taken place in the class-room. He was
very despondent in his experience, and shaded it with a
tinge of melancholy. Bro. Reese, his class-leader, tersely

replied, "John, do you ever expect to see the time, when you can say, well done." The response was instantaneous— "No," and as quick flashed the retort, "well then, stop complaining." But he would soon rally, and his word was a mighty power

Rev. Henry Butler who was at a camp meeting, held on the Calvert Circuit, during the year 1835, heard a sermon of great power and force, which was succeeded by an exhortation from Father Hersey, on the hymn—"And must I be to judg ment brought;"—the effect produced, he says, was electrical, and so powerful was the impression, that years afterwards the solemn admonitions rang in his ears with all the force he experienced when they first fell from the lips of the speaker.

Father Hersey, in 1836, identified himself with the old Light Street Church, and became a member of its Quarterly Conference, and was a member of Brother J. L. Reese's class; the same year he connected himself with the local preachers' and exhorters' association, but owing to his many engagements and extensive missionary travels, he was not assigned in the plan of appointments to any special work; but it was known, that no one was more thoroughly engaged in the Master's vineyard.

During the year 1838, Jacob Gruber was engaged in superintending the erection of the Orchard Street Colored Methodist Church, Father Hersey became interested in this work, and bestowed much of his time and assistance in helping on the enterprise, nor did he desist from manual labor; he was seen handling bricks, passing them to the men who were putting them in position. From the old Dallas Street Methodist Church, he procured a piece of railing, and had it used in connection with the steps leading to the basement; his motive for this act is apparent. He had great reverence for the fathers, and the places where they had held their ministrations. Dallas Street Church, at present the oldest surviving memorial of Methodism in Baltimore, was one of the cradles in which that denomination was rocked in its infancy; within its walls, the sound of Asbury's voice had resounded, and from its altars, souls had been redeemed who are numbered with the inhabitants of the better land. In all the varied responsibilities imposed upon himself, John

Hersey did not forget to trace the tendency of the church, and discuss her proper policy; writing in 1839, upon the signs of the times, he thus expresses himself:

"I am convinced that much more might be done within the pale of the church, than we are now doing; it is mortifying in the extreme to see the church become an object of commiseration to the wicked; we must act independently of the pecuniary aid of the unregenerate, or we must fall; the enemies of the cross may, and will smile in prosperity, but they may also, and will assuredly, stab in adversity. Were we careful to bring into active operation, the sinews of the church, and lop off all our excesses, the kingdom of the world would very soon fall before us, and speedily become the kingdoms of our God and his Christ. A minister of the gospel within the bounds of the Virginia Conference, in the past year, has traveled about three thousand miles on foot, and preached generally six times a week. His entire expenses (exclusive of postage) did not amount to ten dollars; nor was it a desperate effort on his part; for the last four or five years, his movements have been nearly the same; his numerous and kind friends cheerfully gave him his food and raiment, with which every follower of Christ should be satisfied."

We are indebted to the Rev. J. H. Brown, D. D., of the Baltimore Conference, for the following:

"Rev. John Hersey I knew as far back as 1833. When I was first stationed in Baltimore, he was then in the vigor of his age, and in the heighth of his usefulness. I had heard of him before as a man, of great piety and self-denial; I recollect his appointments for preaching at 5 o'clock in the morning; I have heard him preach in different places, and on various occasions, with great unction and power; he visited from house to house, praying with the people, and warning them, not with words only, but by example; I went to the ship to see him take his departure from our shores for dark Africa; he went to Cape Palmas in connection with, or under the direction of the Maryland Colonization Society. In Africa, he remained a short time; he became discouraged from one cause or another, and returned; he seemed persuaded that *his true mission* was to the churches at *home*, to warn them of their worldliness. I was with him at a camp meeting, in

1835, near Fredericksburg, in old Virginia; the meeting was memorable on many accounts. One incident I will mention: The Abolition question had produced great commotion in Virginia; travelers were searched in Fredericksburg and other places, to see if they had Abolition documents about them for circulation; word was sent from Richmond to Fredericksburg, to have Hersey arrested; Dr. Wolford (a most estimable citizen), came to me at the camp meeting, and informed me of it, and requested me to tell Mr. Hersey to quietly leave the ground, and that if anything should occur, he would address the people, and show that Mr. Hersey was no Abolitionist. Bro. Hersey took his departure next morning, and wept, saying, "This is the first time I ever was charged with being an enemy to my country." The next day another order came from Richmond, not to arrest him, that they were mistaken concerning his book on *Slavery*, which was mainly a compilation of speeches delivered in the Legislature of Virginia; they burnt in the meantime, a box of those books in the public square, in their haste and their rage; they admitted they were mistaken concerning the books, and countermanded their order for his arrest, but he was never indemnified for the books.

Bro. Hersey baptised my first-born child in Shippensburg, Pa., which we named Charles Watson; the day will never be forgotten: It was in 1862, I think, when Bro. Hersey came to this city for the last time; he saw the clouds gathering over our national sky, and admonished us of the approaching storm. He saw and felt his end was rapidly coming. He appointed a parting meeting in the Sabbath School room on the south side of old Light St. Church; it was a meeting of preachers: I was present. It was one of those occasions never to be forgotten; Bro. Hersey was weak, extremely weak. He sat during his address; he told us he was going to Pennsylvania to die; it was a marvelous parting. It would have made one of the most impressive pictures; he died in the following November. I wrote, by request of the preachers' meeting, the recorded minutes of his death.

In connection with the subject of Father Hersey's troubles in Virginia, growing out of the slavery agitation, the following letter from him to Messrs. Armstrong & Berry, of Baltimore, his book publishers, of date, September 12th, 1835, has some bearing upon the subject : at that time he seems to have shared with many other patriotic men, apprehension of the storm, that since then bursted with such unrelenting fury over the land; he says, "My way has recently been very much hedged up in selling books : it is almost impossible to form a correct idea of the fearful state of society. I should before this, have left the State, and turned my steps towards Ohio, or Pennsylvania, but have thought it most prudent to remain here until the storm subsides a little, should that ever be. As I have written a book on the black absorbing subject. and distributed them publicly, I have become an object of peculiar hatred; I believe however, that the God, whose I am, and whom I serve, will deliver and protect me from all danger. I only regret that my way is hedged up, and when I have fully delivered my own soul with the people, if my life is spared, I shall leave Virginia. The Lord's will be done : the signs of the times are truly dark, and ominous of evil ; they are not surprising, nor unexpected to me, however ; we are not what we should be, and God will visit us in wrath ; nor is there any way to avert the storm, but by imitating the conduct of Ninevites. May heaven save our own happy favored land ; the Lord in mercy keeps my mind in peace, and stayed on the Lord Jesus.

CHAPTER VII,

CURIOUS BOY.

About the year 1835, a camp meeting was held in a grove situated about three miles north of Barnesville, in Montgomery County, Maryland. The grove was on a beautiful plain, at the foot of the Sugar Loaf Mountain in Frederick County. On Sunday, the day was calm, clear and beautiful ; the majestic blue cone, queen of mountains in Maryland, was arrayed in all its natural glories, as if ready to join in worship; below, its proud summit and the blue hills along the river at its base, were none the less lovely and glorious. Over every hill and along every valley, worshippers poured in toward the consecrated grove. Two circles of tents en-

compassed the inner circle, wherein seats were provided for
the vast thousands who came to worship; on this Sabbath
morning, crowds flocked into this great circle, and occupied
the seats, so that before the hour of ten o'clock, scarcely
another could pass in. Some great interest appeared to
draw the crowd : some great spirit moved it, yet nothing unusual was advertised, no great preacher was expected to hold
forth ; good order and solemnity reigned on the ground, for
a strange spirit marshaled the people.

A curious boy pressed his slim form between two tents, and
gained the inner circle, which was an inland sea of anxious
faces, fanned by gentle breezes, from the summit of the tall,
blue cone of the great mountain. He passed along through
the crowd, and halted at a tree, in full view of the preacher's
stand. In the stand sat about six plain men, whom he took
to be preachers. The crowd thickened, until the observant
boy was about to be forced from his hold on the tree, or to
climb it to avoid suffocation ; he maintained his ground,
however, and the "guards" went out to urge the people to
take closer quarters, which they did, and thousands more
came in with a rush It was now eleven o'clock, and the
presence of the great crowd appeared to be due to the fact,
that a camp meeting was a new thing in this locality. All
eyes, now and then, turned to the rear, as if tired of suspense, yet they saw no stranger object, than a spare, thin
man, whose way was being opened by a "guard." "Who is
that ?" whispers a thousand voices ; the guard has left him,
and he proceeds alone. "Where will he go ?" is the next
inquiry, and "Is he drunk?" is a third ; but he does not heed
the voice of the curious, nor the flutter of a lady's fan-
Look at that old rye straw hat, that blue cotton shad belly
coat, that blue single-breasted vest, and pantaloons of the
same blue material, which reach almost down to the top of
his shoes. "Lock !" exclaims that boy, "he is going down
to the preachers' stand ; we'll have some fun to see the
preachers put him out." There ! he has opened the altar
gate and going in. He is crazy ! now for the fun. Look !
he is into the stand ! he is going up the steps, but the
preachers do not look like they will put him out. Just see !
they shake his hand cordially, and point him to the middle
seat. He places his weather beaten, rye straw hat carefully
under the bench , that old hat has no band on it, and no crape

on the crown. Look! his coat is supplied with "hooks and
eyes" instead of buttons! Now he reaches down for his hat,
he has forgotten something ; from it he takes a madder colored cotton handkerchief, with which he gracefully wipes
his perspiring brow. A preacher rises from his seat, advan-
to the front of the stand, and taking the Bible and hymn
book, hands them to the stranger. Wonder dances on tip-toe,
and the great sea of faces is turbulent. A minister advances
and announces that Rev. John Hersey would preach. "They
are making fun of that old fellow," said the boy, "so as to
induce him to leave without a forcible ejection." Not so
however ; he read a hymn, and it was sung ; he prayed, and
read another ; advancing to the front, he turned his eyes on
the Bible and read—

"Mene, Mene, Tekel Upharsin" ·

He paused and covered the vast audience with a glance,
and wonder arose higher and higher, and the silence which
ensued was oppressive. He relieved it by saying "You will
find the words of my text in the 25th verse of the 5th chap.
of the prophecy of Daniel." "They were written on the
wall by the Spirit of God," said he, "in the language of
heaven. No scholar present at the feast of Belshazzar ever
saw such words in the babbling tongues of the earth. They
were to be found only in the vocabularies of angels of ser-
phim of God."

He enchanted the audience by the words of his lips for
two hours and a quarter; and the writer well remembers what
a thrilling shout went up when Belshazzar and Daniel were
weighed in the balances. "I am ravished with delight," said
the speaker, "down with all glory, down! Daniel out-
weighs the proudest king of the East. To God be all the
glory; amen and amen."

CHAPTER VIII.

MISCELLANEOUS SUBJECTS.

In 1839, Armstrong & Berry published in one volume, several of his works, namely : *"Importance of Small Things"*,

"*Signs of the Times*", *Inquiry into the Character and Condition of our Children*", "*Advice to Christian Parents*", "*Some Remarks on Baptism*," and "*Life of De Renty.*" These works, nearly all of which had previously been published separately, and some of which had run through several editions, were eagerly sought after by the people, anxious to learn the views of this wonderful and inimitable man. They also invoked dogmatic criticism, but their author was their successful defender, and Father Hersey died with the consciousness, though publicly unexpressed, that he had as successfully ingrafted his sentiments upon the religious literature of the country by his pen, as he had paved the way for a new *era* in the theory and practice of moral and perfect christianity by his chaste and logical reasoning—by his upright and truly religious walk and conversation. Most of the works of Father Hersey having gone out of print or being exceedingly scarce, we subjoin some extracts giving his views at length upon lead· ing subjects of social interest, as well as rules for the government of children by christian parents.

On Costly dress.

Upon the subject of costly dress, we opine that Bro. Hersey's crude ideas will not commend themselves to the fashionably dressed audiences of our modern churches.

He thus forcibly sets forth his views :

"Fine and costly apparel is not only forbidden in the holy word of God, but reason and common sense condemn the practice, for a number of reasons, some of which we will notice. It leads to *hypocrisy*. It feeds the flames of *pride* and *vanity*. It *robs the poor, and robs our own souls*. It sets a pernicious example to others. It weakens, if it does not destroy, two of the most important principles of the christian religion—faith and charity. If this view of the subject be correct, then *dress*, is not a trifling consideration, but a point of the deepest interest to every rational, affectionate, human being. Rich and costly apparel leads us into hypocrisy. It is a universal custom among mankind, to judge of strangers by their appearance. If we see an individual dressed in old or coarse clothes, we at once conclude that he is *poor* ; or if he is ornamented with fine and costly apparel, we as naturally conclude that he is rich. Now, there are very few of us who are willing to be *poor*, or even to be thought *poor* by our neighbors, or even by strangers ; hence the ardent desire to *ape* the appearance of the *rich*. It is therefore, an irresistible conclusion, that the *poor person* who assumes the garb of a *rich man*, makes himself a hypocrite.

Do not make or accept of fine caps, red shoes, or variegated frocks, or vests for your children. You would thereby cultivate the poisonous principles of *deception*, whilst you cut up the beautiful flowers and fruits of *innocence* and *truth ;* and nothing can be expected but a crop of shame and disgrace. The deception, however, does not terminate with others, but extends to ourselves. Almost every man, and certainly every child, will think himself better than another, because he is better dressed.

It is not surprising that *fallen man* should wish to pass off a counterfeit upon others; but that he should practice the same fatal deception on himself, is truly astonishing, and shows us clearly how careful we should teach our children in early life to avoid and despise fine dress. Christian parents know full well that God has made of one flesh, the whole human family. The poor man is, in reality, as good as the rich man—they are made of the same materials, and by the same hands; they breathe the same air; and must mingle together in the same grave; therefore; that which induces one to think himself naturally better than another, must naturally lead him into error and self-delusion.

Make as many experiments as you please, and the result will prove this proposition. Dress the slave child in fine clothes, and he will look down with contempt upon those who are dressed in an inferior garb; this will be the invariable result with all classes and conditions in society—the rich, the poor, the bound or the free,

Pride is an abomination in the sight of God. Pride will as certainly shut us out of heaven, as the crime of murder. Will you encourage and strengthen that principle in your children, which must be destroyed, or it must forever destroy them ? Dress your child of two years old in a very fine garb, and then take off those glittering follies, and supply their place with coarse clothes, and the child will discover marks of mortification and displeasure; this fact proves that if they do not engender, at least they feed the flame of pride. A youth will not willingly go into company unless his clothes are as fine as those worn by his companions ; but if they are finer than his associates, he makes no objection, but at once assumes an air of confidence, which proves that he considers himself better than his coarse dressed friends. Nay, make an honest experiment with yourself, put on coarse homespun apparel, a wool hat, and other articles of a similar cast, and then go into the society of your rich and fine dressed acquaintances, and you will feel mortified and degraded. You may say, that this sensation does not necessarily proceed from pride, but from a proper and due respect for the feelings and character of your friends. But whatever may be the source from which it proceeds, you evidently feel *pain* and *mortification* yourself, which proves that there is an unheled ulcer near your heart; this monster may be called pride, or you may give it any other name, yet it is an *impure* and *unholy* affection, which fine dress is calculated to feed and keep alive.

The Lord as a kind and merciful father, provides for the wants and comforts of all his children; some of them are more judicious than others, in the management of his goods; therefore, he trusts one with more, and another with less than enough to meet their real wants, that the fortunate may regard and sympathise with the unfortunate, and administer to their necessities. God has also graciously promised to give a rich reward to the steward who distributes his goods to the poor and distressed part of his children; therefore, every cent we expend in *dress* for any other purpose than to protect us from the inclemency of the weather, is that much taken from the suffering and afflicted part of our heavenly Father's family. Would you like to see one of your children take your money without your permission, and expend it in dissipation, when his sister was in need of food and raiment? Would he not be robbing his sister? Must you not also admit on principles of sound logic, that costly dress robs children? And can a robber be received into heaven? Would you willingly and knowingly receive such a character into your family?

But the evil does not stop with *robbing* the *poor*, it beggars our *own souls!* The time required to make and adjust fine clothes, might have been spent on our knees in humble prayer, or in reading, or conversing about heavenly and divine things, receiving and imparting knowledge: the money required to purchase those articles, might have been expended in the purchase of books, calculated to enrich the

mind with heavenly knowledge, which would throw a rich
and beautiful garment around the soul, that would continue
to shine forever in the eternal world.

Fine dress, however, robs the soul in different ways; it
produces a continual dissipation of thought—a restless dissatisfied mind; it naturally sets us to watching the ever varying
fashions of the day, it disqualifies the mind for solid, serious, profitable reflection, and urges our thoughts and eyes
in ceaseless rounds to see who is looking at us, and what
they think of our appearance.   Oh, thou aerial god of this
world—*dress*; thou fatal, potent snare of the devil, how
many immortal souls hast thou robbed, and plunged naked
into the lake of unquenchable fire ?

Costly dress presents a pernicious example to others. You
are rich, and can afford to dress your children well. Waiv-
ing the argument already advanced, that the silver and gold.
all belong to God, and we are bound in justice to dispose of
it *only* in accordance with His will and direction ; you must
acknowledge that we are social beings, and should not only
consult our individual convenience, or the comfort of our
family exclusively, but we should, as far as practicable,
administer to the happiness of the whole human family—at
least, as far as our influence extends. But if you clothe
your children in costly apparel, because you are able to do so
you exhibit a ruinous example to others.

Many of your neighbors are *poor*, yet they well-know,
that by nature, they are as good as you and your children, and they will *naturally* make an effort to render their
children as respectable in appearance as yours ; some of them
will run in debt, and jeopardise their property, and destroy
their peace of mind, to keep pace with you, to follow your
pernicious *example.*

Others will be unable to procure credit; they will feel discouraged, and sit down in a state of hopeless despair, and
look upon you with a degree of secret envy and contempt;
others again, will be led into acts of dishonesty, to gain those
perishing marks of distinguished folly which your family
bears.   Thus your fatal EXAMPLE *destroys the peace of mind,
and vitiates the morals, and mars the happiness of the whole
neighborhood.* Fine dress has a most unhappy effect on *poor
people*; it not only robs their minds and dissipates their
thoughts, but it inflates them with pride and vanity, which

renders them truly ridiculous in their conduct and appearance. Do, therefore, we beseech you, set them a better example.

Costly apparel has a tendency to weaken, if it does not destroy, two of the most important christian principles connected with our religious character—FAITH and CHARITY.

The Lord Jesus commands us to *deny* ourselves *daily*, and take up *our cross* and *follow Him*, or we cannot be his disciple; neither can we have any confidence, or evangelical living *faith*, if we obey not his words. But there is no *self-denial* whatever, in wearing fine clothes; neither can we *believe* that in this particular we *follow Christ's* example. He was born, and laid in a manger, and said of himself, "The foxes have holes, and the birds of the air have nests, but the Son of man hath not where to lay his head." He was literally, when upon earth, a *poor man*, and acquainted with sorrow, consequently, he could not have dressed either in fine or fashionable clothes; as *poor people,* when they are *consistent* in their character, *never wear costly apparel.* Christ could not act *inconsistently;* consequently, he must have worn such clothes as all *honest consistent* poor people wear. Nor can we possibly say, with confidence, that we even desire *honestly* to follow Christ's example when we wear *costly* or *fine* clothes; therefore, it must *weaken our faith,* and "without *faith*" it is impossible to please God." Unbelief destroys our peace and happiness, and greatly dishonors God. Nearly all of us who profess to be Christ's followers, feel the deleterious effects of this soul-destroying sin; and yet, parents will cherish and strengthen it in their children's hearts every day. Oh! parents, be not so cruel and unwise. But the evil extends still further; costly apparel is calculated to destroy the fairest features in the christian's character—*charity, love.* However necessary and important it may be that our *faith* should be strong and unwavering, it is still more so that our *love* should be *pure* and *ardent,* and constantly burning on the altar of our hearts; but if we *love the world,* the love of God is not in us. Let any individual indulge in the use of fine clothes for a given time—say several years, and let him be called on to give them up, and substitute plain, coarse apparel in their place, and he will clearly perceive that his *affections* are riveted to these foolish and unhallowed things; nor will he part with them withou feeling severe pangs, and very great reluctance Does not this prove that he *loves* them *?* Those who love God, must love their brother also   The beloved disciple says : "If any man say, I love God, and hateth his brother, he is a liar. For he that loveth not his brother, whom he hath seen, how can he love God, whom he hath not seen."

Costly clothes operate as a barrier to our love, especially for poor people; if we love them, they cannot love us. *Reciprocity* cannot exist without *seeming* inferiority.   Honorable love admits of no distinction ; perfect love is incompatible with anything but perfect equality of character. Fine clothes draw an *unholy* line of distinction between those who wear, and those who cannot procure them.

The principles, dispositions and affections which we cultivate and establish in life, cannot be laid aside in death.   In heaven there will be no distinction—there all are *cne,* and God is *all in all.*   Poor Lazarus is there, and all the pious, holy poor people, who ever lived on earth.   Your dress drew a line of demarcation in this world.   Here you would not, there you possibly cannot associate with them.   Jesus says, "Whatsoever you do to one of the least of these, my brethren, you do it unto Me."   In dressing to gratify pride, and public sentiment, do you not set at defiance, the command, and reject the love of the Lord Jesus Christ.

It is therefore a rational and inevitable conclusion, that costly dress has a direct tendency to destroy our *charity* ; *to divide and impair* and consequently, extinguish our love for man and *God.*

On Early Rising.

Father Hersey was one of those most industrious of workers.   He arose and performed his morning devotions, usually lasting one hour, before the early dawn.   His journeying to and fro over his circuits, were discarding the usual methods of conveyance, performed on foot, and when not eating or sleeping, he was invariably engaged in reading, writing, or other profitable and useful employment; but he taught not only by example, but laid down some excellent precepts upon the subject, which we subjoin for the edification of our readers:

"Diligently teach children to avoid the sluggard's bed ;

teach them to consider *idleness* as the principal source and
parent of every evil. *Disgrace* and *misery* and *poverty* and
ruin, are the legitimate fruits of indolence. Carefully guard
them not to approach this dead lake, whence thousands have
been swallowed up in destruction. Idleness is not only the
direct road to poverty and shame, but it leads to dissipation of every kind—to gambling, drunkenness, theft and
murder; therefore, receive your Divine Master's counsel,
and do not lay up treasures for your children, nor suffer
them to be attended by servants; teach them, from their
infancy, to wait on themselves—to give no trouble to any
one."

A modern writer makes some trite remarks on this subject—he says "And as to *love*, it cannot live for more than
a month or two towards a LAZY WOMAN, in the breast of a
man of spirit. No beauty, no modesty, no accomplishments,
are a compensation for the effects of laziness in women ;
and of all the proofs of laziness, none is more unequivocal,
as that of lying late in bed."

"Make any sacrifice on earth, rather than raise up an idle
child to be a pest to society, a disgrace to mankind, a reproach to his Creator, and a curse to himself and all connected with him."

"Industry is the certain road to *wealth* and *wisdom*, to
virtue and *happiness*; teach them to believe this doctrine,
and they will be the better prepared to practice it."

"Among all the unfortunate and unhappy beings on earth,
perhaps there are none more so, than those whom we generally term *poor gentlemen—to dig they cannot*, and to *beg* they
are *ashamed*. For them there is generally but one alterna-
tive—either *suicide*, or *robbery*; the latter profession *generally, if not always* commences at the *gambling tables*."

"Therefore, whatever else you may omit in the management of your children, endeavor by all possible means to
instil into them, habits of industry."

On Economy.

Whilst Bro. Hersey inculcated the fundamental principles
of economy by precept, and illustrated it by his practice even
so vigorously as to incur the suspicion of parsimoniousness,
he did not fail to hold views on generosity which he not only

expressed, but practised in a manner which does honor alike to his head and heart. He says, "Great care must be taken that while you are diligently engaged in cultivating the principles of economy in your children's hearts, that the bitter, poisonous weeds of parsimony and covetousness do not spring up and grow in the same soil. The character and ultimate prospects of a miser are more despicable and desperate than even the character and prospects of the spendthrift "

"Guard against selfishness; develop and increase a noble, generous disposition. Our Divine Master taught his disciples that it was "more blessed to give than to receive." Never receive a present, however small, even an apple, without dividing it. Think nothing little or unimportant which will have a tendency to create or confirm one of the most noble and excellent principles connected with our fallen nature; when the principles of benevolence and generosity are wanting, there can be no genuine honor or greatness of soul. A mean, contracted, parsimonious disposition, withers and blights with the frost of death, that soul which God made in His own image, that it might bloom forever in immortal beauty. While you are engaged in inculcating the principles of rigid economy, do not forget to teach your children, that it is not for their benefit exclusively, but for the benefit and comfort of all the family; while you are inculcating the noble principles of generosity, you must not at the expense of the more important one of justice."

"Economy consists in doing that only, which is right and proper to be done, and doing it in the best and most judicious manner, and at the very time it should be done. Do not run in debt for anything; there is more waste and extravagence connected with the system of credit, than people are generally aware of. Credit frequently induces us to buy, when we would not otherwise do so, and always at an enhanced price; but pay day must come, and with it frequently comes much vexation and trouble; therefore, teach your children early in life to observe that wholesome scripture precept, "owe no man anything." If you wish to enjoy peace of mind, and peace with your neighbors, carefully observe this excellent precept; in the course of a very short life, a large amount may be saved in this way alone, besides the peace and comfort it must afford every honest heart. Let your motto be, "Let nothing be wasted." Do not suffer your children to waste even a crumb of bread, nor to throw anything, even a piece of paper or a string, into the fire; but parents, whilst you teach your children by precept, do not, by your example, teach them a different lesson. Do not waste your father's money for useless ornaments, either in your houses, or on your persons : real economy admits of no negligence, or carelessness, as these lead to waste. Every article should be in its proper place ; everything about your house and person should be sweet and clean. Our conduct and appearance will generally form a correct index of the heart."

"A rational principle of economy will admit of no waste of time, or money, or property. We should be as economical of our words as of our goods ; the gift of speech is a blessing, which should not be abused : we should be swift to hear, but slow to speak."

On Justice.

"Be just before you are generous," is a motto aptly illustrated by Father Hersey's action. In early life he failed in business, leaving considerable outstanding liabilities. From that time, he practiced the most rigid economy of dress and diet, he indulged in generosity judiciously, until by abstemiousness and frugality, he saved enough to discharge the long standing obligation, which he did, much to the astonishment of the heirs of his creditor, who had been so long dead, that his claims upon Bro. Hersey were unknown to his representatives. In discussing the claims of justice, Bro. Hersey says : "The principle of *justice* cannot be *impaired* innocently ; therefore, great pains must be taken to implant it permanently, and to cultivate it assiduously in your children's hearts. Explain and enforce the principle very clearly and carefully ; show them that a *desire* to get more for any article they may have to sell, than its real value, or to purchase anything for less than its worth, discovers an unjust and dishonorable principle in the sight of God, their heavenly Father. Suffer them never to equivocate, nor use many words in their transactions one with another ; let them know that to ask any honorable man to take less than the price he asks for an article they may wish to purchase of him, should be considered an insult, and a dark reflection upon his character. Do not suffer them to take even a pin, or button from any one without permission, under any circumstances.

Some men do not pay their *just* debts, and are yet *generous* in contributing to charitable purposes; this is neither just, nor reasonable. Others are so unjust and cruel, that they refuse to give anything to their Father's poor children, because they are in debt, and never intend to be otherwise. Teach them to avoid subterfuges and evasions, as they would the bite of a serpent. The noble sentiment expressed by the Athenians to Aristides, should always be their motto, *i. e.*, "Let justice prevail if the pillars of heaven should fall." This Divine principle should be impressed with great care, upon their minds every day. Teach them that to take only the value of one pin, or one cent by force, or by fraud, or to detain it improperly in their possession when it is demanded by those to whom it justly belongs, will as certainly mark their character, with the black mark of dishonesty, as if they had stolen one million of money. The eternal principles of justice are stern and inflexible, and will admit of no compromise or evasion.

If after having established good, virtuous and pious principles in your children's minds, unless you sacredly and judiciously guard and regulate their intercourse with others, all your labor will be in vain—your children must ultimately be ruined; therefore, we beg you to be careful in selecting your children's company.

On Marriage.

Bro. Hersey's views on marriage, are well worth reproducing in this day of hasty and advantageous connubial co-partnerships.

He says: "Having discharged your duty faithfully; having trained up your children in the way they should go, you will naturally feel a deep solicitude respecting the connections they will form in their marriage."

If you have been as judicious as you should have been in selecting their society, there will be but little difficulty in acting your part in reference to this momentous step. If they have never associated, either at home, or abroad, with improper company, you need not fear that they will select an unsuitable companion for life.

Those who live right will be sure to die right. In all other things you can judge better for your children, than in their matrimonial connections. It is and ever must be, love, pure unsullied love, which alone can smooth the rough paths of life, and render the conjugal state desirable and happy.

You had much better bury than marry your children, when this exalted principle is wanting; of this you can be no judge; you can, and should counsel, but you should not command. You would not be willing to impose on your daughter, a burden more cruel than death; why then wish to compel her to marry your choice, and not her own? If, however, after all you can do, your children will form matrimonial connections which do not meet your approbation, you must treat them with parental regard and affection: much evil, and perhaps no good has ever been affected by treating offending children in this particular with great severity. It should be carefully and permanently engraven on their minds, that *industry* and *piety*, good sense and virtue, are pre-requisites which should never, no, never, be dispensed with in chosing a companion for life. There should also be a perfect congeniality of sentiment and disposition; genuine *love* cannot long exist where this is not the case; hasty matches, therefore, are ever fraught with danger.

There should also be, as far as practicable, a perfect equality of condition, and of circumstances in life. Teach them that to marry an individual who has much more *money*, or education, or intelligence, or beauty than themselves, is to place a thorn in their pillow, which will pierce occasionally, if not uniformaly and painfully. Their religious sentiments should be the same. The Apostle's injunction should never be violated—"Be not unequally yoked together with unbe- lievers." This practice is disgraceful to God and to the church, and to our shame be it spoken is entirely too common. There certainly is a far greater difference between a child of God and a child of the devil, than there is between a white and black person. How would such a union corre- spond with the laws of harmony and order, which God him- self has established? "It is a sin in itself," says J. Wesley, "and indeed a sin of no common dye. According to the oracles of God, it is no less than spiritual adultery. All who are guilty of it, are addressed by the Holy Ghost in these terms. 'Ye adulterers and adulteresses;' It is plainly violating our marriage contract with God, and as it is a sin in itself, it is attended with the most dreadful consequences. It frequently entangles men again in the commission of those sins, from which 'they were clean.' It generally makes them partakers even of those sins which they do not commit themselves."

It gradually abates their abhorrence and dread of sin in general, and thereby prepares them for falling an easy prey to any strong temptation. It lays them open to all those sins of omission whereof their worldly acquaintances are guilty. It insensibly lessons their exactness in private prayer, in family duty, in fasting, in attending public service and partaking of the Lord's Supper. The indifference of those who are near them, with respect to all these, will gradually influence them, even if they say not one word to recommend their own practice; yet their example speaks, and is of more force than any other language. By this example they are unavoidably betrayed, and almost continually, unto unprofitable, yea, and into uncharitable conversation, till they no longer 'set a watch before their mouths and keep the door of their lips' till they can join in backbiting, talebearing and evil speaking, without one check of conscience; having so frequently grieved the Holy Spirit of God, that he no longer reproves them for it." How great is the darkness of that execrable wretch, who will sell his own child to the devil; who will barter her own eternal happiness for any quantity of gold or silver. What a monster would any man be accounted, who devoured the flesh of his own offspring? And is he not as great a monster, who by his own act and deed, gives her to be devoured by that roaring lion? As he certainly does, who marries her to an ungodly man. But he is rich, has ten thousand pounds. What if it were a hundred? The more, the worse; the less probabilities she have of escaping the damnation of hell. With what face willt thou look upon her, when she tells them in the realms below, thou hast plunged me into this place of torment. Hadst thou given me a good man, however poor, I might now have been in Abraham's bosom."

CHAPTER IX.

WILL THE MACHINE BE GOING?

Many anecdotes are related illustrative of the subject of our sketch. From among which, we reproduce the following:— From the Baltimore American, of Saturday, Nov. 30th, 1861.

Will the Machine be Agoing? The Rev. John Hersey is well known as one of the most eccentric and self-denying ministers of the Methodist Episcopal Church, and has so many good traits of character, that he has endeared to himself to host of friends, in and out of the society. But his prepossessions, sentiments and proclivities are strongly in unison with that element of primitive Methodism, which forbade the preachers from giving Love-feast tickets to those who wore huge bonnets, who held high heads, who put on gold and silver, laid up treasures upon earth, and were guilty of softness and needless self-indulgence The following anecdote of Father Hersey, as he is respectfully called, illustrates his character. It is well known that the regular appointed minister of the Charles Street Church has long been absent in the land of "Dixie," and Mr. Hersey was called upon to administer to the people on Thanksgiving day. Before giving his consent, however, he called upon one of the stewards, when the following colloquoy took place: "Brother Job," said Father Hersey, "I am willing to preach in the church, but will the machine be agoing?" He was told that if the machine (the organ) was objectionable, it could be stopped; whereupon, he consented to preach, and did so, in a very effective manner. This will explain to the large congregation present, the disappointment experienced upon the absence of the choir, who very good naturedly abstained from the exercise of their vocal powers, which are acknowledged to be unsurpassed in the city. The leader, the organist, the bellows blower, as the good father termed them, and the sterner sex, released from their obligations, had, therefore, a good opportunity of enjoying the day in a manner different from what was anticipated, whilst the the ladies, (may heaven bless them,) who are foremost in the work of benevolence and charity, were busy and active in relieving the necessities of the poor and needy, at the "Home of the Friendless," and other kindred institutions.

To morrow, the choir wish it to be understood, that "The machine will be agoing" as usual,

Anecdote of the Buttons.

It is related that whilst attending a camp meeting at Ball's camp ground, Va., in the Fall of 1826, Father Hersey preached a powerful sermon, in which he inveighed against the then becoming to be fashionable practice among the ladies, of wearing earrings; insisting with great force, that the wearing of useless apparel or ornaments, was questionable, if not sinful. After service, an amiable and accomplished sister, whose heavy gold pendants had made her the "observed of all observers," during Father Hersey's sermon, approached the Reverened gentleman, and said, "Father Hersey, before discarding my earrings, as unnecessary, be kind enough to inform me what use those two buttons on the back of your coat are designed for." For a moment, a blush mantled the good man's check, but it was for a moment only, for seizing a knife he quickly removed the offending buttons, exclaiming, "Sister, let the buttons go with the jewelry," and from that day, till that of his death, Father Hersey as sedulously eschewed buttons as the lady did ornaments.

City Missionary.

Whilst City Missionary in Baltimore, Father Hersey on a cold, snowy December day, in going his accustomed round of duty, soliciting for the suffering poor, in whom he always manifested the liveliest interest, stopped in, at the store of a Hebrew gentleman, who was more noted for profanity, than charity. The clothier, who was busy waiting upon a lady customer, had never met Father Hersey, and supposing from his coarse though neat garb, that he was a mendicant, roughly querried, "Old man, are you a beggar?" "I am begging to-day," quietly rejoined the Missionary; then roughly replied the merchant, "You had better get out of here, and go to work" adding, "that is the way I get my clothes, and you might have better ones, if you were industrious, without begging me for them." "I do not want clothes," quietly responded the unselfish minister; "I am amply supplied by He whom you crucified on Calvary.' but you are angry, and I can't leave until you get cool, when I will talk to you." Astonished at the unruffled demeanor and dignified manner of the thinly clad, and insulted stranger, the merchant quer-

ried "Who can he be?" "That" whispered the lady, "*is
Father Hersey*;" he is the only wholly unselfish man, that
I have ever met; rejoined the merchant, "and now sir"
addressing Father Hersey, "after begging your pardon, tell
what are your wants and they shall be supplied." Look at
my coat, you see I need none, I want nothing for myself;"
but there is a poor woman near you, who is suffering for the
common necessaries of life, and you must relieve her." "I
will," returned the merchant, and turning to the best blankets
in the store, he directed his clerk to wrap up as many as
Father Hersey should deem necessary, whilst he armed the
good Missionary with an order upon his grocer, authorizing
him to draw upon that tradesman for the remainder; the order
covering in amount whatever sum in Father Hersey's judgment should be required to meet the widow's necessities.

On the observance of the Sabbath.

On the observance of the Sabbath, Father Hersey says:

"There has recently been much controversey in the christian world, respecting the Sabbath day, whether its obligations are binding on christians, or not. It is incorporated in
the Decalogue, and for us, one of the commandments delivered to Moses, by the hand of God himself. Christ's gospel,
is admirably adapted to the wants and conditions of all mankind, and must ultimately prevail in every clime on earth;
therefore the Sabbath day has been wisely passed over in the
New Testament, almost in silence, lest vain jangling and idle
controversey about forms and shadows should engage the
minds and engross the time of dying mortals. The custom
of the fathers, and the inferences of the Gospel, are sufficient
to establish fully the right of christians to enjoy one day in
each week devoted to rest and worship. The inhabitants of
the frozen regions, and Torrid zone, may equally claim and
enjoy the unspeakable blessing of devoting one-seventh
part of their time, exclusively to the service of the Lord,
and whether it be the first or seventh day of the week, can
make no difference to God, who is a spirit, and must be worshipped in spirit and in truth. It is very much to be feared,
that those who cavil with so much rigidity about its formal
observance, know very little about God's holy law, which is
love, or of his worship, which is spiritual in its nature, and
delightful in its operation. Not long since, I spent the close

of the week with an old and respectable member of the church. On the Sabbath morning, almost the first sound that reached my ear, was the axe; I reasoned with my kind friend on the impropriety and awful consequences of such conduct. He frankly acknowledged his faults, but alleged that his servants were to blame—he could not control them—it was an express violation of his orders. As he could not prevent it, he supposed he was innocent himself. Do you think, said I, if there was a fine of ten dollars only, for cutting wood on the Sabbath day, that those ungovernable servants would be guilty of a violation of the law, and compel you to pay the ten dollars every week? He promptly and frankly replied, no sir, I am sure it would not be the case. Suppose the President was to issue a proclamation offering to every one, who would observe the fourth commandment for one year, fifty thousand dollars, do we honestly believe that we should be as careless under such circumstances, as we are now? Would there be the sound of an axe heard on our premises? Would our servants be laboring on that day, preparing a sumptuous repast, against we returned from a social visit? Would we talk business and politics, sooner than divine love and law? No sir, I think we could very well fare on cold food for fifty-two days in a year for that amount, it would be near a thousand dollars a day—it would soon be over, and then we would be comfortable for life. If we would keep the day more strict to get fifty thousand, or fifty millions of money, than we do under present circumstances, we have no hope of heaven.

One Cent Beggar.

Many, very many years ago, Father Hersey met on the highway, an old grey-headed man, who asked him for *one cent*. From the stranger's language and address, he perceived that he had seen more prosperous days. Father Hersey asked him what benefit one cent could be to him? He replied, that he was far from his friends and home, and occasionally had to pay ferriage and other incidental expenses; he did not, however, complain, or intimate, that he was unkindly treated by the public. Father Hersey then inquired what his prospects were in regard to another world.— They were certainly very gloomy in the present. From his reply and the simple, but pointed relation of his experience, he had every reason to believe that he was then in possession of the "pearl of great price," though an earthly beggar; he paused and pondered the circumstances over in his own mind; here is a child, thought Father Hersey, of my heavenly Father, an old grey-headed pilgrim of the cross, a stranger in a strange land, far from any earthly friends and comforts, who respectfully solicits *one cent* to aid him on his toilsome journey.

Father Hersey says, "I examined myself from head to foot, and found that I had expended many dollars for what might have been dispensed with, without depriving me of one real benefit, or comfort.—first, several dollars might have been saved in my *hat*, and something from every part of my dress. I thought of the poor widow who gave two mites, and reflected upon our Saviour's command to gather up the fragments, that nothing might be lost.—I thought upon the crown of thorns, that another stranger in this cold world wore for me. I was ashamed, I was condemned—I found this man's blood upon me; the money with which these unnecessary things were purchased, belonged to this poor old man's father. Was I not a robber? And what was my gain?—Pride, that master sin was fed and strengthened. And what was my motive? Evidently to recommend myself to the sons of Belial, my Divine Master's deadly enemies. I saw them and still believe that one cent expended to gratify the passions or appetite exclusively, or for any article not really useful and beneficial, is a departure from the high and honorble standard of *mercy*: *"except ye deny yourself daily*, and take up your cross, and follow Me, ye cannot be My disciples."

I then resolved to adopt the dress, and endeavor to conform more closely to the practice of a christian.

Stain on the Floor.

Father Hersey used to relate the following anecdote, which he alleged made a powerful impression upon his mind, and which he intended should have a good effect upon the minds of those to whom he related it.

"Being unwell at the house of a friend, where everything was neat and clean—the floor of my chamber being unusually white,—the servant brought in a small mug, containing a

preparation for me to take as I retired to bed. It was set on
the hearth—a brand fell and upset it, part of the contents
ran on the floor ; I removed it as soon as possible, but felt
not a little mortified at the careless occurrence. At four
o'clock when I arose and lighted the candle, the floor attracted my first attention, and to my great surprise and gratifica-
tion, there was no stain to be seen ; it was dry and white.
With the light of the candle, I could distinctly see to read
very small print. When the sun arose, and shone into the
room, a *plain stain* was quite perceptible on the floor. By this
accident, I was led to the following reflections : with the
light I now use, all appears to be well—no stain is perceptible, but when the light of eternity shines forth upon my
soul, will there be no stain, or dark marks to be seen ? Do
I now honestly bring the light of God's holy word and spirit
to bear · on my heart and conscience ? Is there nothing
which that standard enjoins which I omit; nothing which it
forbids that I indulge in ?

On Begging Money from the Irreligious.

Father Hersey's views on begging money from sinners, do
not accord with the practice now so prevalent. He says :

What must sinners think of us when we declare faithfully
to them, that they must be turned into hell, and then ask
them for pecuniary aid. What would be thought of the soldier
who in time of conflict, sought to obtain among his enemies,
the means to continue the war against their leader ? Would
they not rejoice to get rid of such tormenting neighbors ?
Reason and honor declare aloud that the church should keep
within her own borders, in collecting money for any religious
purpose. Our nakedness is by this course sometimes completely exposed.

I was sometime since, eye witness to a mortifying scene,
which is a case in point, strengthened both my fears and
supposition. A minister of the gospel, at a three days'
meeting, observed one or two advertisements on the side of
the church, he immediately removed them from that place—
very soon he was called on by an enraged sinner to know if
he had taken down his advertisement, the preacher replied
mildly in the affirmative. The insulted child of Belial, per
emptorily demanded them of him ; he had thrown them away
but they were picked up and given to the rightful owner, he

then in a boisterous, profane manner declared, that he had paid his money towards building that house; consequently, he had as much right to it as any other man, and in an open, daring, insulting manner, hammered his paper up to the house again, in the presence of a large concourse of people, and triumphantly dared any man to touch them again. The poor insulted servant of God, was compelled to see his Father's house, the Lord's Sanctuary, degraded to the level of a common tavern, or ordinary sign-post, or fight the devil on his own ground.

By the unguarded and indelicate course of begging from sinners, we place ourselves within their power. All God's children are—they must be honorable people; nothing could be more painful, and mortifying to a high minded sinner, than to be compelled to ask a favor of his enemy; surely our sense of honor is not more obtuse, than that of those who are regarded by the Lord Jesus, as children of the devil."

On Apostolic Prayer.

"For this cause I bow my knees unto the Father of our Lord Jesus Christ, of whom the whole family in heaven and earth is named.

That he would grant, you according to the riches of his glory, to be strengthened with might by his spirit in the inner man.

That Christ may dwell in your hearts by faith, that ye, being rooted and grounded in love, may be able to comprehend with all saints, what is the breadth, and length and depth and heighth.

And to know the love of Christ, which passeth knowledge, that ye might be filled with all the fullness of God.

Now unto him who is able to do exceedingly abundantly above all that we ask or think, according to the power that worketh in us.

Unto him be glory in the church by Christ Jesus throughout all ages, world without end. Amen."

The above, says Father Hersey, is the sublimest intercessory prayer on record, embodying the supplication for those blessings in language, the most magnificent that ever issued from human lips.   Here we find the full length and finished portrait of intercessory prayer.

Father Hersey thus photographs the Apostle to the Gentiles :

"If ever there was a man, who lived for others, not himself—willing to endure any suffering by which the sufferings of others might be soothed, and in promoting the happiness of others, supremely desirous to find his own—that man was St. Paul.

If ever there was a human heart in which the divine spirit of christian benevolence was enthroned, and had brought every feeling, affection and passion to bow beneath its sceptre of love, it was the heart of the great Apostle of the Gentiles.

If ever there was a character moulded in every feature after the adorable Redeemer's, and reflecting in beautiful clearness, the image of him who was the incarnate manifestation of divine love, it was the character of this greatest of merely human philanthropists, and if ever there was a life of mere man, which might be considered but as one embodied and unbroken exhibition of disinterested zeal for the advancement of human happiness, it was the life of St. Paul, from the moment he met Jesus on the way to Damascus, and fell to the ground, beneath his piercing expostulations, till the moment, when, as the dying testimony of his gratitude to that Jesus, he bowed his head beneath the murderous axe,"

Will the reader not join with us in asserting, that if in more modern times, there has lived one who deserved and earned the application of the above pen portrait—that man was John Hersey. We cannot better present Father Hersey to our readers, than by copying entire the following vigorous epistle from an eminent and able member of the Philadelphia Conference. All who ever met Father Hersey will recognize the picture :

CHAPTER X.

My Dear Brother:

My acquaintance with that memorable man of God, of whom you speak, Rev. John Hersey, or John Hersey without the "Reverend," (as he preferred to be called,) was not very close and intimate, though it covered a tolerable long period.

The first time I ever saw this unique man, was in my boyhood. The year I have forgotten, and have no means of refreshing my memory.

He was at my father's house in the village of Trappe, Talbot County, Maryland, which was the regular home for the preachers. I had been accustomed to the sight and conversation of preachers, from my earliest childhood; but this was a *preacher* differing from all others. He was a thin, spare, stoop-shouldered, sharp featured man, with keen, penetrating eyes, and quick movements, whose whole aim was to publish Christ, to live Christ, and to bring men to Christ. This was evident to the most casual observer, who was with him for the briefest period. This was the atmosphere he breathed, this was the food he ate, this was the dominant— the ever-present thought and effort. I can recall how my young heart was awe-stricken by such intense and all absorbing consecration to God. I reverenced ministers, but here was a man who made me tremble in his presence.

He wore a suit of gray, the fabric was coarse and inexpensive; the cut, plain; the shad-belly coat, having a standing collar; there were no buttons on his coat or vest. Hooks and eyes were less conspicuous, and less expensive, and served as well the intended purpose, which was not show, but use. A clean turn down collar gave him the appearance of scrupulous tidiness, but no cravat encumbered the neck. Coarse, strong shoes protected his feet, and a palm leaf hat with a twine string band, covered his head.

At table and everywhere, his conversation was spiritual and religiously edifying, with a small sprinkling of anecdote.

His food was simple, nutritious and abstemiously used. He slept (according to his own request), upon a straw bed, and often, I believe, on the floor.

He had books of his own writing, and others I believe, of his own compiling, which he offered for sale, but did not urge any one to buy. I remember I took a fancy to one— his extracts from Wesley—and with the consent and the aid of my father, bought it. This man all afire with the constraining love of Christ deemed every moment designed for the holy use. He was in his room writing; through the village visiting and praying ; in the stores, the shops, the family preaching. I well remember a question he asked my father, "Is there any family for whom others do not care ?" My father told him of an abandoned family, living in a long deserted house, on the outskirts of the village, where rum and prostitution had full sway. To that place, this man of God went, carrying as well as I remember, some useful article of food for them in their family, amazing the people of the village, and those outcasts, by his condescending tenderness. At five o'clock in the morning, the old church was vocal with his clear penetrating voice, as he preached Jesus and the resurrection to no inconsiderable multitude. Tarrying thus for a few days, he left to bless other towns, villages and rural neighborhoods. After an interval, he returned to our village. When I heard of his prospective visit, I recollect how anxious I was to finish reading "Extracts from Wesley," in order that I might have some valuable knowledge of the book, for I was very sure he would catechise as to the use I had made of it. Years elapsed before this marvelous man made his appearance again. He had been to remote points, ever busy and full of work for Christ. Wherever John Hersey was, he could say with something of the spirit of Jesus (more, probably than any man I ever knew), "Wist ye not, that I must be about my Father's business."

I remember one cold Sabbath day, when the wind and storm kept the people away, how he talked to the few who were present, on the text: "Fear not, little flock, for it is your Father's good pleasure to give you the kingdom." He put his hands up to his ears, in a gesture peculiar to himself, and which he used only when intensely interested in what he was saying, and rung the charges on "little flock" and pointed us to the "Kingdom." So close was his preaching, so awfully appalling was his proclamation of the truth in its sterner aspects, so perfectly opposite to anything latitudinarian, that when we were returning from church, where he had defined to us the way of life, the young lady with whom I was walking, asked me "Are there any christians?" Just here I think was a defect in his ministry; he was not sufficiently Jobian to give a gospel of hope: it was almost a gospel of despair. And yet, God owned his ministry at times wonderfully.

At Royal Oak camp meeting in Talbot County, somewhere about 1841, he preached a woderful sermon, "Casting four anchors, and waiting for day;" he seemed inspired. Spry Downs, a wealthy citizen, rather advanced in years, with others, many others, came to Christ, under the influence of his wonderful appeal. Assisting Rev. John Bell and Rev. John Rutter, he preached on Talbot Circuit, at a meeting in St. Michael's. The religious interest chiefly under his ministrations was so intense and all absorbing, that people quit business, stores were closed, farmers left their work, the house of God was crowded all day, during the week. Religion was the theme. Dr. James Dawson fell, and was converted, whilst Father Hersey was preaching.

Commencing my ministry on Talbot Circuit, in 1851, under the Elder, Thos. J. Quigley, with Rev. Jas. A. Massey, as my colleague; we had a camp meeting at the Bayside. Father Hersey was with us; he preached a powerful, eloquent and deeply impressive sermon, on "The wicked spreading himself like a green bay tree."

The last time I saw Father Hersey was in Green St. Church, Philadelphia, in 1861 The pastor, Rev. Wm. N. Brisbane was sick and died not long after. As his neighbor, I was requested to administer the Sacrament of the Lord's Supper to his people; Father Hersey being in the congregation, I requested him to assist in the solemn service, which he did. He was more tender and subdued in manner than I had ever seen him; less abuse of worldliness bristled in his address: he was sweet and full of love, but he could not forbear condemning flowers, feathers and jewelry.

About the time I have covered in these reminiscences, Isaac Taylor wrote: "The Methodism of the eighteenth

century has ceased to have any extant representative among
us." If he had known John Hersey, I doubt whether he
would have made as sweeping a declaration. John Hersey
had his faults; my impression is, that he failed at a cardinal
point, in failing to make religion a genial, attractive and joy-
ous experience. He was too much of an ascetic. He acted
too much as if he served a hard master. His manner of life
and preaching did not recommend christianity as joy-giving,
but for deadness to the world, entire devotedness to Christ,
intentness, or making the most of his opportunity for doing
good, intensity of effort at all times and in all places, to save
souls and to bring men to a knowledge of salvation through
Christ. I do not remember ever to have seen John Hersey's superior, nor even his equal.

With kind remembrance, I remain your brother in Christ,

JOHN F. CHAPLAIN, D. D.
Phila. Conference.

CHAPTER XI.

Labors on Church Hill Circuit.

Thus, might have mused Father Hersey, as he wrote from
Orange Court House, Va., Sept 12th, 1835: "My way has
recently been hedged up; I should, before this, have left the
State, and directed my steps towards Ohio or Pennsylvania,
but thought it most prudent to remain here until the storm
subsides, should that ever be. I have been an object of peculiar hatred; I believe however, the God "whose I am and
whom I serve," will deliver and protect me from all danger
When I shall have fully delivered my own soul with the people, if my life is spared, I shall leave Virginia; the Lord's
will be done; the Lord keep my mind in peace and stayed on
the Lord Jesus."

Father Hersey had made up his mind to change the field of
his operations; how long after writing the above he remained
in Virginia is unknown, but he is found at his spiritual work
in Pennsylvania, Delaware, and on the Eastern Shore counties
of Maryland during some subsequent years.

Rev. E. J. Way states, that during the year 1839 he was preaching and selling his books in Accomac county, Virginia; that he occasionally met him and was assisted by him in his fields of labor. There can be no doubt that the Eastern Shore counties were among the most successful fields of his ministerial success: throughout their breadth his name is precious as ointment. He was frequently employed as a supply on different circuits within the bounds of the Philadelphia and Baltimore Conferences.

About the year 1840 (although the precise year is not altogether certain, it cannot however, be later than 1842), he traveled the Church Hill Circuit, Queen Anne's County, where he was hailed with joy, and was instrumental in accomplishing much good; for a time he journeyed to his appointments on foot, but finally was persuaded to buy a horse; then it was insisted that he should provide himself with a buggy, his health being endangered by the rays of the sun in summer, and the cold and rain of winter; finally he acceded to this wish, and provided himself with a gig of his own construction; the top covering consisted of white muslin. Thus equipped with a traveling conveyance, for the spiritual warfare, he went forth; (those who saw Father Hersey's vehicle, will recall its appearance;) on the road he met two sisters belonging to one of his congregations; they were driving towards town, he from it. Their horse became frightened at the sight of the singular equipage, and ran away, threw them out of their carriage, injuring them badly but not seriously; the good old man was highly mortified over this mishap, and at the earliest opportunity, he procured lamp black and oil, which he applied bountifully to the white covering of his gig.

While at Church Hill, he resided with a poor widow who had a family of children, dependant upon her for support; she was also afflicted and without the means of relieving her want. It is said of him that he was generous to the poor, and this widow shared largely of his bounty; nor did he forget her when the time for his departure from this circuit was at hand; having no further use for his horse, he proposed selling him; brother H——, willing to buy, asked the purchase price, and upon being answered the same as he had paid for him, *provided*, good care would be taken of the animal. Brother H—— rejoined that the amount asked, was not enough by several dollars; whereupon, Father Hersey stopped him saying, "I am not a horse trader, and don't want to get more than I paid for him;" after the price was agreed upon, brother H—— proposed to give his note for future payment, but Father Hersey point blank refused it, and said, "When you get the money, pay it to Mr.——, a merchant in the town, who will supply the needy with groceries to the amount you owe me." In this arrangement he did not forget the widow, whose humble home was his circuit parsonage, and she shared largely in the distribution.

It is stated during a Quarterly Meeting held at Centreville, on this circuit, that an official brother who had charged usurious interest on a sum of money loaned by him, invited Father Hersey to his house for dinner, to which he quickly replied, "That he could not break bread with any one who had charged unlawful interest." He was averse to seeing rooms adorned with picturers and on viewing them, would repeat with peculiar emphasis the commandment—"Thou shalt not make unto thee any graven image, or any likeness of anything that is in heaven above, or that is in the earth beneath, or that is in the water under the earth" Upon dining with a friend, he ate heartily, and upon being pressed to take more, accompanied with the statement you have not ate anything, he expostulated, "Don't speak an untruth."

On one occasion he was preaching to a large congregation, many of the ladies wore their hair braided in front. Father Hersey regarded the innovation (for it was a new fashion) with dislike, and remarked, "Here you are with your hair in all sorts of vain styles, some even plaited up like town ladders."

He visited a friend in Easton, Maryland, who had recently refurnished his house, in modern style; throughout was luxuriant and costly furniture, and nearby stood the church, with its spire pointing heavenward. Father Hersey after a few hours in his friend's domicile, feeling ill at ease amid its costly furniture, went to the door for relief, when lo and behold, the first sight his eyes rested upon, was the church with its steple; calling to his friend who quickly joined him; Father Hersey threw up his hands and exclaimed, "Brother, that church has gone to seed

The foregoing anecdotes have their point, and are no trifling circumstances in enabling us properly to ascertain the
character of the godly man to whom they refer. He did not
hesitate to rebuke sin, whether of avarice or pride, and with-
all he gave alms; what he taught, he practiced; he was a
model of his own honest profession, at all times true and
loyal to his ministerial calling.

Labors on Dorchester Circuit

In 1841, Father Hersey attended a camp meeting at
Ebenezer, Cambridge Circuit, in Dorchester County; in
attendance, there was also a gay young man from the city of
Baltimore; he had been trained in the fear of and admonition of the Lord, but had departed from the true faith, and
adopted the doctrines of Universalism. On the Sabbath
day, Father Hersey preached one of his argumentative sermons; the congregation was enraptured, the young man's
attention was closely riveted, and the effect produced was so
convincing, as to cause him to return again to the acceptance of the views of his father. He was converted and
became a useful member of the church. The shadows are
now gathering about his path, and the close of his life's day
is nearing. Oh, how he rejoices that it was his privilege to
have heard that Sunday sermon, in the blissful hope of an
immortality beyond the grave, and a reunion with Father
Hersey in the spirit land; he is consoled as he nears the
valley of death. In this same year he was made a life member of the Maryland State Bible Society, by contribution
raised at the camp meeting on the Cambridge Circuit. He
also was present at the camp held at Wheatley's, in the
upper end of Dorchester County; here he also preached on
the Lord's day, and his sermon was attended with marked
results: among others, John Clements' heart was powerfully
effected, his entire being trembled under the power of the
word; he returned to his home, complained of sickness and
sent for the doctor; but it was not a physician he needed for
the body, and the doctor so told him; rather was it one for
the soul. Brothers William Allen, Mace M. Mezzick and
S. Williams, were called into his presence, and found him
agonizing under deep contrition for sin; they prayed and
exhorted with him and had the great satisfaction of witnes-
sing his happy conversion; his body now rests under the sod,

waiting the judgment day, but his spirit with the sainted
Hersey's is at home in the kingdom of God.

The sermon above referred to made a decided religious
impression, and was long remembered as Hersey's grubbing
sermon; manfully did he labor that day: eternity will reveal a proud record as its result. (The writer was present
on that occasion at the camp meeting.)

In 1849, Father Hersey was appointed Bible Agent, for
Washington County, Maryland; in the Spring of 1851, he
visited Vienna, Dorchester County, where the writer then
resided, and became his guest. An account of this visit
will not be without some interest.

Upon his arrival, he stated that he had been directed to my
house by brother Brindle, who had told him that I was a
plain Methodist, and in the family of such an one, he wished
to spend a few days, he did not expect to go to heav-
en in silver slippers; he was accorded a hearty welcome,
and made to feel perfectly at ease and at home, The visit
was one that recollection dwells upon with fondness, and was
of great spiritual profit; it cannot be forgotten, the humble
attitude he assumed, when addressing the throne of grace—
morning and evening, calling down upon us all our Father's
benediction in language of rarest simplicity. At bed time,
upon ascertaining that a couch of feathers had been prepared
for his repose, he called, "Sister, remove the feather bed, I
prefer the under one;" things being adjusted to his liking,
he retired. At an early hour in the morning, he was heard
at his devotions; they were continued until he was summoned
to breakfast, when all joined with him in family prayer.

After he had partaken of his morning meal, he at once
entered upon his Master's work, visiting from house to house
throughout the entire village.

At this time the Baptists were erecting a church; accord-
to their usual custom, brother B—— their pastor had
preached several sermons on the subject of immersion. I
asked Father Hersey to discourse on the same topic from a
Methodist standpoint, which he consented to do; our denom-
inational church was well filled on the occasion of its deliv-
ery—in a clear firm voice, he impressively gave out the
hymn—"O, for a closer walk with God." His text was "I

will sprinkle you with clean water." The sermon was a concise logical effort, and those who heard it were convinced that on the scriptural subject of baptism he was no novice.

Friday morning he informed us, it "was his usual custom on that day to abstain from the use of food—that he feasted on prayer, faith and humble love."

When the time for departing was reached, he called the family together, read and explained the scriptures, and all kneeling, he reverently invoked the blessings of the triune God to rest upon us all: when we were risen, he presented my wife a book of which he was the author—*Advice to Christian Parents*, also, *Family Rules;* a work of his own composing, and an acrostic on each of our three children; he then took his departure, commending us to God, and the word of his grace, which is able to build us up and give us an inheritance among all them which are sanctified.

As a specimen of his style, this chapter is concluded by appending two of the acrostics, and his *"Family Rules,"* which were printed in convenient form for framing.

ACROSTIC.

Will Jesus bless this little boy,
Impart to him both peace and joy,
Live ever in God's holy fear,
Learn that all wisdom centres there
Improve each moment as it flies,
And you shall be both good and wise,
May thus gain the pearl of great price.

May you in life's clear early morn,
All virtues shining paths adorn:
Then you will learn to watch and pray,
That in her pathway you may stay,
Honor God and walk in wisdom's way;
Each word you say be kind and mild,
With all your thoughts still undefiled.

Must learn to pity those who need,
And soothe the sick; the hungry feed,
Remember Christ may say to thee,
In heaven your great reward shall be,
Now in Christ's Kingdom you shall shine,
Eternal life shall there be thine.

The fear of the Lord is the beginning of wisdom, and the knowledge of the holy, is understanding.—PROV. ix, 10.

If you would be wise and honorable and happy, you must have the fear of the Lord always before your eyes; this divine principle must dwell in your heart, regulating and influencing all your thoughts, words and actions.

You must fear to offend the Lord at any time; therefore, you must keep all His commandments always. You should fear to grieve the Holy Spirit of God, either by word or deed. You must have a new, pure heart, to enable you to live the life of the righteous. Please God and get to heaven.

Never forget that solemn truth—Thou God seeth me; and avoid all idle and wicked company, and pray much in secret.

Vienna; Md , March 7th, 1851. J. H.

ACROSTIC.

Those babes, Christ takes into his arms.
Here smiles, and gives to them new charms.
O parents train him in God's fear,
Make him his Saviour's words to hear,
And as his days shall glide away,
Still teach his infant lips to pray.

Prepare him Lord for life's rough sea,
Righteous and pure, still may he be,
In Jesus, all God's goodness see.
Christ says, of such my kingdom's made,
Each one shall have my care and aid.

May he be kept by power divine,
And in his Saviour's image shine.
Remember Him in riper years,
In mercy Lord, dry up his tears.
No clouds of sin obscure his sky,
Each breeze still waft him up on high.

"But when Jesus saw it He was much displeased, and said unto them : Suffer the little children to come unto Me, and forbid them not; for of such is the Kingdom of God."— MARK x, 14.

Parents bring your child to Christ, in the arms of faith and prayer, teach his infant lips to lisp his Saviour's name, in accent's of prayer and praise.

"Train him up in the way he should go, and when he is old he will not depart from it;" the way in which he should go, is the way of holiness: nor are you qualified to teach him those things with which you are yourself unacquainted.

"Therefore, be ye holy, for I am holy saith the Lord."
Remember that you must meet Him in the day of judgment.
O may it be with joy and not with grief.

Vienna, March 7th, 1851.   J. H.

FAMILY RULES.

"For I know him, that he will command his children, and
his household after him, and they shall keep the way of the
Lord, to do justice and judgment."—GEN. xviii, 18.

"But as for me and my house, we will serve the Lord."—
JOSH. xxiv, 15.

RULE I.

Our time is a precious talent, and must be improved.
Idleness paves the way to poverty and vice ; therefore, we
are determined to be diligent in business, and also fervent in
spirit, serving the Lord. We will indulge in no unprofitable
or uncharitable conversation, but in that only which is good
to the use of edifying, ministering grace to the hearer. We
say nothing concerning the flying news of the town, nor the
business of others, for we desire to hear of the things pertaining to the Kingdom of God. Nothing is to be said respecting the faults of others ; nor will we at any time say
anything respecting absent persons, which we would be unwilling to say in their presence.

RULE II.

The family shall be dedicated anew each morning to God
in prayer. All the family in health, over five years of age,
shall be present. Also each evening this solemn duty shall
be attended to, at an early hour, before the children and servants become too drowsy to hear what is said profitably,
that God's blessing may rest upon our family, morning and
evening.

RULE III.

Except in case of sickness, or other preventing providen-
ces, our regular meals shall be served up at stated hours ;
and no member of the family shall be permitted to make any
remarks at the table respecting the food, its quality or its
preparation ; each one must eat that which is set before him,

or her, asking no questions, and making no comments, either for or against.

RULE IV.

The Lord's day must be kept HOLY. We will neither receive nor pay visits on that day; neither will we indulge in any worldly conversation, nor compel our servants to labor for our sensual gratifications; therefore, no cooking will be allowed, except in case of sickness. Our children and servants shall be carefully instructed, and not suffered to pass the day in idleness or dissipation. In a word, we will do, or say nothing during the day, which we would not do or say, if the Lord Jesus was personally present. Works of piety and necessity alone shall be attended to.

RULE V.

The poor are respected and pitied; therefore, no unkind censure, or invidious remark respecting them, will be allowed. Although we do not intend to encourage idleness, or dissolute practices, yet the poor shall never be turned empty away from our door. No waste, or unnecessary expense will be indulged in, while so many of our Heavenly Father's children are suffering for bread. We will visit the abodes of want and poverty, and as far as it may be in our power, we will impart unto them spiritual, as well as temporal comfort.

RULE VI.

In our intercourse with our friends and others, we are resolved to use all possible openness of manner and expression, having no secrets of which we would feel ashamed, or that may shame or condemn us in the day of eternity. When we meet and when we part with our friends, it shall always be, if practicable, with prayer.

RULE VII.

As it is pleasant and desirable for brethren to dwell together in unity and love, we earnestly desire any one to reprove us in a spirit of meekness, when we shall deviate from any of these rules; so shall we be as guardian angels to each other on earth, until we shall be permitted to form a part of our Father's family in heaven.

CHAPTER XII.

REMINISCENCES BY REV. S. W. THOMAS.

We are indebted to Rev. S. W. Thomas, of Philadelphia Conference, for the following sketch :

I became acquainted with John Hersey in the year 1851; he came to, what was then Church Hill Circuit, to visit the people. I felt some fear in the dear good man's company; but it soon wore off, as we went from house to house, praying with the people. Bro. Hersey would speak very plainly, but kindly, to all the people in the house; inquire how their souls prospered, &c.

I was told by the friends in Beaver Dam, that while he was stopping at the house of Dr. B.——, he requested Mrs. B—— to·order the servants to take off the feather bed and give him a hard straw bed to sleep on; the room was very large, and two double bedsteads were in it. Rev. Geo. Barton was sleeping in one, and felt provoked at Father Hersey for putting the friends to so much trouble; especially as the night was bitter cold. But enjoying his feather bed and ample clothing he soon fell asleep. About midnight, Father Hersey aroused brother B—— out of a deep sleep, asking the privilege of sleeping in bed with him, because he was so cold; at first brother B—— refused, but after the most earnest entreaty, he granted the ·request In the morning Bro. B—— spoke of the matter, and censured Bro. II—— for his course; the subject being an unpleasant one, it was dismissed.

Dr. B—— and family, ever sought to make Methodist preachers happy; it was a home indeed for the weary itinerant. Father Hersey was watchful for his brethren, and when opportunity offered, was not slow to censure, or reprimand them. Rev. N. W——, of Chestertown, Md., always gave Father Hersey a cordial welcome, but the dear good man was just as faithful with those who treated him with marked attention as those who regarded him with disdain. Bro.

W—— having purchased for his daughter a piano, was
severely censured for the act, and caused no little stir in the
house by his repeated reference to the spirit of worldliness
that was creeping into the church, and even among those
who stood at the head of affairs.   Bro. W—— determined
to avoid unpleasantness, and made no reply; but several
months after, Father Hersey wrote to Bro. W—— to meet
him at the boat from Baltimore, at a given time; Bro. W——
awaited the arrival of his guest, but before allowing him to
enter his house, he said: "Bro. Hersey, I don't want to subject you to any unpleasantness, or embarrass you as to your
surroundings, but least you may feel at liberty to administer
reproof to me in the presence of my family, I wish to inform
you before you enter the house, that I have purchased for my
daughter, a new suit of furniture of a new pattern, and
which I regard as very good; this furniture is in the room I
have set apart for your use, during your stay in Chestertown;
now, if this is displeasing to you, and will cause you unhappi-
ness, I must prefer that you seek other quarters; but if you
are willing to accept what I have, without remarks of a dis-
agreeable sort, no one can give you a more cordial welcome."
Father Hersey made his home with Bro. W—— ever after
when he came to the town, and always abstained from remarks of the sort referred to.

I was invited to take tea with Father Hersey in company
with several other Methodists, at the house of Bro. Sherwood,
in Milford.   The godly man was in one of his happiest
moods, and gave us his views on various subjects, greatly to
our edification and profit, for every one honored and rever-
ed him.   Some one remarked, that his was a singular life
for him to lead, constantly on the wing, always separating
from friends, and that if he made friends, he had but little
time to test them.   Oh! said he, "perhaps that is best; for
one of my oldest friends has given me the greatest trouble,
and especially at a time when I most needed him; we lived
together for years and years in the same house, we slept together; indeed I may say that for years he was with me by
night and by day; the more I felt the necessity of his friendly offices, the more he complained; indeed matters grew so
serious that there was no living in peace with him.   I tried
my utmost to soften his merciless complainings; I threatened
if he did not desist, I would resort to extreme measures.

The neighbors began to notice the effects of our mutual struggle; at last I could not bear it any longer; true, he was almost the last of a company of friends I had, still I said look at my disfigured face, it tells a story that no words of mine need express, and if I were to tempt it, I could not, for the pain it gave me, to think of parting, and the cruel treatment I had received from him, still, I consoled myself with the reflections, that for fifty years and more, there had never been a disturbing thought; perfect peace and good feeling between us. Dear friends, I assure you it was no trifling matter, for two such old friends after so many years of intimate friendship, to part, and that to, by the most violent means."

The whole party deeply sympathised with the dear good man, and were commenting upon the wickedness of so ungrateful a friend, who would thus turn against one who they knew to be so good and holy a man, and were about to request the name of the wretch, whence he opened his mouth and showed the place from whence an old stump of a tooth had been drawn out.

He once reprimanded Bro. W—— for allowing a servant to chop some kindling wood early one Sabbath morning; Mr. W—— said, "It was against my express orders, but I don't think it was any worse than selling books on Sunday;" Father Hersey said, "It shall never be said of me again that I sold books on Sunday."

On entering the mansion of a lady in Virginia, which had been beautifully furnished with pier glass and rich tapestry and elegant furniture, he raised his hands in holy horror, and stepping back from the parlor door, he said: "Sister! sister! do you expect to take these things to heaven." The sister replied, "Why Bro. Hersey, you surprise me, I take such mean stuff as this to heaven, never! Golden paved streets, jasper walls and pearly gates would so outshine such trash as this, that I would be ashamed to have it about; no indeed, I never thought of taking it to heaven." The dear old man had nothing to say to her reply.

He used to rise at midnight to pray, greatly to the annoyance of his brethren who slept in the preachers' tent. One of them said: "Father Hersey, I really think your course is damaging to religion rather than a help to it, for it seems that you

cannot trust God for one whole night, but rise at midnight,
to ask God to keep you for the remainder of the night. Why
said the brother I can say my prayer, go asleep and never
wake until morning. I can trust God for a whole night."
"So can I," said he, "But I cannot trust myself, I want to
keep very near Jesus."

When in Philadelphia the last time, he called upon and
tarried with several of his old friends, among them was dear
Bro. Solomon Townsend, who lived in fine style on one of
the principal streets. He enjoyed his hospitalities; but when
he came to Rev. S. W. Thomas' to stay a short time, he remarked "Bro. Townsend, I think does very wrong to keep
two girls to serve his family, when he has daughters well
able to do the work." Mrs. Thomas said, "Father Hersey, I
think you do very wrong in censuring them, for you must
see that they are doing a great service to these young women;
they are fully able to keep two girls, and thus give them a
good home, and enable them to procure an honest and honorable livelihood. Just think of the good Bro. Townsend is
doing, and I think you will not find fault." The dear old
gentlemen leaned back from the table and paused for a
moment, seemed to be thinking seriously about what had
been said; then resuming the conversation, he remarked,
"Sister Maggie, my dear child, I am sorry I said what I did
about Bro. Townsend; I thank you for your suggesting
another view of the matter, and I fully subscribe to it."

It is generally known that he failed in business, and that
his economical habits grew out of his purpose to save every
cent, until his debts were paid. The last debt that remained
unpaid, was due to Garret & Co., Snuff manufacturers, in
Philadelphia. Having gathered the amount due, both principal and interest, he found their place of business: years had
elapsed since the debt had been contracted and the account
had been charged off to profit and loss, or if not, was regarded as a suspended debt. When Father Hersey called, and
asked for a bill, they said they had no knowledge of such an
account, and enquired as to the time when the debt was
made; he told them, and they answered let it go, the books
have been closed long ago, and we know enough about you,
to know that you need the money more than we. "Oh no," said
Father Hersey, "I have paid everybody but you, and left yours
because I thought it was for the most useless articles, but I

must pay principal and interest," and he did, at least I am
so informed.

I asked him if he thought other persons ought to dress
and live like he did. "No" said he, "I would not have others·
to follow my example in my manner of dress. My necessities first required me to save all I could, and after the·
necessities did not exist, I was perfectly contented with my
way of dressing, and should not have been happy had I
changed it. Still I think christians ought to be simple and
plain in their way of dressing. It is a grief to me to see
the flowers in the sisters' bonnets, and the jewelry they wear;
it is not, in my judgment, in harmony with their profession."

A Friend Writes:

"In answer to your inquiry concerning my personal recollections of the Rev. John Hersey, I enjoyed the pleasure of
his acquaintance, and ever esteemed it a privilege to enjoy
his company.

On one occasion at a camp meeting held at Bacon Hill,
Cecil County, Md., he narrated to us how ready the laity
were to go off into exaltation, whilst he was exhorting in one
of the large tents, but when I brought the law home to them
they all 'dried up.' The punctilious life observed by Father
Hersey was often criticised, but though his "eccentricities"
as the people used to call them, were often subject to severe
criticism, yet we never knew his piety to be brought in
question.

We were rambling through Tide-water, Virginia, just before the late civil strife, and put up with a thrifty farmer
over Sunday; among other subjects which engaged our
conversation, was a recent visit of Father Hersey, to that
neighborhood. He had refused to eat wheat bread, while a
guest of this old planter, and on being interrogated for not
eating wheat bread, his reply was, "I will not eat of it until
all my Father's children can partake alike with me of it."
The venerable man was known and respected; perhaps no
one had more sublime influence as a gospel minister than he.

During a visit to Fluvanna, Va., it was announced he
would preach on the Sabbath of his sojourn. As might be
expected, the announcement brought out a large concourse
of people; when the service was over, a prominent man of

the district, who had rode some distance to hear the sermon, was asked what he thought of Father Hersey—he is credited with saying—"·If that is the gospel, heaven will be thinly populated."

The frailty of human imperfection, beheld its own dwarfed insignificance by a contrast with his perfect life, and we have ever thought the censoriousness of his critics, was more to hide their own folly, than to carp at his blameless, spotless life."

Father Hersey on one occasion preached at Franklin St. M. E. Church, at 11 o'clock ; Rev. Bro. B. had an appointment in the country, at Ridge Chapel, at 3 o'clock, and invited Father Hersey to accompany him, which he did, and preached, and walked back to the city, and preached at night at Strawbridge ; at this time Bro B—— was very fond of his Cavendish ; Father Hersey was equally as great an enemy. Bro. B—— was well supplied with the weed for the journey, but when the sermon ended and they left the house of God, to the great annoyance of Bro. B—— unknown to Father Hersey, he happened to lock arms on the side where the plug was deposited ; the supply was cut off ; those who use the article, and knew Father Hersey's hatred to the same, can realize the situation Bro. B—— was in.

Father Hersey, on the subject of colonization to Africa, in the second edition of his book, published by Armstrong & Plaskit, in 1833, writes :

"An experiment has been made which more than realizes the expectations of its friends. The colony which has been settled at Liberia, on the shores of Africa, is in a more flourishing condition than any new settlement of the same nature and age ever before made in any part of the world ; our own country, the United States, in their progress ; in the increase of their population ; their improvement in the arts and sciences ; in the diffusion of christian knowledge, stands without a paralled on the page of history ; yet, in their origin, in the dawn of their existence, this powerful independent nation was far less successful than has been the little vine planted at Liberia. The first settlers reached the shores of Africa, in June, 1822 ; they are now in a prosperous condition ; three churches have already been erected ; several schools are in successful operation ; they have a newspaper, conducted by a colored man. Many of the new settlers are becoming wealthy; the population numbers about three thousand souls; they are extending their territory along the shores of the Atlantic; also, into the interior, among the natives, with whom they are on friendly terms, and highly respected by the savages.

The whole amount of money received by the Colonization Society up to the 20th of June 1832, is $155,912.52; with this small sum of money, a new world has been purchased—a new nation has been settled, and the prejudice of thousands respecting the colonizing our slaves in Africa has been wiped out. Surely never before was the same amount of money, so judiciously expended."

Rev. J. Pasterfield, Philadelphia Conference, writes:

Shenandoah, Schuylkill Co., Pa., Dec. 31st, 1878.

DEAR BRO. MARINE:

Yours of 28th inst. is at hand. In response, would say, that concerning the memory of Rev. John Hersey, I have many hallowed recollections; was with him in his last sickness, and officiated as one of the speakers at his funeral.

Before I mention my last meeting with him, I wish to speak of some personal interviews, when in health.

I remember on one occasion we roomed together in Dorchester county, Maryland; next morning, he was up at four o'clock, bathing in cold water, and rubbing briskly with a coarse towel; then he prayed ferverently for one hour; then he opened the Bible on a chair, and knelt and read and prayed until day. He was very abstemious in his diet. He always spoke humbly of his spiritual attainments. His was not a boastful piety, it was rather of the Apostolic type.

In my diary of Sept. 23d, 1853, I find the following entry: "I have just had an interview with Bro. Hersey—a man of God; he preached for me at Beckwith's, last Wednesday night, from these words: 'I have seen the wicked in great power, &c." It was a solemn sermon. God bless the preacher, and give him success. He is the *plainest man and preacher I ever knew.* O Lord help me to follow them, who through faith and patience inherit the promises."

The above interview and preaching was in Dorchester county, Maryland, September 23rd, 1853.

My wife speaks of an incident, that occurred some years after this in Talbot County, Md., at a place called Royal Oak; he had just preached, and my wife said to him, "Bro. Hersey, where are you going?" "Going to heaven" was the reply, with a smile. He afterwards told her where he would sojourn; this, however, was characteristic of him, and showed the bent of his mind.

He died at Penningtonville, Pa., in 1862; and summing up the "Greenspots" of the year 1862, I find this entry in my diary: "The aged Father in God, Rev. John Hersey passed away this year, and I was at his funeral, at his request, as one of the speakers. He is buried in the grave-yard of the Methodist Episcopal Church, at Penningtonville, Lancaster County, Pa.

In an interview, I had with him just before his death, the following testimonials he spoke—"One thing I regret—I have not been charitable enough to my fellow men. I have accused them of excess in eating, and I am dying with dyspepsia." After I prayed with him, he exclamed, "Victory! Victory!! Victory over self!!!" And if any man ever had victory over self, he had. Peace to his memory. May we follow him, as he followed Christ.

CHAPTER XIII.

CITY MISSION IN 1853.

Father Hersey's field of labor was so extensive, and his time so fully occupied, during his earlier ministerial life, that his views are not preserved to us as copiously, as during the last ten years in the cause of his Master; advancing years forced him, in order to have an interchange of views with distant friends, to resort to the pen; thereby fortunately preserving his matured thought in ample expression—with a rich and varied experience, coupled with a thorough and sublime faith; he kept a brief record of passing events, of which fragmentary portions are only obtainable.

During the year 1853, while laboring in Baltimore as

City Missionary, near the corner of Light and Winder streets; he had built a chapel, which was paid out of his own resources, and by him free of all charges, presented to the board of trustees of the William Street M. E. Church; they accepted of the gift, and in honor of the donor, it was called "Hersey Chapel." Modern innovationists, who are every now and then, leveling some old land-marks, have caused this temple to disappear; but it was dedicated with due religious ceremonies. On Sunday, May 1st, Bishop Waugh preached in the forenoon at 11 o'clock a fine discourse, from John, 3rd chap., 16 verse; in the afternoon at 4 o'clock, Father Hersey powerfully held forth, basing his remarks on the 24th verse of the 20th chap. of Exodus; in the evening at 8 o'clock, that most estimable and useful local preacher, Isaac P. Cook, preached from Isaiah, 56th chap., 7th verse.

Father Hersey in writing of this circumstance, says: "May this temple be accepted of God, and rendered useful to the people, for Christ's sake. Amen."

All through this year, Father Hersey worked with unabated and enthusiastic zeal; he also caused to be built one other chapel, for colored worshippers, on Biddle alley; avoiding ostentation and in a spirit of meekness, (although his means wrought the work.) The transfer of title to those for whom the edifice was intended, was made in the name of the Rev. Joshua Wells to the trustees of the Orchard Street M. E. Church, his name no where appearing. This chapel yet stands a monument to his modesty and honor. By this, and many other benefactions, he endeared himself to the colored people, and the old generation that is passing away, hold his name and memory in enduring remembrance.

When the writer was gathering together material for this sketch, he chanced to pass an old venerable colored woman upon the street, a presentment that she might impart some information, caused him to address her, when the following colloquy occurred: "Aunty, did you know Father Hersey?" La me, I know Father Hersey? Yes away back, honey, when he preached at a camp meeting from the text—"Righteousness exalteth a nation, but sin is a reproach to any people." O, but he did preach. I knew Father Hersey—he has eat many a meal in my house; why, he built us a church in Biddle alley, and the colored people purchased him a house, but he refused its acceptance, because, he said, if he took it, he couldn't sing the hymn :—

The things eternal I pursue,
A happiness beyond the view
  Of those that basely pant,
For things by nature felt and seen,
Their honors, wealth and pleasures mean,
  I neither have, nor want.

I have no babes to hold me here :
But children more securely dear
  For mine I humbly claim,
Better than daughters, or than sons,
Temples divine, of living stones,
  Inscribed with Jesus' name.

No foot of land do I possess ;
No cottage in this wilderness ;
  A poor way-faring man,
I lodge awhile in tents below,
Or gladly wander to and fro,
  Till I my Canaan gain.

Nothing on earth I call my own,
A stranger to the world unknown,
  I all their goods despise,
I trample on their whole delight,
And seek a city out of sight,
  A city in the skies.

The old lady was in ecstacy, when told that a sketch of Father Hersey was preparing for publication, and said, "I want that book." During our talk. she informed me, she was 102 years of age.

There was a most remarkable and marvelous cure, in answer to Father Hersey's faith and prayer, this year, which took place at the home of his friend W——. Father Hersey writes, Saturday, July 30th :

Called to see Bro. W——'s family, who are deeply afflicted ; their little son seven years old, the last time I was there, had lost the use of his lower extremities, both feet and legs ; the doctor said he never would recover. I prayed with the family and for him ; he arose and threw away his crutches, and walked as usual. The boy thus cured by faith and prayer offered up to God, by Father Hersey, is no less a person than the Rev. James P. Wilson, of the Baltimore Conference, who is now stationed at Frostburg, Md. He informed the writer at Conference in March last, of this marvelous cure.

In 1854 Father Hersey traveled much, and during the year visited the scenes of his childhood; we hear of him preaching at Red line Camp Meeting, near Elkton, Md., and other places; his sermons were vivid and impressive, heightened no doubt in their intensity by his mental retrospections of other days.

In 1855 he was employed as Junior preacher on West Harford Circuit, Md., by the Presiding Elder as assistant to the Rev. F. McCartney.

In the Spring of 1856, after a short stay in Baltimore, he visited Philadelphia, also Cincinnati, and attended the General Conference in Indianapolis. He returned to Baltimore in June; in the Spring of this year as he jocosely told Bro. Reese, he was appointed by the P. E. *young* preacher on Cochranville Circuit, Chester Co., Pa.; at this time he was seventy years of age: on this circuit he proved very efficient; doing a good work, and endearing himself to its people.

He was in Baltimore a part of the year 1857. In 1858, he visited New York, and paid off a debt, contracted when a wholesale merchant in the District of Columbia, and thereafter returned to Baltimore, in May, 1858. He visited Staunton, Va., in 1859, and other points in the South, accompanied by a friend, who paid the expenses of the trip.

We hear of him in Greensboro, Ala., December, 1859; in Jackson, Tenn, 1860. During this time he made an extensive tour through the South and West, visiting the places of his earlier days; he returned home in 1861. From that time to the closing up of his mortal career, was spent his most anxious years; he had a presentment that his days were rapidly drawing to a close; he had more work than time to perform it in; he pressed with vigor on, until at last the weary wheels of nature ceased to roll, and we hear him say, the Master is about to call me home, and I have no objection to go.

Sainted man of God, how grandly comes the close of thy life's day; your work is all well done; no more will you tread the dusty road afoot in the Master's cause, no more will the hail and snow of winter encrust thy locks and beat against thy brow. Your sacrifices are all made; your reward is at hand.—"Mark the perfect man, behold the upright, for the end of that man is peace."

Father Hersey during these years, made his home with his kind and benevolent friends, Bro. William Welsh and lady, who resided at 142 Pearl street, where he always found a kind, welcome and hospitable home.

Good sister Welsh fitted up to this patriarch's liking, a room in their home, which was always known as Father Hersey's room, and no one was allowed to occupy this room but he whom it was set apart for, and to which he had all his correspondence directed; and this was the home to which he bent his steps after his toilsome journey ended, where he would recount to sister Welsh his sorrows and triumphs.

I shall not soon forget my first interview with this dear aged sister and former friend of Father Hersey. I called to see her for scraps of information; although for years a child of severe affliction, at the mention of her old friend Hersey's name, she had to be taken out of bed and sat by my side, and said she "The dear old man, I did love him; he would when he came home, tell me about his journeyings, especially his trip to Africa, his indian agency, his business failure, and in different places where he traveled, but I cannot remember now particulars, only when he was leaving my house for Pennsylvania to die; I shall never forget the parting: it was and will be memorable long as life lasts; he handed me a few dollars, which he said, he had drawn from the savings institution, and wished me to apply it for him, to his Lord's poor, for whom he had spent his life in their service, which I did as he directed, ("precious man," she added,) and he took his departure for Pennsylvania where he died." Brother and sister Welsh expects soon to have a reunion with Father Hersey in the kingdom of heaven. They were not forgotten by him in his last hours, for he directed Bro. Reese, after his death, not before, to correspond with his old friends, and let them know he had passed over safely to the shining shore. Bro. Welsh kindly furnished me the letter, which is to be found in this volume, to which the reader is referred.

CHAPTER XIV.

LETTERS FROM MINISTERS.

We have in our possession many letters from ministerial and other friends, which, whilst not properly a part of the biography of Father Hersey, still, coming from those intimately acquainted with the departed saint, cannot but possess a fascination to the general reader. The poetry which introduces the letters, was held by Bro. Hersey in kind remembrance; he carried them with him on his evangelistic tours, distributed them wher cever he went, wrote them in his book of prayer, and this copy was found among his effects after death; we here insert it, as applicable to his own state of mind. He writes in his book on prayer:

"Madame Guyon was imprisoned about ten years in the Bastile and other French prisons. During this period she employed herself chiefly in writing her life; four volumes of poems and other writings, were the result; the following is a translation of one of her poems, it illustrates her state of mind in her affliction."

SENTIMENTS

WRITTEN BY

Madame Guyon in Prison.

———

A little bird I am,
  Shut from the fields of air;
And in my cage I sit and sing
  To Him who placed me there;
Well pleased a prisoner to be,
Because, my God, it pleases Thee!

Nought else have I to do;
  I sing the whole day long,
And He, whom most I love to please,
  Doth listen to my song;
He caught and bound my wandering wing,
But still he bends to hear me sing.

Thou hast an ear to hear;
  A heart to love and bless;

And though my notes were e'er so rude,
  Thou wouldst not hear the less;
Because thou knowest as they fall,
That love, sweet love inspires them all.

My cage confines me round,
  Abroad I cannot fly;
But though my wing is closely bound,
  My heart's at liberty.
My prison walls cannot control
The flight, the freedom of the soul.

O, it is good to soar
  These bolts and bars above,
To Him whose purpose I adore,
  Whose providence I love;
And in thy mighty will to find
The joy, the freedom of the mind.

Father Hersey out West..

Rev. Dr. D. R. McAnally, Editor of the St. Louis Christian Advocate, publishes the following, which we copy
from that paper of October 15th, 1879.

"A book is in press, entitled, 'A Sketch of the life of
Rev. John Hersey, by Rev. Fletcher E. Marine,' a local
preacher of this city. Mr. Editor, did you ever know the
pious and eccentric John Hersey? He travelled extensively
through the Middle States, and even in the Southern States,
preaching and warning the people constantly, everywhere he
went, for 42 years. He generally traveled on foot. He
wore the plainest clothes, and lived on the simplest, coarsest
fare. He was a great friend to the poor, in visiting and
giving largely to their relief. He was a very prayerful man,
and intelligent preacher. He died in 1862, aged 76 years.
Mr. editor, you can use this communication as you please.
God bless you and the St. Louis Christian Advocate."

W. R. MONROE, M. D.
Baltimore, Oct. 4th, 1879.

Dr. McAnally editorially replies as follows:

"It was my pleasure to know the Rev. John Hersey
quite well. First met him at a Conference in Virginia, in
1832. In 1861 he was here in the West, frequently in my
office, and at my house, and to-day, I have a grateful recollection of his prayers for me and my family, offered at our own

fire-side. A wonderful man, not so very eccentric after all, rather straightforward, pure in his purposes and true as steel to his convictions. Notwithstanding a dash of eccentricity that seemed to be mixed in his nature, he seemed to live as near to the Divine Master as any man I ever knew. In my library are copies of several books and tracts, he caused to be published more than 40 years ago; and I shall look for the forthcoming sketches with more than ordinary interest."

Believe me, dear sir, yours truly,

ED. ADVOCATE.

Letter of Rev. L. Scott, Bishop of the M. E. Church, whom I had hoped would have written the preface to the book ; he writes me,

Odessa, September 10th, 1879.

F E. MARINE, Esq.—Dear Brother :

"Yours of 3rd inst , is before me. It is quite out of the question for me to comply with your wishes ; I am already overburdened, and having great difficulty in writing at all, owing to the almost entire failure of my sight. I wish you success in your undertaking, and want a copy of your work when it is published. I knew Bro. Hersey long and tolerably well, but never intimately. I saw him frequently and heard him preach several times. He was a good, but eccentric man ; many doubtless, will rise up and call him blessed.

He is now far above the praise or blame of men.

Very truly,

L. SCOTT.

Letter of Rev. J. C. Keener, Bishop of M. E. Church (South).

New Orleans, Sept. 7th, 1879.

MR. F. E. MARINE.—Dear Brother :

"Your favor is at hand, asking for items in regard to Rev. John Hersey ; I regret that I am unable to supply you with any. I knew him as a preacher, calling at my father's house, when I was young and just from school ; and I afterwards entertained him here in New Orleans for a week or two, before the war, where he preached in our churches ; but of his history, I know nothing special, or reliable He was a delightful man, exemplifying the beauty of holiness, for years, wherever he went, and an able minister of the New Testament."

Yours truly,

J C. KEENER.

The Rev. W. R. Monroe, M. D., a distinguished minister of the Local Preachers' Association, writes :

"Some of us knew the eccentric John Hersey, who during his ministry never wore broadcloth, but dressed in rough, home-spun, grey kersey. Father Hersey as he was reverentially called, was a very devoted man of God, an indefatigable christian worker, and a most earnest local preacher for forty-two years. He was so self-sacrificing, that he slept but little, and then generally on a hard mattress, or a bare floor, covered with a blanket. He ate the simplest food, and never indulged in any luxuries, except those of prayer and preaching . He traveled long distances on foot. He preached one forenoon in Washington city, then walked nearly forty miles to Baltimore, where he preached the same night. He occasionally supplied vacancies on the circuits, and would walk at all the appointments and preach, and would visit every family within the bounds of the circuit, on foot, and pray with them, and exhort with them to seek Christ. For a number of years he was the City Missionary in Baltimore, preaching on the streets, and in the chapels ; during those years he was made a blessing to thousands, both temporally and spiritually."

A good Quaker physician of Georgetown, D. C., who prescribed for Father Hersey on one occasion, being so impressed with his deep piety, said to a friend, concerning him, "That when he died, he would go up like a rocket."

Father Hersey often preached in private houses, where a few neighbors could be assembled. Occasionally my father-in-law would take him out to his country-place, a few miles from the city to spend a night, when a few neighbors would be informed of the fact, and would gladly come to hear him preach. After my father-in-law's death, I have taken him out to the same house, where he most earnestly and faithfully preached Christ to a few glad listeners. Perhaps the last

time I took him out to the country with me, just before
arriving at our place, I informed him we would stop a little
nearer, as we had built a new house, and were occupying the
same, on a new avenue, that had recently been opened. He
immediately began to rebuke me by saying the former house
was sufficient, without building a new one. Soon after
entering our house, he called for all about the place, to come
into prayers, as his custom was. After reading the Scriptures, he engaged in prayer, and prayed most fervently for
my wife and self, saying to the Lord we had almost gone to
ruin, and praying for our forgiveness.

He lived to an advanced age, and was greatly beloved for
his devotion to God, and his success in saving souls ; peace
to his memory."

Rev. T. M. C. writes :

January 8th, 1879.

F. E. Marine.

"Yours of the 30th inst. came to hand. I have letters
received through the course of several years, from my highly esteemed friend and Bro., Rev. John Hersey, which I did
not intend to part with, but if any good can be accomplished by placing them in your hands, you shall have them."

On Feb. 22nd, Bro. C. writes : "If you succeed in collecting sufficient matter to write a short history of the life
and labors of our dear Bro. J. H., it will afford me great
pleasure. I have often wondered, why some member of the
M. E. Church, of which he was an honored member, did
not give to the church and the world, a history of the dear
old servant of our Master; while the history of many, not
more deserving, have been scattered broad-cast over the
land. I have not the honor to be a member of the M. E.
Church, but an Elder in the M. P. Church ; but a part
of my family are members of the M. E. Church, but my
love and theirs differ not for that dear old man, who was
for many years a visitor at our house, and an honored and
welcome guest ; perhaps the last visit he ever made to Har-
ford-County, was to our place. He was no longer able to
preach, but was calmly waiting for his discharge from service to reward. I often think of him during that visit : my
wife and children did all they could to make his stay with us

as pleasant as possible; his appetite had failed, and his limbs were swelling, so that he was very feeble, yet he was as cheerful and happy as a school-boy, after the confinement of the day is over. We all enjoyed his visit, and sorry when he left, for we all felt that we should never see him again in this life. He wrote to me after he reached Penningtonville, but one letter, as he lived but a short time; in his last letter, he spoke of the great kindness shown by all the denominations of that place; this was all right, for our dear old friend was no bigot, but a companion of all them that feared God

Father Hersey seldom indulged in anecdotes, but being very intimate with me, he would sometimes relate one concerning himself. He told me that he was preaching one day in a neighboring State, in a church where one of the members, a gentleman, who was very rich; you doubtless remember how he used to pepper the rich; while preaching on that occasion, he touched that rich brother's feelings, and he hung his head, resting it on his hands; Bro. Hersey's shot fell thicker and faster around him, until this rich brother forgetting himself, threw up his head and exclaimed aloud in the congregation, "Good Lord but that is hard;" but said he, "Bro. Hersey you are right, go on."

Greensboro, Caroline Co., Md , Jan. 23rd, 1879.

DEAR BRO. MARINE:

"Your letter comes in a bad time for me, as every moment of my time is so taken up in my extra meetings, that I can scarcely find a moment to recall past events connected with my dear friend and brother of former days—John Hersey. I will however, give you a few incidents illustrative of that departed minister."

"On one occasion occasion I was invited with him and a certain M. D., who was a very fashionable man, known to be living beyond his income, and could not pay his honest debts, to dine with a poor man whose wife had made a great display in the culinary department. Meats of the choicest description, and oysters prepared in the varied and most approved style only relieved the sumptuousness of the delicacies under which the table fairly groaned, as we advanced to partake of this inviting repast. Bro. Hersey got one glance at the table thus prepared, when stepping back, he asked to be excused from participating in the meal, adding that he could not conscientiouly encourage such extravagance. The doctor undertook to reprove him, when Bro. Hersey said : "Now if I wore fine clothes, rode in a fine carriage, wore gold glasses, and indulged in similar luxuries, whilst I did not pay my tailors', or butchers', or provision dealers' bill, I would be a deceiver and a hypocrite, and upon the same principle, by partaking of this dinner, I should encourage this brother's extravagance, and would be equally guilty before God." He subsequently told me, that the doctor had no use for him afterwards, avoiding him on all occasions.

Whilst I was stationed on the circuit, on one occasion Bro. Hersey preached for me. After the sermon, a good sister, the wife of a merchant who sold liquor, and who had usually entertained the ministers, invited him to her housefor dinner. Bro. Hersey asked her, "Where do you live"? she replied, "At the store." He enquired, "Do you sell liquor there ?" She answered, "Yes." 'Then" said he, turning away with a look which she never forgot, "I never eat bread that is obtained in that way." The sister returned home weeping; whereupon, her husband inquired the cause of her distress, when she told him that her feelings had been wounded, and related what Bro. Hersey had said to her. During the afternoon the husband appeared to be in deep thought, and when on the next day his son went to the city to purchase a bill of goods, the article of liquor in all its forms was omitted therefrom.

Thus by the straightforward, plain, consistent course of this venerable man, was the stream of evil cut off, the workings of intemperance narrowed and abridged. Yet such was his modesty and unselfishness, that he never alluded to this circumstance, which was therefore only known by the family of the merchant.

Brother Hersey once visited me in Cambridge, where I took him to some of my friends, one of whom, an official member of our church, had a luxurious home, costly furnished and decorated with fine portraits of members of his family. Bro. Hersey asked our host, how he could take his Lord's money and spend it for such things, when his heathen brethren were in perishing condition. The brother said he placed a great estimate upon the paintings, for they recalled to his mind, the departed. Bro. Hersey looked at him smilingly and said: "Are we not strange creatures, to forget how our *dear* ones looked *when* they lived."

The brother then said, "Bro. Hersey, I think you would be far more useful, if you would change your manner of dress; our preacher, I think dresses about right". "Yes," rejoined Bro. Hersey, "I suppose he does to suit you.?"

At the dinner table, on one occasion, my wife remarked that she never had a desire to be rich. Then rejoined Bro. Hersey, who was dining with us, "You should have no desire to *appear* rich, which you do by wearing a dress which betokens that condition; I am a poor man, and my clothes show it: I dress according to my circumstances."

I have often wished some one would write the life of Bro. John Hersey. May the Lord bless you in this good work, is the sincere prayer of my heart.

Your Bro. in Christ,

J. A. BRINDLE,

Wilmington-Conference.

Bridgeville, Delaware, Feb. 13th, 1879.

DEAR BRO. MARINE:

Yours of the 8th was duly received. I will be glad to serve you in gathering *Herseyan,* so far as I can. I know but little about him myself, and nothing at all about his early life, except that I have heard it said, that he was a gay wild young man; that extravagance caused him to break in business, and that after his conversion he adopted his very frugal and extreme way of living, to save means to pay his debts, and that it grew upon his ascetic nature and disgusted spirit, until great self-denial became a habit and a passion.

He was in my place of business, in Camden, Del., in 1857, and knowing his extreme opposition to wearing gold and costly apparel, as well as all fashion following, I said to him: "Father Hersey, I have thought it would be a wise thing, for the evangelical church, throughout the whole world, to hold a General Convention, on *dress,* and by a judicious committee, adopt a permanent style of dress, both for ladies and gentleman, that will be at once most simple, beautiful, comfortable, convenient, appropriate and economical." He replied, "Ah! my brother, if we get the inside right, the outside will be right also." He did not believe in getting the world right, by the mere action of christian conventions. I will see what I can learn for you at Conference. But nearly all the fathers from whom might be gathered reminiscences have passed away. The now reigning Pharoah knew not Joseph. Can't you visit Conference yourself, at least for a day or two? Let me suggest a title for your memorial or biography: "The voice of one crying in the wilderness." Was he not in some respects, cut out by the pattern of John, the Baptist?

Kind regard to your family,

Yours in Christ Jesus,

J. T. VAN BURKALOW,
Wilmington Conference, M. E. C.

Conshohocken, May, 1879.

BRO. MARINE:

I knew Bro. Hersey personally. When I was a boy he frequently came to my father's house, in Wilmington, Del., and I remember to-day, very distinctly, his searching inquiries and impressive advice. At the time, the words of the holy man were not a pleasant sound to me. They made my hair fairly stand up, and seemed to give me an untimely taste of the judgment, I little thought then, that I would travel a few years later the same circuit (Cochranville) upon which Bro. Hersey died; yet so it was. I found that the people on this circuit, preserved a very distinct recollection of Father Hersey's loyalty to his country, and also of his searching appeals from the pulpit.

An amusing incident in connection with Father Hersey's earnest manner of addressing his hearers, was related to me by Bro. Fox, now dead, but formerly of the Scottsville M. E. Church, then on Cochranville Circuit:

Bro. Fox, who was a farmer, had entertained Father Hersey over Saturday night, prior to his preaching in the Scottsville Church, next morning; observing that Bro F. was not preparing for church, Father Hersey inquired if he were not going. "I think not" said Bro. F——; "I have labored so hard during the week, and feel so wearied this morning, I know I would go to sleep, and in that case, you would reprove me." Father Hersey after a moment's reflection, said, "He thought he would not admonish, or reprove, under the circumstances;" and Bro. F—— concluded to attend the service. It was not long before Bro. Fox was lost in forgetfulness of all surroundings. Father Hersey on the other hand, was warming up with his theme, and reaching a point where he felt called to exhort the people to arouse themselves, he cried, "*Wake up, I say.*" The effect upon Bro. F—— was most arousing; thinking the dreaded reproof had at last come, he almost bounded from his seat and opened his eyes, to find that he had made a spectacle of himself before the people, and that the good man, true to his word, had simply exhorted to a spiritual awakening.

During his later days, Father Hersey was compelled to change somewhat in his acts of self-denial. The last night I remember to have seen him at my father's house, my mother knowing his indisposition to seek ease even in slumber, and that he had before shown an aversion to feather beds, exclaiming, "The Son of man had not where to lay his head;" inquired whether she should substitute a mattress therefore in the spare room. He replied that his suffering from rheumatism was such, as to make it necessary for him to accept the softer bed. But even in this no one who knew him, will doubt that he had first assured himself that it was right before God.

W. A. JOHNSON,
Philadelphia Conference.

June 16th, 1879.

DEAR BRO. MARINE:

Father Hersey about the time the war broke out, had arranged for a trip through the South; the war clouds were fast gathering, and his friends tried to persuade him to abandon his plans and remain in Baltimore. He answered them that he had been impressed that it was his duty to go, and that he was not responsible for the existing state of the country, and would therefore, keep on, going about his Father's business; desirous of making provision for the poor, whom he had been helping, he went to his friends and committed them to their care.

A poor woman with two children, lived in the vicinity of Emory Church, of which I was then pastor; handing me some money, he said: "Here brother, use this, and if more is needed, please continue to help; if I return I will repay, if not, the Lord will settle the matter with you, no doubt to your satisfaction." He went, and on his return, resumed the care of them until they were enabled to do so themselves.

The extent of his charities cannot be known, until the Great Day shall reveal them. He practiced rigid self-denial that he might help the poor.

GEORGE. W. COOPER,
Baltimore Conference.

Father Hersey always regarded the South as a field opened before him, who as a herald, would advance the Maker's cause; he was fond of visiting that section. Just a few years before the late civil war he preached in Greenville, Virginia, a remarkable sermon; on this occasion he seemed to have allowed his dormant power of eloquence to escape from his grasp; he described Satan in pursuit of the sinner and crying at every step, *death! death!* After a painful suspense, with an electrical thrill, he reversed the position and proclaimed aloud, that while Satan pursued and shouted the sentence of doom, a voice from Calvary proclaimed *life! life!* that this was music in the sinner's ears, who found a refuge in the rock—Christ Jesus.

Brother Wilford Downs, of the Baltimore Conference, M. E. Church, who has a vivid recollection of the aforementioned sermon, was visited at his home in Frostburg, Maryland, by Father Hersey, during the year 1861. While his short stay lasted, he at different times preached with great unction and power, and as was usual, visited and prayed with the families of the place; when he came across those who were in want, they were the recipients of his charity. Whilst at Bro. Downs' house, he spoke with great earnestness to him of the approaching storm of civil war, the dark clouds of which were gathered above the nation's existence.

The first battle of Bull Run had not then been fought; it was his belief, that the war would last four years, and with perfect faith in his prediction, he cited certain passages from the book of Revelation, to sustain his position ; subsequent history when its periods were all rounded up, showed that he had not calculated amiss.

He also good humoredly, narrated the part he had personally taken in the "Races at Bladensburg," as the battle of that place was, years ago, familiarly called. He was at that time a merchant in Georgetown, and when recounting the part he took in that action, said with considerable zest : "Our troops ran, and I ran too ; at that time I was a proud young man, and with others went out to make the British run, but they turned the tables upon us;" and here followed a laugh, so hearty and real, and withal so unusual, as to seem marvellous.

There is also the same authority for the statement, that at a quarterly meeting, held at Bel-Air, Maryland, during the time that Father Hersey was junior preacher on that circuit, a heavy snow had fallen, and the sleighing was excellent ; after the Monday morning appointment, the preachers present, who were F. McCartney, Father Hersey and W. Downs, were seated in the sleigh of a good brother, and driven several miles out in the county to his house to dinner ; while on the way, Brother Downs remarked, "Father Hersey, what would you think if on my return to Baltimore, I should state that you had been out sleighing ;" this was a poser : his countenance showed that he felt some inward emotion; the effect of which was to prevent any further reference to the subject.

An esteemed brother writes of Father Hersey—"How shall we that are dead to sin, live any longer therein."

St. Paul said—"I am crucified with Christ, nevertheless, I live, yet not I, but Christ liveth in me."

If any man, since the days of St. Paul, was truly crucified with Christ, that man was John Hersey ; for he was more like a man from the spirit world, than of the earth. He was as dead to sin and to the spirit and customs of the world, as if he were not living in it. And he was so spiritually alive to God, as if he were among the "Spirits of the just made perfect." His conversation was in heaven. It was clearly apparent to those who knew him best, that his citizenship was in heaven. He dwelt in love, and consequently, dwelt in God. He abided in Christ, a living branch to the true Vine. He lived in the Spirit, yea he also walked in the Spirit.

The love and goodness of God as manifested in Christ to fallen men, occupied all his thoughts, and all his hours. His uniform custom was to rise very early in the morning, even "a great while before it was day," and commune with God, in reading His word, and in prayer for several hours.

Being thus endued every morning with power from on high, he became fully prepared to spend the whole day in going out among the poor, in ministering to the sick and needy, and in helping all by his counsels, his sympathies and his prayers.

He was the most self-denying and self-sacrificing man I ever knew. He slept but little ; he ate but little, and that the simplest and most easily digested food ; he wore the plainest and cheapest clothing, and consequently, gave away to the poor, all that was ever given to him, except barely enough to procure the coarse clothing he wore. Often he would procure and carry with him provisions to feed the hungry, and garments to clothe the naked. He would visit the sick and those in prisons, and minister unto them.

His preaching was scriptural, close, heart-searching, convincing and powerful. The Spirit of God was in his holy utterances of Divine Truth. Many were awakened and converted to God, under his preaching ; and many were comforted and strengthened in their faith and love to Christ.

Multitudes in the humble walks of life were blessed by the visitations, counsels and prayers of Father Hersey. He kept a book in which he wrote hundreds of names of those persons who had requested his prayers : and that book, he would open before God, present every name, with every request in the name of Christ. He "visited the fatherless and the widows in their affliction, and kept himself unspotted from the world."

In the meekness and boldness of his Master, he was always ready in his uncompromising spirit with the world and sin, fearlessly to reprove sin, fashion and worldly-mindedness, and extravagance in dress, furniture, food, or in any thing else. The christian community looked upon him as being extreme and eccentric ; yet if he were eccentric and as-

cetic in his way of living and teaching, he was on the safe
side, for he was conscientious in his convictions upon this
subject.   The love of Christ constrained him in all he said,
and in all he did.   He felt it his duty to denounce the spirit
of the world, the lusts of the flesh, and pride of life, especially among professors of religion.

His conversation was always of the most profitable kind, for
it was seasoned with the grace of God.   No doubt multitudes
whom he helped, will arise up in the day of Judgment and
call him blessed.

CHAPTER XV.

RECOLLECTIONS OF FATHER HERSEY, BY BRO. ROBT. TURNER.

"He had eyes lifted up to heaven; the best of books in his
hand; the law of truth was written upon his lips; the world
was behind his back.   He stood as if he pleaded with men,
and a crown of glory did hang over his head."

Bunyan's Pilgrim's Progress.

We quote the foregoing picture as a true portrait of Father
Hersey, as we thought of and viewed him in life, which was
a lesson and a treasure in our home.   Never did we feel so
honored, as when our roof sheltered him.   This was a privilege granted us frequently during the latter years of his life.
Consistency was one of his prominent characteristics; he not
only preached righteousness, faith, charity, peace, self-denial,
but he practiced these virtues.   He rebuked all that he believed to be sinful, in love, not in anger.   His example reflected more fully the lovely image of his Master, than any one
I have ever known.   His gentle refinement, and affectionate
nature, won, not only the highest respect, but the love of every
member of our family, as well as every domestic; each and all
feeling that Father Hersey was interested in their welfare.
His explanation of the scriptures at family prayer, was particularly interesting and instructive, and when he prayed that
we might have an abundant "entrance into the better land,"
we felt that he had done us good; believing that true prayer
reaches up to heaven.   .

An incident occurs to my mind just now in connection with Father Hersey, which I will relate. Some years before his death, he called upon me, and remarked that he owed some three hundred dollars which was a debt incurred in his early business, and that whilst legally exonerated from paying it, he still felt morally bound to cancel the obligation.

Having heard that two of the children of one of his creditors who had been many years dead, were living in New York, in reduced circumstances, he was determined to find them, and pay to them the amount which he had owed to their father. I said to him, "Father Hersey, do you suppose you can find anybody living that would take from you that sum?" He replied, "I feel it is a religious duty, and must be performed." I said, "Father Hersey, if you find the parties to whom you refer, I want you to draw on me at sight for the amount;" he replied with a smile and "God bless you." I heard nothing from him until some time after, when having occasion to visit New York I met him at the New York East Conference; being curious to know whether he had fallen in with the children of his creditors, I inquired into the matter. He answered, "Yes, and I have their receipt in full; I have paid them and whilst they hesitated, still they did receive the money, remarking that they 'were now convinced that father was not mistaken in his often repeated assertion, that John Hersey was an honest man.'" This tribute to his virtues was richer than any earthly honor, however exalted, that could have been bestowed.

During his stay with us, when his health seemed to be failing, and the physician assured us that he could not recover from his debilitated condition, yet, could be rendered more comfortable by conforming to certain rules prescribed, I succeeded after some difficulty, in convincing him that it was a religious duty which he owed to himself as well as his friends, to yield a little from the abstemious regimen which had been his habit through so many years of his later life. The change of diet for a short time seemed to revive him; and gaining strength, he resolved to finish some books which his impaired health had compelled him to abandon. For this purpose, he retired to a quiet rural village about fifty miles from Philadelphia, Pa., now called Atglen, but then known as Penningtonville, where his books were completed, and his pious and useful life ended.

My last connection with him was to receive over one hundred dollars, the receipts from the sale of books which he had left with his friends This money, thus left by Father Hersey, was designed by him as a sacred legacy to the poor. For many years I have been conscientiously endeavoring to execute this duty in the spirit of him who devised it, by distributing it to necessitous cases, such as were the objects of Father Hersey's care, when able to attend personally to its distribution; and some how or other, this legacy, like the widow's cruse of oil and barrel of meal, has never been exhausted, but is yet being distributed in Father Hersey's name, and is placed to the credit of the Hersey Fund.

I will here mention an incident connected with the death of our child Lily, which made an impression that can never be effaced from our memory. She was baptized by Father Hersey, when a few weeks old, who ever after evinced the deepest solicitude and affection for her, speaking of her as the best of the family. As her age increased she became fond of him, hailing his coming with delight, and always called him "Father Hersey." She died when two years and three months old, some months after Father Hersey's death, whom she had not seen for a year, and whom we supposed she had forgotten, in consequence of her tender age. When dying, she reached forth her hand, and in a tone of salutation, exclaimed, Father Hersey!

Is the vail which separates child—like innocence and purity in this world, from matured spiritual perfection in the next so thin, so transparent, that this little innocent could peer through the gloom, and recognise her departed friend in the beyond? Can the redeemed saints be introduced into the spiritual world before life is extinct in the material? We *know* not, yet believe, what St. Paul inferentially declares, "Are they not all ministering spirits sent forth to comfort the heirs of salvation." We believe that the purified vision of our angel child saw and recognised the sanctified image of the departed father, who wrote the following lines on Lily, just 6 months and 10 days before he went to heaven.

ACROSTIC.

Each babe, Christ folds within His arms,
Loves and imparts to them new charms,
In mercy saves them from death's alarms.

Zion's children are clothed in white,
And shine their radiant stars more bright;
Behold for those what Christ hath done !
Each one exhalted to his high throne,
There to wear an everlasting crown,
Honored above earth's smiles, or frown.

A cruel Herod said they must die,
Save Lord, and hear a mother's cry,
His cruel hate, O turn away,
Let our children live and learn to pray.
Each mother now rests secure,
Your babes shall live to die no more.

Then mother you must act your part,
Unite with Christ to mould her heart.
Rise and lead her to the throne of grace,
Now teach her to love that holy place,
End then life's day and reign above,
Renewed in everlasting love.

' Suffer the little children to come unto me, and forbid them not; for of such is the Kingdom of God."—MARK x, 14.

"Mother, bring your child to Christ in the arms of faith and love; train her up in the way in which she should go, and when she is old, she will not depart therefrom. The way in which she should go is the King's highway of holiness—the way of obedience, of love, and reverence for God and her parents. Never permit her to disobey your word, no never, or she will be emboldened to disobey the word of the Lord, which must result in condemnation. Remember, you are not qualified to teach her those things with which you are yourself unacquainted; therefore, be ye holy, for I am holy saith the Lord."

Baltimore, May 7th, 1862.   J. H.

CHAPTER XVI.

LAST DAYS ON EARTH.

We approach the end of Father Hersey's earthly career; his sun set without a cloud. He was much given to musings during his last days, and lived over his entire life in retrospection

The following lines—the familiar song of the writer's departed pious mother, which she was most desirous should be preserved—contains sentiments very often expressed by the aged patriarch ; they are here assigned a place, as doubtless expressive of his experience at this matured time of his life.

A NEW SPIRITUAL SONG.

Come christians join with me to praise
  The Lamb on Calvary ;
Who shed His blood upon the cross,
  So free for you and me :
And by the virtue of the same,
  To heaven I hope to rise ;
And there to shout redeeming love,
  With angels through the skies.

Deep waters here I do pass through,
  My Father's face to see ;
O ! children to your Father pray,
  For to remember me.
A pilgrim here on earth I am,
  Bound to fair Canaan's shore,
The land of rest, the saints' delight,
  Where sorrows are no more.

Oft' times my Father I have asked,
  My soul to sanctify,
That in his church among the saints,
  That I may live and die ;
But pride and unbelief has been
  Injurious to my rise ,
And by my passions oft I fell,
  Which clouded much my skies.

One more request my Father's flock,
  I have to ask of thee ;
That when you are at the Throne of Grace,
  There to remember me ;
That when with you I no more meet,
  I may in glory be ;
That when you are received home,
  To shout along with me.

Companions there in heaven we'll have,
  Just suited to our mind ;
No turning back, no aching heart,
  No crosses there to find :
No more the people of our own,
  Our enemies shall be ;
And gushing tears are wip'd away,
  From pain forever free.

Before my song I do conclude,
  Sinners—A word to you;
I pray you to receive the Lord,
  For He hath died for you; ·
I want you all to go with me,
  Not one to stay behind;
But let us join and travel on,
  Jerusalem to find.

And if I faint upon the road,
  Don't you one moment stay;
But live to God, and march along
  To everlasting day.
I hope when I shall come to die,
  My rest to have in view;
Live near to God, and watch and pray,
  And He'll take care of you.

Hail happy souls, how fast you go,
  And leave me here behind:
Don't wait for me for I do know,
  The Lord is good and kind;
Go on, go on, my soul says go,
  And I'll come after you;
Tho' you're so fast, and I'm so slow,
  I'll sing hosanna too.

God give me grace that I may go,
  And guide my steps aright,
Tho' you're so fast and I'm so slow,
  You're not yet out of sight;
When you get to that world above,
  And there God's glory see:
When you get home—your journey's end,
  Then look you out for me.

For I will come fast as I can,
  Along that way I'll steer,
And through God's grace, I shall at last
  Be one among you there;
There all together we shall be,
  Together we shall sing;
Together we shall praise our God
  And everlasting King.

Heaven is the place I hope to see,
  Then, all my trials over;
I'll hail my old cross-bearing friends,
  And be with Christ forever;
There we shall meet no more to part,
  Around the Eternal Throne;
Where sin shall all be done away,
  And sorrows never come.

Hard trials here I do pass through,
 But Jesus is my friend;
What, tho' I meet with trials now,
 They all shall shortly end;
Then I shall bid this world adieu,
 Away my soul shall fly,
And wing away to worlds above,
 Where pleasures never die.

At some period in the year 1862, he wrote the following, which is among the latest efforts of his mind and pen:

"God in mercy has spared my life until I have well nigh reached my seventy-sixth year on earth, and I feel sensibly that my lengthened days on earth are fast drawing to a close. Until within a few months past, I have seldom felt any bodily fatigue, though I have generally preached twice or thrice each Sunday, and nearly every night in the week. I have not for many years laid down in the day time, unless in case of sickness, which has seldom occurred. God in mercy has given me strength to walk most of the circuits I have traveled, some of them being very large. The Culpeper Circuit, which was the first I traveled, was two hundred and forty miles around, with but one rest-day in four weeks. The last two circuits which I traveled only a few years since, West Harford and Cochranville, were about the usual sizes, in these modern days. Two Sabbaths I filled three appointments five miles apart, and generally led two classes, seldom retiring to bed feeling any more fatigued, than when I arose in the morning. This, for one over seventy years, may appear to be incredible. I attribute it all to the goodness and mercy of God alone. It is true, that I lived a self-denying life, rising every morning at four o'clock, and using no animal diet of any kind, no tea, no coffee, for more than forty years, yet all this would be ineffective without a pure heart filled with love for God and all mankind. I desire to magnify the grace of the Lord Jesus further, for the encouragement of our young brethren in the Lord. I have never asked any one for one cent of money for myself, nor have I contracted a debt for many years to the amount of one cent, which I conceive to be in strict obedience to the gospel injunction—"Owe no man anything;" and yet within the last few years (under the most exciting circumstances,) I have traveled several thousand miles in the Southern and Western States, visiting Alabama, Mississippi, Louisiana,

Tennessee, Missouri, Kentucky and Ohio, preaching Christ
crucified in simplicity, being everywhere received with confidence and affection. We have a rich Father, and a kind
Master; therefore, we have nothing to fear from men, or devils, or earthly contingencies, if we love God fervently, and
serve him with a perfect heart and a willing mind. We
have a bond that makes us rich, yea, richer than the Roths-
child's, viz.: "All things shall work together for good, to
them that love God." This fully meets every righteous demand, and supplies every christian want; therefore, one
anxious thought about to-morrow, about what we shall eat,
or drink, or wear, dishonors God, and disgraces our own
character as children of God. One dissatisfied feeling, one
distant murmur weakens our faith, and stains our spiritual
garments, disqualifying us for a place at the marriage supper of
the Lamb. From the present condition of our country and
of the church, I fear we are guilty of the crime charged
against the rulers of the Jews. God says: "Ye have healed the heart of my people slightly, crying peace, peace when
there is no peace."

JOHN HERSEY.

Although his health was failing, he preached in the month
of January, 1862, no less than seventeen times; in the
month of February, nineteen times; in the month of March,
he was present during the session of the Philadelphia Conference, and preached that week and till the 16th of April, no
less than twenty-three sermons, in Philadelphia and vicinity.
This was his last visit to the church of Philadelphia. Opening his commission at Wharton street, from Numbers 35 : 12
and closing it at Central, from Gal. 6 : 14. After leaving
Philadelphia, he preached but eleven sermons. During the
month of March he preached twenty-one times; in April six-
teen times; in May but four times; in June and July he was
unable to preach; in August he preached on the 6th, at
Denton Camp Meeting. After this he preached but twice:
on the 24th, at Georgetown, from Luke 11 : 32, and on September 28th, 1862, at Fayette st. M. E. Church, in Baltimore,
Maryland, Psalms 139 : 23-24.

Being convinced that his end was near, he sought a place
of rest and quiet, away from noise and bustle, in which to

close his days; such he found in the hospitable home of
Charles Reese, of Penningtonville, Pa.

How like the patriarchs of old, recognizing that the time of
his departure was at hand, breathes the following expression
of his feeling, and wishes in regard to the rapidly approaching, yet recognized end of life, in a letter to Brother Reese.

Baltimore, August 18th, 1862.

DEAR BRO. REESE.

    The Lord in great goodness and mercy, has laid His
kind hand of affliction upon his very unprofitable servant,
with whose manners he has borne long, lo, these many
years, and I desire to feel as grateful for the rod, as for the
staff, for affliction as for health, well knowing that God has
done, and will do all things well. He has spared me to a
good old age, and has dealt bountifully with me. It would
therefore, be ungrateful in me, not to receive affliction with a
thankful heart.

I have no objection to closing my long career on earth,
except that I feel ashamed of myself, that I have been so unprofitable a servant; yes, I also regret the wretched condition of our highly favored country, and the worse condition
of the church, but as I am too old to reform myself, and can
do very little for the real benefit of the church, or State, I
bow submissively to the mandates of Heaven, and say, good
is the way of the Lord. To depart and be with Christ is far
better than to remain in this sin disordered world. I feel a
comfortable assurance that that God who has been my un-
ceasing friend, will, when heart and lip shall fail, be the
strength of my heart, and my portion forever. I look forward with fearful apprehension to those things which are
coming upon the world and the church. Indeed the church
will be doomed to drink the bitterest cup of God's wrath,
which must be poured out upon our wicked world before
Christ's Kingdom shall be established in universal peace and
righteousness, when all mankind shall dwell together as one
great family of God, when there will be no discordant sound
heard upon earth, when righteousness shall cover the earth, as
the waters cover the sea. That glorious day must and will
come. The character of your Redeemer, demands it, and
the mouth of the Lord has spoken it. But a moment's

thought will convince the reflecting mind that the present rubbish of sin and folly, of pride and vanity and worldly-mindedness, with a thousand other dark traits of briers and thorns must all be consumed, must be burnt up when Jesus Christ shall be revealed from heaven in flames of fire, taking vengance on them that know not God, and obey not the Gospel of Christ. Oh may we be ready for that fearful day. The farmer does not expect to make a crop until he has cleared the ground and burned up the brush; neither can universal purity prevail and abound, until all the rubbish is destroyed. Christ says: *"Ye are the salt of the earth."* If therefore, God has provided salt to save the world, and it is not saved, the salt is the cause. And Christ says, if the salt has lost its savor, it is henceforth good for nothing, but to be cast out and trodden under foot of man. This declaration should arouse and alarm the church. Oh may the watchmen take the alarm, and may the trumpet no longer give an uncertain sound. When in my affliction my whole physical system was almost paralyzed, when I had no energy left to read or write, not even a letter to a friend. greatly alarmed at the aspect of things. I sat down to write without previous plans, without meditation, without books (save the Bible), or authors for my guide. I wrote with more ease, than I had ever done before, until I had written enough to make a small book, which I am preparing for the press, and intend to leave behind, as my last warning to a wicked world, and a corupt church. As I can have no personal or pecuniary interest in the matter, I hope it will do good, especially to the ministry, which I am sure it will, if they will condescend to read it. As I am laid by, unable to preach, and can hope to do but little more on earth, and must very soon render up an account of my stewardship, I feel a desire to retire from the bustle and vanity of this wicked world, and close my earthly career in peace and quietness. In thus reflecting upon the condition of the cities (sinks of corruption,) and our distracted and degraded country, I have thought of no place where I could realize my desires as fully and as comfortably as under your own roof.

If therefore, you have a little room, where you could place me, and will consent to accept a suitable compensation for my trouble, it would be grateful to my feelings, in my declining hours. Please write and let me know if such an arrangement would meet the approbation, fully of yourself and sister R——. I leave all however, beyond the present moment, where it should be, in the hands of that God, who number the hairs of our head, saying I hope understandingly—"Thou shalt guide me with thy counsel, and afterwards raise me to glory." Amen.

Yours affectionately,

JOHN HERSEY.

Brother Reese writes: "In reading the above letter to my family, every ear was listening, and every heart beat for joy, to know that his request would be complied with. So immediately I wrote and gave him a hearty welcome, which he gratefully accepted."

Below will be seen the letter of acceptance of the great good man, who it will be seen would not for a moment consent to be a charge to any member of a church which he had served so long and faithfully.

Baltimore, September 1st, 1862.

DEAR BRO. REESE:

Your very kind and affectionate letter of the 28th ult. has been duly received. I feel more than thankful to you for your very kind proposition of christian love and friendship. It is more than I deserve, and what may be deficient on my part, I hope my merciful Father in heaven will supply.

There is only one omission in your letter—You say nothing about the remuneration for the trouble I shall make you. David said that he would not offer a sacrifice that cost him nothing; neither can I impose on my friends for nothing. This however, I presume, can be adjusted when we meet. I am here in the city against my will, where I have many kind friends, whose homes are freely offered to me; but the place and the worldly feelings of my friends here, renders it an unpleasant home for my old age and fast declining years.

I am attending to the publishing of another book, and the printer has disappointed me so often, that I do not know when I can be released from this earthly encumbrance, perhaps not for several weeks. But as soon as I can, I will retire to Penningtonville, and seek a shelter under your hospitable roof.

My health is still very feeble, with no prospect of being better, yet should it be at all restored, I must occupy my time until the Master comes. All the future, however, I leave where it should be, in the hands of Him, who knoweth all things, and say, I hope understandingly, Father, "Thy will be done." If my health should improve, which at pres- is very doubtful, I can use my time in your county as well perhaps, as elsewhere. Let all behind the curtain remain. Amen.

I hope that you and yours will ever be found *striving* to enter in at the straight gate which leads to that holy city, whose inhabitants never die—where sin has never entered, and suffering and sorrow and death are unknown—where war's blood stained banner will be forever furled, and uni- versal peace and joy abound. May that be our home, our rest, our joy. There may we meet to go no more out for- ever. Amen.

"Who meet on that eternal shore, shall never part again."

My kind respects to sister R——, and all the family. The good Lord bless you all for Christ's sake.—Amen.

Yours affectionately,

JOHN HERSEY.

Father Hersey before leaving Baltimore, preached on the 28th of September at Fayette street M. E. Church, what proved to be his last sermon. On the next day he appointed a parting meeting, in the Sabbath School room, on the south side of old Light street Church. It was a meeting of preach- ers, and one of those occasions never to be forgotten. Fath- er Hersey was weak—extremely weak. He sat during his address; he told the meeting that he was going to Pennsyl- vania to die.

I am a poor way-faring stranger,
   A journeying through this world of woe ;
Through sickness, sorrow, toil and danger,
   To that bright world to which I go.

I am going there to see my Mother,
   I'm going there no more to roam,
I'm just going over Jordan,
   I'm just going over Home.

I know dark clouds may gather round me ;
I know my path is rough and steep ;
But beauteous fields lie just before me,
Where God's redeemed their vigils keep.

I'm going there to see my Father,
I'm going there no more to roam,
I'm just going over Jordan,
I'm just going over Home.

I want to sing salvation story
In concert with the blood-washed band ;
I want to wear a crown of glory,
When I get home to that Good Land.

I'm going there to see my brethren,
I know they are near my Father's throne ;
I'm just going over Jordan,
I'm just going over Home.

I feel my sins are all forgiven ;
My thoughts are fixed on things above ;
I'm going away to that bright heaven,
Where all is joy, and peace and love.

I am going there to see my classmates,
They have gone before me one by one,
I'm just going over Jordan,
I'm just going over Home.

I'll soon be free from every trial ;
My body will sleep in the old church yard ;
I'll drop the cross of self-denial
And enter on my Great Reward.

I'm going there to see my Saviour,
I'm going there no more to roam ;
I'm just going over Jordan,
I'm just going over Home.

It was a marvelous parting ; it would have made one of
the most impressive of pictures.

On the 30th of September, bidding a final farewell to his
friends in Baltimore, he started for Penningtonville, which
he reached in safety.

Bro. Reese says when he arrived. he was very weak, suffering much pain in his stomach ; his disease was dyspepsia.

One week after his arrival, he penned the following lines
to a dear friend in Baltimore : an air of christian resignation
and sublime faith, is evinced in every sentence.

Penningtonville, October 6th, 1862.

DEAR. BRO. R. T.

Through the very great mercy and goodness of God, my Saviour, I am still permitted to enjoy a place among the living, though much more connected with the dead and dying. My health is now much as it has been for some time past; at times apparently better, again evidently worse, so that my onward march is constantly tending to the grave. Nor should I object to that most reasonable result, after a long life, blessed with every comfort that any reasonable being could wish or desire. And though I have been a very unprofitable servant, God has mercifully borne with my imperfections and has given me many and kind friends, wherever I have been, nor will he cast me off in the day of eternity.

When I could be no longer useful to my fellow mortals, I concluded to retire from the public scenes of folly and vanity, and spend the close of my life in peace and quietness. God in mercy has directed my steps to such a place.

The family I am now with, are the most pious and peaceful family I have ever known. Not a loud or unkind word is heard at any time, and yet everything moves like clock work; each one has his or her duty to perform, and it is done pleasantly and perfectly. The only difficulty is they press me down with personal kindness—each member striving to see who can render me the greatest service, and make my life the most agreeable and pleasant, as far at least, as my suffering will admit of.

I do not know why it should be so, but all through my christian life, God has given me kind friends, and while it is most pleasing to flesh and blood to enjoy those privileges, yet it is also most dangerous. Smiles are more likely to lead us astray than frowns. O may not the smiles of friends on earth, lure me away from the arms and favor of the sinners' friend, who says: "If any man will be my disciple, let him deny himself, and take up his cross and follow me." But, alas, our fallen nature and the smiles of friends, do not sympathise with the *cross.* Pray for me brother, that after I have preached plain gospel truths to others, I may not myself be a castaway.

That jewel (a pure heart) is very valuable and precious in the sight of God, and none but the *pure in heart* can see

God, can possess and enjoy him forever. That which is *pure* will admit of no admixture—no self, no worldliness, no double-mindedness, no love of the world—its honors, or its pleasures can exist in a *pure heart*, that pearl of great price. May this be our treasure and glory Bro. T——, that when Christ comes to make up his jewels, ours may be found *pure*. Even the little queen of England would not wear a mock jewel, in her earthly crown, which must soon fall to the ground and be mingled with the dust; how unreasonable then to suppose the Lord Jesus, the King of kings, and Lord of lords would place an impure gem in his eternal crown of power and splendour and glory.

My dear brother, let us be careful so to live, that when the Master comes to demand an account of our stewardship, we may be prepared to respond promptly, when He asks the question, "Why have you done this thing to please the Lord Jesus, not self, not the world, but to please Him, who died to save our souls from death and hell?" Your principal danger like my own, lies chiefly in the smiles of the world, and in ardent love for your family. How hard, oh how hard to resist the importunity of those we love; and how hard to see in them even one blemish. To act faithfully and impartially in the fear of God, in these things will require the constant aid of God's Holy Spirit, and the grace of our Lord Jesus Christ to enlighten our minds and strengthen our faith. I hope the good Lord will have you and all your kind family in His holy care continuously, and reward you all richly for your unremitting and almost unlimited kindness to one of the least of your Master's servants on earth. Oh may we meet in our Father's house above, beyond the reach of war, of sin and death, where not a cup of cold water given to Christ's least disciples will be forgotton.

Please write to me in my obscurity, when you can find leisure to do so. Grace, mercy and peace from God, the Father, and from our Lord Jesus Christ, be with you and yours evermore. Amen.

Yours affectionately,

JOHN HERSEY,

A few days later, he wrote the following cheerful letter to his friend:

Penningtonville, Chester Co., Oct. 10th. 1862.

DEAR BRO. T. M. C.

Through the forbearing and wonderful mercy, and goodness of God, my poor life is still spared, I hope for some wise purpose, which none but He who knoweth all things knows. I greatly desire to lie at the foot of the cross, having no will or desire of my own, either for life or death, either for sickness or health, but Thy will, oh God be done.

I have retired from the noise and bustle and folly of the cities and towns, and have found a quiet and peaceable spot to close my earthly days, where I find a greater opportunity of doing good, than in the cities—where the ministers of the church shut up the! way to heaven, not willing to go in themselves, nor suffer others to enter by that only door, *Christ crucified.*

Here many call to see me to whom I can speak freely and profitably. Both Baptist and Presbyterian ministers have been to see me, manifesting the greatest regard for me, for which I feel thankful, and point them to the narrow way, in which few are willing to walk. The family with whom I stop are *plain, pious* industrious people; everything works like clock-work, yet not one loud or unkind word is ever heard. My greatest difficulty is, that they weigh me down with kindness. This however has been my doom all through life. Oh, may not the smiles of friends on earth lead me away for one moment from the arms of the sinners' Friend in heaven. Pray for me brother, that after I have preached plain gospel truths to others, I may not be myself a castaway.

Oh may I be permitted to meet all my kind friends, including you and your family, in heaven, when the storms of this wicked world shall all have blown over. We live in an evil day, when it will require more faith and watchfulness and zeal and faithfulness than at any former period of our world's history. Our privileges mount up to heaven, and yet I fear our sins and follies out-top them all. Oh may we who at least in part see the way, the old path, be enabled to walk therein, through the grace of our Lord Jesus Christ, that thereby we may enter into that rest, prepared for the people of God. May you and I and all your little family

meet there to go out no more forever. I presume we shall
meet no more on earth. Well it will not be long that flesh
and blood, and hills and dales and distance will separate the
friends of Jesus. Be thou faithful until death and Jesus
says, "I will give thee a crown of life." Amen. Lord help us
to act wisely and promptly and faithfully that we may hear
the Righteous Judge of all the earth say, "Well done good
and faithful servant, enter into thy Father's joys in heaven."

Write soon and often. My health is so feeble that writing
exhausts my little strength. My kind respects and love to
sister C—— and children, Bro. M—— and family, and all
my christian friends. The good Lord bless and save you all
in His everlasting Kingdom for Jesus' sake. Amen.

Yours in love,

JOHN HERSEY.

About four weeks before his decease, being much better,
he concluded to go to Philadelphia, thinking perhaps he
could obtain some medicine from some of the physicians that
might do him some good; his purpose was to go to the
preachers' meeting, and give them his dying advice, but he was
so feeble that he was unable to attend the meeting. He also
intended to spend a few days with his half sister in Delaware
City; his health continued to get worse, and he had to abandon the visit and return to his home in Penningtonville to
wind up the toils of an eventful life.

Shortly after, his health rallying, he paid a visit to Philadelphia, and writes his last letter to his friend Reese. His
physical weakness is apparent in every sentence.

Philadelphia, October 17th, 1862.

DEAR BRO. REESE :

My health still continues very feeble, sometimes it appears to be better, again, evidently worse, so that my steps
are bearing me steadily and rapidly down to the brink of
Jordan. Oh may I be prepared to cross over like Joshua, or
Elijah, and leave this wicked, warring, rebellious world behind. Amen. I have not yet deemed it prudent to go down
to Delaware City, Delaware, to see my sister, and have con-

cluded to remain in this city, until next week, when it is my wish, if able to attend the preachers' meeting, and give them a few plain words of counsel. Perhaps a word from the lips of a dying man, may be attended with beneficial results. If my strength will permit of it, I design going to Delaware City next [Monday evening, or Tuesday, where I may remain only a day, or two, after which I shall endeavor to return home. There I expect to close my long earthly career under your roof and in the bosom of your family, with whom I shall confidently hope to spend an; unending eternity beyond the reach of war and sin and suffering of every kind, when and where alone you will be rewarded for all your kindness shown to one of the least of all your Master's servants on earth. Oh may we meet there, and all will be well forever.

> "Who meet on that eternal shore,
> Shall never part again."

Thank the Lord, bless and praise His holy name forever. Should nothing prevent, you may expect me home sometime next week. I say *home;* I have no other on this side of the swelling tide, but I humbly hope to have a better home, when all the storms of this evil world shall have blown over. Amen.

Let us meet there, where there is room enough and to spare, where not a cup of cold water given to one of Christ's disciples will be forgotten I am very weak and must say farewell.

My love to all your kind family. The good Lord bless you all.

Yours respectfully,

JOHN HERSEY.

Before starting on his return to Penningtonville on the evening of October 21st, 1862, he wrote the following letter to a dear friend in Baltimore. This letter written less than four weeks before his death, breathing in every line and sentence, his consciousness thereof and his acquiescence therein, assumes somewhat the character of a last will and testament, and invokes the attention as it challenges the admiration of all who admire consistency in a man, fidelity in a friend, devotion and untiring energy in a minister, and sublime faith the nearest unquestionable approach, certainly since the days of the Apostles, to perfect santification in a christian.

Philadelphia, Oct. 21*st*, 1862.

DEAR BRO. R. T.

Please apply the amount of the enclosed check of $35.88 to my account, to be disposed of after my decease as previously arranged, for the benefit of the poor. Money from the sale of books, comes in slowly. Many are afraid to read the new book, others are prejudiced against the source from whence it originates. If however, the present gloomy scenes being transacted in our country, and I may add in the whole world, continues much longer, the people will begin to think that the hand of God is upon us for evil, which may cause them to investigate the cause and cure of our disasters. I have been in Philadelphia for eight or ten days past, but expect to return this evening to my home on earth for a few days, or moments. My health is no better, and if no change for the better takes place, must very soon close my long and unprofitable career on earth. I have given my kind friend, Chas. Reese, directions to have my poor earthly remains laid away, with as little expense and parade as possible, and have requested him after my decease, to let you know the amount that will be due for my board, and all other necessary expenses. He is a good and faithful man, and will not make an improper statement. I am sure you will take pleasure in attending to this matter. I have now but few desires, or wishes to gratify; the first would be to see the church which Christ has purchased with his own precious blood, made pure and holy and spotless, walking in perfect unity together in all the commandments and ordinances of the whole earth, unblameable and unreproachable in His sight. This would soon save the whole world, and transform our poor distracted, wicked world into the Paradise of God on earth. My second desire would be to see all my more than kind christian friends, who have ministered freely and bountifully to all my earthly wants, filled with all the fullness of Christ's redeeming love, richly clothed with the garments of salvation, and covered with the robes of righteousness, and then in heaven rewarded with a crown of undecaying glory, and hear the Righteous Judge say, "In as much as ye have done it unto one of the least of these my brethren, ye have done it unto Me."—Amen. So may it be.

Give my kind respects and love to sister T—— and the children, to father and mother and friends in the Lord. Oh, that I may see you all, in a brighter and better world. For Jesus' sake. Amen.

Yours affectionately,

JOHN HERSEY.

The last work of his pen is the following unfinished letter addressed to Rev. C. B. Tippet, deceased, late of the Baltimore Conference, bearing date October 31st, 1862. A part of this letter was written by Father Hersey one week before his death ; realizing that he was too weak to finish it, he wrote on the margin, the words "'Tis too late."

Penningtonville, Oct. 31st, 1862.

DEAR BRO. TIPPET:

'*Tis too late.*

"So I thought and believed a few days since I had promised to write to you, but like poor sinners, I had deferred to do so until I believed it was too late, and even now I write more like a dead man than a living man. But after much suffering, the God of all grace and truth, hath (as He has done all through life) dealt bountifully with his unprofitable servant. Through the mercy of our Lord Jesus Christ, He has not only enabled me to demolish that most dangerous idol —*self*, not only to cast him to the ground, but to have him *crucified*; as certainly as Christ was literally crucified for us, so must we be as certainty crucified with him. I awoke in the night from the arms of death, and was enabled by the grace of our Lord Jesus Christ to despise and condemn all—*yes, all* my good works, and trample them all under my feet, in holy triumph, giving to God, through our Lord Jesus Christ, all— *yes all*, the merit, or good works I have ever done, and by the omnipotent arm of faith claim perfect redemption through the blood of our Lord Jesus Christ. Though I was too weak to stand up without support, yet, in the midnight hour, I felt not only like shouting victory to God and the Lamb, but as though I could shake the empire of darkness through the unlimited power of Jesus' grace. If therefore, you hear any one say that your old friend J. Hersey, expected to

reach heaven, through the slightest degree of merit attached
to his own works, you may give it an unqualified contradiction, or if you hear any one say that myself, or any other
person will ever enter into heaven with one spot or wrinkle
upon their garments—that will be equally untrue.   I fear
God and honor the King.   I preach Christ as an all-sufficient
Saviour; that his blood applied by faith, can and will wash
out every stain, even the slightest spot or stain of selfishness
or pride, or ambition.   The *love of the world* in any of its
modifications must and will shut us out of heaven, even a desire to shine as an orator; ambition can no more be received
into heaven, than the love of the world—its gold, or silver,
or honor, or desire of applause.   These all belong to the
beast, and where they are found in any degree, they will
identify us with Satan, and exclude us from God, and the
word of his power forever.

Surely God has dealt bountifully with his unprofitable
servant."

Bro. Charles Reese, by letter, gives the following information of his last days; "He came to my house Tuesday, Sept.
30th, 1862; the Sabbath morning after, he was very ill indeed.   We thought for a while he would die, but soon he
revived and was much better.   The Presbyterians had their
Sacramental occasion that Sabbath; he said he appreciated
the Sacrament very much, and would like to receive it once
more, before he went hence.   I got a carriage and took him to
the church; he communed with them.   After the communion,
he gave a short but pointed address.   In the afternoon he went
over to our church and heard Brother Jones (our young
preacher.)   He also spoke after Bro. Jones with a good deal
of energy.   This I believe was the last of his public speaking.   He led in the family devotions, morning and evening,
in his usual manner, exhorting all present after reading, then
a fervent prayer to the throne of grace for a blessing.   He continued to do so until within two weeks of his death, he being
too weak to continue it any longer.   He was very thankful
for any little favor done; he would say, "Thank you."
When the family was about to retire he would take all by
the hand, and pronounce a blessing on them, and impress a
holy kiss on each, and bid them good night.   I would then
take charge of him during the night; I shall never forget
those nights.   Among his sayings, I have preserved the fol-

lowing : at one time in the middle of the night, the Lord blessed him most powerfully. He said, "Oh that I had strength and voice to shout the praise of God. Hallelujah, hallelujah, praise the Lord, oh my soul, and all that is within me rejoice and bless His holy name. Oh that I could stand on some eminence, and with the voice of an angel proclaim salvation to a lost world." Thus we can see that the burden of his heart was for the salvation of the world. In conversation, he said he was sure he had not run before he was called (meaning his call to the ministry,) for said he, I felt when a sinner, I should be a Methodist Preacher, and that seemed to mortify my pride. Again, "How unworthy I am; but Christ alone is worthy; poor, poor; rich, rich; having Christ, I have all things. Oh that I had a congregation and strength, I would preach Christ and hold Him up before them as an all-sufficient Saviour, and the only refuge for poor fallen men."

On November 13th he asked what day it was; he was told it was Thursday. He replied, "Oh, I think I shall spend my Sabbath in heaven."

In bidding farewell to some friends who had called in to see him, he said to them, "Farewell, hold on to Christ. God bless you."

During the day he seemed very happy, but frequently said "Unworthy," and would exclaim, "Thank God I have been enabled to take self down; yes, from the very stump, and Christ set up."

On November 14th, when asked by my wife if he would have a little supper, he replied, "I shall sup in my Father's house above. Jesus smiles and bids me come."

> Where everlasting Spring abides,
> And never withering flowers;
> Death, like a narrow sea, divides
> This heavenly land from ours.

"Oh sister, what a shout there will be when I see you come up there"

In one of his spells of suffering, he said, "Farewell, vain world, I'm going home." He frequently would ask us to sing one hymn he seemed to love so much, and said sing

WHEN FOR ETERNAL WORLDS I STEER.

When for eternal worlds I steer,
And seas are calm and skies are clear,
And faith in lively exercise,
And distant hills of Canaan rise ;
My soul for joy then claps her wings,
And loud her lovely sonnet sings,
   I'm going home.

With cheerful heart her eyes explore,
Each land-mark on the distant shore,
The tree of life, the pastures green,
The pearly gates, the crystal stream ;
Again for joy she claps her wings,
And loud her lovely sonnet sings ;
   I'm almost home.

The nearer still she draws to land,
Each moment all her powers expand
With steady helm and free bent sails,
Her anchor drops within the vale :
With holy joy she folds her wings,
And her celestial sonnet sings ;
   I'm safe at home.

The last word we heard him speak, that we could understand, when he was dying, was "Salvation ;" he tried to say more, but could not.

This unique document is the last will and testament of the departed divine.

JOHN HERSEY'S LAST REQUEST.

It is my wish and positive instructions, that should I be permitted to close my earthly career under the roof of my kind friend, Charles Reese, that he will have my poor earthly body enclosed in a very plain pine, or poplar coffin, and deposited (if there be room) in his lot in the Methodist grave yard, in Penningtonville, and as few people to attend, as will be sufficient for the occasion, or at least with as little show and parade as possible. I wish no funeral sermon preached on the occasion, but a few appropriate remarks when the body is interred.

I also wish and direct said C. Reese, to take what money he may find in my pocket book and purse, for the payment of all expenses, and should there not be enough to defray all expenses and compensate for his trouble, I request Robert Turner, merchant, South Frederick st., Baltimore, to pay promptly the balance. After these things are attended to and not before, let Wm Welsh know of my death and burial. I wish *especially* that my watch shall be sent by some safe conveyance to Robert Wilson, whose mother lives at No. 434 West Lombard street, Baltimore.

I further request that Bro. Reese and his family love and fear God and keep all His commandments, and meet me in heaven.

JOHN HERSEY.

I will endeavor as far as practicable, to comply with the above request and directions.

Signed,   CHARLES REESE.

The following letter conveyed the sad tidings of his demise, to his sorrowing and anxious friends in Baltimore.

Penningtonville, Nov. 21st, 1862.

MR. WM. WELSH.—Dear Sir :

In accordance with the request of our venerable friend and father, John Hersey, I hereby inform you that he departed this life, on Monday morning the 17th inst., at twenty minutes past twelve o'clock, in full triumph of a blissful immortality and eternal life beyond the grave. His remains according to his directions, were quietly and peacefully interred (in my lot which had never been broken,) in the burying ground connected with the M. E. Church of this village. His suffering was very great, especially during the last four weeks, continuing until the forenoon of the Sabbath, which was his last.

He slept soundly and was only awakened at intervals by intense pain, but in the after part of the day, and at night there was no more sleep, for suffering ; yet there was not a murmur escaped his lips, whilst all praises were given to his Redeemer. It was evident to all after night set in (indeed we looked all day for him to die), that the vital spark of life was about to go out, yet it continued to burn until the turn of the night as stated before.

At one time, in the middle of the night, some two weeks before his death, he sat up in his bed, no one being present but myself (for I was with him in his room, and watched and attended to him, during his sickness, I mean in the night), when the Lord blessed him and made him happy. He shouted aloud and said, "Praise the Lord, oh my soul, and all that is within me bless His holy name, hallelujah, hallelujah. Oh that I had voice and strength to shout the praise of God." Then would I say, "Poor! poor! poor! rich! rich! rich!"

Again, would he say, "Farewell, vain world, I am going home; my Saviour smiles and bids me come."

On Friday, my wife asked him if he would have something to eat; shaking his head, he replied, "Oh no, the next meal, I shall eat at home in my Father's house above, "Where everlasting Spring abides, and never withering flowers; death like a narrow sea, divides this heavenly land from ours." And oh sister, what a shout there will be, when I see you come up there." Many were his precious sayings, the last of which, when dying, was 'Salvation.' He tried to say more, but could not. There was no struggle in death; just a little move of the muscles of his face, and all was over. Thus, was the end of the good man of God. He now rests from his labors. "Blessed are the dead, who die in the Lord."

Yours affectionately,

CHARLES REESE.

N. B.—I could say much more, but enough has been said. He was perfectly rational to the last. He often spoke of the kindness of yourself and wife in ministering to him, whilst with you. Oh let us all try to meet him in heaven. May God help us so to do,   Amen.

C. R.

We subjoin the following letter from the Rev. I. R. Merrill, which will commend itself to the attention of our readers:

COATESVILLE, DEC. 5th, 1862.

An hour with the Rev. John Hersey, twelve days before he left the Kingdom of Grace for the Kingdom of Glory.

When I heard that the Rev. John Hersey was in my neighborhood, and was not expected to live long, I availed myself of the first opportunity to visit him. When I arrived at Bro. Reese's house, in Penningtonville, Chester Co., Pa., where he had come to spend the remainder of his days, I was inform-

ed that his physician had forbidden persons seeing him, yet,
when my name was announced to him, (he being a little
better,) I was, by his direction, invited in. When I entered
the room he was sitting on an easy chair; as I approached
him, I said, "I am happy to see you sitting up. I hope you
are better." "Yes," said he, "I am better, thank the Lord;
but I am very feeble." He loooked me in the face as I held
his hand, and said with peculiar emotion and emphasis, "I
am glad to see you, take a seat." I felt I was in the presence of the true Christian Philosopher. I asked him if he needed
anything for his temporal comfort; for, said I, "You have many
friends who would gladly minister to your wants, if they but
had an opportunity." A tear of gratitude rolled down his
cheek, and he said, "Thanks to the Lord for friends. My
wants are all supplied. I have a friend in Baltimore who
will take care of me the remnant of my days, and see that I
want no earthly comfort." I then asked him what was the
state of his mind in a spiritual point of view. He replied,
that, "Through the abundant mercy of God, in Christ Jesus,
he felt that he was accepted of God. My brother, I have only
one regret, that I have not done more for my Lord and Master." This remark led me to ask him some questions in reference to ministerial usefulness, or what course we, as ministers, should pursue, to make us more useful: admitting that
the minister is truly called of God, and has the anointing unction from the Holy One. He paused, and said, "Pastoral
visiting in the true spirit of a minister of Jesus Christ; tal-
king religion to the people; reading and expounding the word
of God, with prayer, as we have opportunity in their families,
is a means of usefulness, and cannot fail to render a minister
more acceptable to, and useful among his people." Then
said he, "Brother, we have too much formality in the pulpit,
and out of it. We want more simplicity and spirituality in our
preaching. We want more of the merit that was in Christ
Jesus, more of the spirit of true christian sacrifice, more
self-denial, &c." I then asked him if he had his arrangements made for his funeral in the event of his death. He
said he had directed to be put away in as plain a manner as
possible; "I wish as little formality as can be: I dread formality. I don't wish any sermon preached at my funeral.
If you can be present, I wish you to make a few remarks."
He named the Rev. Mr. Bunker, of the Baptist Church, Pas-

terfield and others, whom he desired to be present and partic-
ipate in the funeral exercises. He then said, "My strength
is failing, have prayer with me." I took the Bible, and
read a part of the eighth chapter of Romans, commencing
with the fourteenth and closing with the twenty-eighth verse
of the chapter, "And we know that all things work together
for good to them that love God, to them who are the called
according to his purpose". I asked him what he had to say
to that. He replied "It is true, it is true." We then engaged
in prayer and truly our fellowship was with the Father and
the Son and the Holy Spirit.

> The opening heaven around us shone
> With beams of sacred bliss;
> Whilst Jesus showed his mercy ours,
> And whispered we were His."

I then helped him to his bed and said, "Peace be with you."
He replied, "The Lord bless you. Come and see me again."

Rev. W. T. Bunker of the Baptist Church, writes as follows.

During the last illness of Father Hersey, I visited him frequently, and always found him to be what you all know he
was—a matured christian in his judgment, his views and his
character Christ crucified was his continual theme, and salvation through unmerited grace his homely song. His hope
of acceptance with Christ, he said, was unshaken, though
temporary clouds flitted across his mind. His sufferings were
intense, and I ventured to suggest, that possibly, his physical
disease might have something to do with his momentary
gloom; to which he replied in his characteristic manner,
"Perhaps, and if so, it is a part of my Saviour's discipline to
make me meet for His Kingdom;" quoting at the time these
two beautiful passages: "Whom the Lord loveth, He chas-
teneth;" and "Our light affliction which is but for a moment,
maketh for us a far more exceeding and eternal weight of
glory;" laying particular and peculiar emphasis on the phrase
"maketh." The last interview I had with him, when I understood what was apparent to me, that his last hour had nearly
come, and quoted for his encouragement, the dying words of
the sainted Payson; he looked up smilingly, and said, "God
has given me a Paradise to live in, and a Paradise to die in."
My interviews with Father Hersey were to me always mel-

ting, instructive and encouraging. It seemed to be getting out of this world into the vestibule of heaven to get into his chamber. I need not state the impressions I received from different interviews with Father Hersey, were precisely the impressions that another christian would have received, that John Hersey was Christ's, and Christ was John Hersey's.

The following letter from Father Hersey's pastor, at the time of his death, will be read with interest.   -

DEAR BRO. MARINE:

In compliance with your request sent from Baltimore Dec. 28th, 1878, concerning Rev. John Hersey, I will send you a few reminiscences, which occur to my recollection.

I was only occasionally privileged with an interview with the dear old saint (for he was truly one of the best men and christians I ever knew). My first acquaintance with him was in the City of Baltimore, in the year 1853, in the month of May, in Armstrong & Berry's book store. I was introduced to him by the Rev. I. P. Cook.

Being then a young minister, and junior with Rev. H. K. Freed on the Springfield Circuit, in Philadelphia Conference, which, I think Bro. Hersey had once traveled, as assistant preacher. He seemed especially interested in my success, giving me much good advice. He left an indelible impression on my mind. His tall manly figure—broad brimmed hat, linsey-woolsey clothing—his earnest, spiritual conversation—his affectionate, kind address—all led me to feel a singular veneration for him.

My next interview with him was in Hedding M. E. Church, Philadelphia, at the tent meeting, under the supervision of Rev. A. Manship. Again at a camp meeting, held near Pennsgrove, New Jersey, whilst in charge of St. George's Circuit, Philadelphia Conference.

Bro. Hersey was visiting his half sister, Mrs. Nickelson, in Delaware City, and seeing me there in my carriage, he proposed going home with me, and in riding along together. I was delighted and profited by his conversation. Having visited us while I was in charge of Crozierville station, Delaware County, Pa., in 1858, two or three times, he was not a stranger in our family. On Sabbath he rode with me to my appointments—preaching at Red Lion and Glasgow. We had just finished and dedicated the new church at Glasgow, and of course he took exception to several things making up the furniture of the new building. After service in the afternoon, we rode to Bro. Isaiah Staunton's house, for supper, where we spent the night together, he having a separate bed. The next morning we rode over to Salem M. E. Church, then on Newport Circuit and not far from Christine, in New Castle County, Delaware.

Bro. Hersey recognized the grave-yard, connected with Salem, as a hallowed spot, containing the precious remains of his parents and ancestry, After lingering there for a little time, he returned with me to my home in St. George's, and soon left to attend to his Master's work—"going about doing good."

In the Spring of 1862, I was appointed to Cochranville Circuit, Pa., and in the month of October, I received a letter from Bro. Charles Reese, who lived in Penningtonville, a small village, six miles from Cochranville, and on the line of the Pennsylvania Central Railroad, which was also one of my appointments, concerning Bro. Hersey, who having traveled this circuit as an assistant, had formed some special acquaintances, and now having received premonitions of death, selected Bro. Reese's house as his last earthly home.

Here he was most tenderly and kindly cared for, from Tuesday, October 2nd, until Sabbath night, November 16th, when just twenty minutes past twelve o'clock, Bro. Hersey died, shouting salvation! repeating the word several times; and placing my ear close to his lips, he attempted the utterance of salvation again, succeeding only in articulating the first syllable, when his sainted spirit fled.

There were present at this solemn, yet happy hour, Rev. Alexander M. Kemble, one of my local preachers; Bro. Reese, wife, son and niece; sister Ruth Anna Brosius and myself. Then and often since, I have thought of the couplet:

"The chamber where the good man meets his fate,
Is priviledged beyond the common walk of virtuous life,
Quite in the verge of heaven."

was and is a truthful representation of the dying scenes and associations of the saint of God, leaving the earthly tabernacle: The impression and memory of that Sabbath night will never be forgotten by me, or the rest who were present. "It was good to be there."

I send you a transcript of the letter that Bro. Reese sent me, on Bro. Hersey's arrival at his house in Penningtonville, Chester County, Pa.:

Penningtonville, Oct. 2nd, 1862.

DEAR BRO. DARE:

The old Israelite has come (I mean Father Hersey). He landed safe on Tuesday evening. Not being able to get out of the cars in time to get his trunk, they took it on to the city, which worried him very much. I wrote a note describing it, and gave it to the baggage-master, requesting him to bring up the trunk, which he did the next morning, to the great satisfaction of Father Hersey—who is very anxious to see you, as soon as you can conveniently come. He is none the worse of his ride on the cars, but is feeble—not able to walk much—his feet being very stiff and paining him very much. Come soon.

Respectfully yours,

CHARLES REESE.

I hastened to see him, and was permitted to repeat the visit several times before his death. My esteemed colleague, Rev. Robert W. Jones, spent much time with him—more than I could—as his boarding house was in that village. In my frequent visitations, he was continually giving me good instructions, which has ever since been a stimulus in my work as a minister of the Lord Jesus.

There were occasionally seasons of depressions with Bro. Hersey, because of the wicked world and the lack, or want of zeal in the church. Yet the last were among the happiest weeks of his eventful life.

I called to see him on Sabbath, Nov. 16th. After dinner sang with him, his favorite hymn—"When for eternal worlds we steer, &c., &c." and then joined with him in prayer.

After his death, a new suit of clothes which some kind brother had given him, was put upon the body, which, as he had requested, was placed in a neat coffin, made of poplar

wood, by Bro. Charles Reese. He had requested me to superintend the funeral services, which he desired to be without
pomp or show. He wished no sermon to be preached, but
leaving it at my option to invite several brethren, which I did.

Appropriate remarks were made by nearly all the brothers
present, after which we followed the precious remains to the
lot surrounding the Penningtonville M. E. Church, and on
the East side of the building was placed all that was mortal
of Rev. John Hersey.

Very truly, yours in Christ,

JOSEPH DARE,

Wilmington Conference M. E. Church.

The remains of Father Hersey were taken from the home
of Charles Reese, where he died, to the church, on Wednesday afternoon at 2 o'clock, where the funeral services took
place. The pall-bearers were Rev. Joseph Dare, preacher in
charge of the circuit, Rev. Robert A Jones, junior preacher,
Rev. J. Pasterfield, Rev. Wm. Burrell, Rev. George W. Lybrand and Rev. I. R. Merrill, Methodist preachers and Rev.
Wm. T. Bunker and Rev. Charles Young, Sr., Baptist
preachers.

Revs. Jos. Dare, Robert A. Jones, Jeremiah Pasterfield,
Wm Burrell, George W. Lybrand, I. R. Merrill, Wm. T.
Bunker and Chas. Young participated in the services, all delivered short addresses, except Revs. Chas. Young and Robt.
Jones; Rev. J. Pasterfield read as a Scripture lesson, the
15th chapter of First Corinthians. The opening hymn was
sung, being announced by Rev. I. R. Merrill.

"Servant of God, well done, &c."

Doxology was then sung, and benediction pronounced by
Rev. A. Hooke.

The attendance by the citizens of the place and surrounding country and from the other churches on Cochranville circuit was large.

The remains were buried in Penningtonville (now called
Atglen,) cemetery, adjoining Atglen Church.

The dust of this venerable servant of God being sealed from
the sight of the living.

Happy the spirit released from its clay;
Happy the soul that goes bounding away,
Singing, as upward it hastes to the skies,
Victory! victory! homeward I rise.

Many the toils it has passed through below.
Many the seasons of trial and woe ;
Many the doubtings it never should sing,
Victory! victory! thus on the wing.

There lies the wearisome body at rest :
Closed are its eyelids, and quiet its breast.
But the glad spirit on the pinions of light,
Victory! victory! sings in its flight.

While we are weeping, our friends gone from earth,
Angels are singing their heavenly birth ;
Welcome, oh welcome to our happy shore ;
Victory! victory! weep ye no more.

How can we wish them recalled from their home,
Longer in sorrowing exile to roam ;
Safely they passed from their troubles beneath,
Victory! victory! shouting in death.

Thus let them slumber, 'till Christ from the skies
Bids them in glorified bodies arise ;
Singing, as upward they spring from the tomb,
Victory! salvation! Jesus hath come.

The following epitaph marks the last resting place of this venerable saint.

JOHN HERSEY,

MINISTER OF THE GOSPEL

OF THE

M. E. CHURCH.

Died November 17th, 1862, aged 76 years, 3 months, 15 days.

(Earth exchanged for heaven.)

Behold God is my salvation,
I will trust and not be afraid ;
For the Lord Jehovah is my strength and my song.
He is also become my salvation.

ISAIAH : xii chap., 11 verse

When the report of Father Hersey's demise reached Baltimore, a meeting of the preachers was called, when, by unani-
mous request, the following minutes were written by Rev.
J. H. Brown, D. D.

"Rev. John Hersey who has recently been taken to his
everlasting rest, was a remarkable man. We shall not soon
see his like again. His name will live in the remembrance
of God's people, wherever he journeyed as an Evangelist,
for his self-denial, his great labors both in public and private
preaching the word, and visiting from house to house; for
his primitive habits and for his unworldly and holy example.
He seemed to be raised in the providence of God, to be a
living rebuke to the worldliness of the churches, especially
our own. Those who knew him best, esteemed him most.
He was kind in his reproofs, agreeable in his intercourse and
amiable in his spirit. In the times which came over him,
he did justly, loved mercy and walked humbly with God.

This body of christian ministers will not soon forget his
parting address; he was extremely feeble. It was to be his
last interview; it was an occasion when words sank deeply
into the listening ear. How impressive and patriarchal the
remark, "My Master is about to call me home, and I have
no objections to go."

It told of an intercourse above—a divine commission
known to a sort of God's dear children, who walk in perfect-
ness. He died in the Lord on the morning of the 17th of
November, 1862, in Penningtonville, Chester Co., Pa, in
the kind family of Bro. Charles Reese. He has left us a
monument, more enduring than the chiseled stone. His life
is a living testimony, and his death gloriously triumphant
through the grace of our Lord Jesus Christ. Therefore,

Resolved, That the life and labors of this devoted servant
of God and laborious Evangelist, shall ever live in our
remembrance.

Resolved, That his diligence in the improvement of time
and opportunities shall not be without their notes of admonitory reasoning to us in our future ministry.

We extract the following from that excellent newspaper,
" *The Daily Baltimore Sun,*" under date of November 25th,
1862.

DIED

At Penningtonville, Pa., on the 17th of November, 1862, Rev. John Hersey, in his 77th year. It will be gratifying to his numerous friends to be informed, that he died in great triumph.

(Delaware and Missouri papers please copy.)

From the local columns of the same journal we glean the following :

"DEATH OF REV. JOHN HERSEY. The numerous friends of Rev. John Hersey, will learn with regret that he departed this life at Penningtonville, Pa., on the 17th inst., in the 77th year of his age. Mr. Hersey was a local minister of the Methodist Episcopal Church, but traveled extensively in various States of the Union. He also visited Africa some years since as a Missionary. In this city he labored for several years as a Home Missionary, and extended valuable relief to the poor and destitute. He was the author of several volumes, embodying his views of religion and practical economy. Recently, being impressed that his end was near, he prepared his last publication, and bidding an affectionate farewell to his Baltimore friends, he repaired to the residence of a friend to spend his last days, where he died in peace, and was interred in the Methodist burying ground. His manner of life was abstemious and marked by great self-denial. His piety was of the most decided character, and his benevolence knew no bounds, except his limited means.".

A singular coincident is found in the fact that upon the same day that "Satan unmasked, or the human heart unveiled ; the mysteries of the Book of Revelation explained," was offered for sale through the columns of the *"American,"* at Baltimore, Md., its author, Rev. John Hersey, died at Penningtonville, Pa.

We copy from the *Christian Advocate and Journal,* of Jan. 8th, 1863, the following notice, by Rev. G. W. Lybrand.

Rev. John Hersey died at the house of Charles Reese, Penningtonville, Pa., on Monday, Nov. 17th. He was born in New Castle County, Del., August 2nd, 1786. His family were identified with the early history of Methodism ; his parents, Isaac and Jane Hersey, lived west of Christiana,

Del. As early as 1771, they opened their house to the
preachers ; here a society was raised up and afterwards a
church called Salem was built about 1809 ; this is one of the
oldest appointments in Delaware. "The house of his uncle,
Solomon Hersey, was the first place at which Mr. Asbury
preached on the Manor, Cecil County. Md." He had the
preaching at his house for a number of years, and though the
first Methodist preaching on the Eastern Shore of Maryland,
was in Kent County, yet the evidence in the case leads to
the belief that the first society on the Shore was formed at
Bro. Hersey's in 1772. This society is still represented at
the Manor Chapel. Another brother, Benjamin Hersey, was
the leading spirit, if not the father of the Union appointment on Smyrna Circuit.

Our departed brother enjoyed from these connections,
marked early religious advantages, He often referred to the
influence of mothers, and spoke in his illness of his precious
mother, and that in answer to her prayers, he was brought to
Christ. She in early life was a Friend, and when she became
a Methodist, she retained the simplicity of manners and plainness of dress that characterizes that people. Highly favored
as he was, he spent the earlier years of his manhood, as a
man of the world.

At what period he gave his heart to God, I have no data.
For upwards of forty years he was an itinerant local preacher ; as an Evangelist, he traveled through nearly all the
States, besides visiting the colony of Liberia. He often
preached every day in the week, and frequently on the Sabbath thrice. He was ordained deacon by Bishop Soule,.
April 10th, 1825 ; elder, by Bishop Roberts, March 1st,
1829. He thus refers to the goodness of God in the preser-
vation of his health and life through a long period of service:
"God in mercy has spared my life until I have well-nigh
reached my seventy-sixth year on earth, and I feel sensibly,
that my lengthened days on earth are fast drawing to a close.
Until a few months past, I have not felt any bodily fatigue,
though I have generally preached twice, or thrice each Sunday, and nearly every night in the week. I have not for
years laid down in the day time, unless in case of sickness,
which seldom occurred. God, in mercy has given me strength
to walk most of the circuits I have traveled, some of them very
large ; the Culpeper circuit, the first I traveled, was two

hundred and forty miles around; and one rest day in four weeks, and no more. The last two circuits which I traveled only a few years since, West Harford and Cochranville, were about the usual size in these modern days. Two Sabbaths I filled three appointments, five miles apart, and generally led two classes, and seldom, if ever retired to bed feeling more fatigued than when I rose in the morning ; this for one over seventy years may appear to be incredible ; the cause I attribute to the goodness and mercy of God alone ; the first indication of failing strength, was at the close of last year." He spent the watch night at Kenton, Del. After this he preached some seventy-nine times, mostly in January, February, March and April of this year. His last sermon was preached in Fayette St. M. E. Church, Baltimore, Md., on Sabbath, Sept. 28th, from Psalm, 23, 24.

Convinced his end was nigh, he sought a place of rest and quiet, away from noise and bustle, to close his days ; this he found in the hospitable home of Charles Reese, of Penningtonville. He reached this on Tuesday, Sept. 30th, 1862.

He was able on two occasions afterwards, to go to the house of God, on one of which he worshipped with the Presbyterians at the Communion season, assisting in the same ; the last service in which he took part, was an exhortation, at the close of a sermon in the M. E. Church on the same day, just six weeks before his death. His faith triumphed gloriously in the final struggle.

Bro. Reese who was constant in his attendance, and who, with his family, nursed him as a child, thus writes : "He was very thankful ; any little favor done, he would say thank you; when the family was about to retire, he would take all by the hand and pronounce a blessing on them, and impress a holy kiss on each, and bid them good night. At one time in the middle of the night, the Lord blessed him most powerfully ; he said, 'O that I had strength and voice to shout the praise of God !' but, said he, 'Hallelujah, hallelujah, praise the Lord, oh my soul, and all that is within me bless His holy name ; oh how unworthy I am, but Christ alone is worthy.' Again, he would say, 'Poor, poor, rich, rich, rich, having Christ I have all things.' O that I could stand on some eminence and with the voice of an angel proclaim salvation to a lost and ruined world !"

The Rev. I. R. Merrill visited him during his sickness, and thus writes: "I then asked him what was the state of his mind in a spiritual point of view? He replied that through the abundant mercy of God, in Christ Jesus, he felt that he was accepted of God; and said he, "My brother, I have only one regret; that is, that I have not done more for my Lord and Master."

The Rev. Mr. Bunker of the Baptist Church, writes: "The last interview I had with him, when I understood his last hour had nearly come, I quoted for his encouragement, the dying words of the sainted Payson. He looked up smilingly, and said, 'God has given me a Paradise to live in, and a Paradise to die in;' thus it was till the last; the last words uttered were "Salvation." He gave directions, in reference to his burial "That his remains be inclosed in a very plain pine or poplar coffin, with as little show and parade as possible; no funeral sermon preached, but appropriate christian remarks, when the body is interred." His wishes were complied with and on Wednesday, November 19th, 1862,-in the presence of his brethren in the ministry and laity, his remains were deposited in the burial ground of the Penningtonville M. E. Church. The impression of all, in his life and death, "That John Hersey was Christ's, and Christ was John Hersey's"

Soldier of Christ, farewell, thy race is run,
  Thou hast kept the faith, and nobly served thy Lord,
Fought the good fight, the glorious victory won,
  And now hast entered on thy Great Reward.

Departed saint! and shall we mourn thy flight,
  Or bid our breasts with holy triumph swell,
To greet thy entrance on the realms of light,
  Check the full tear—the bursting sigh repel.

The crown of righteousness is now thy own;
  Thine to behold our God's unclouded face;
With heavenly harps before the eternal throne,
  To join the Wesleys in the Songs of Praise.

Yet why from numbers drops the gushing tear,
  Hersey, your valued friend has Jordan crossed.
Yes, weep, ye children of his faith and prayer,
  Another father hath our Israel lost.

But no—hold fast your hope unto the end,
  You shall be stars to glitter in his crown,
You shall with him the heavenly mount ascend,
  In God's Great Day—His ministry to own.

The Lord who first our spreading churches raised,
  Will still vouchsafe his all-sufficient grace,
To bless the assemblies where his name is praised,
  And bid another fill our *Hersey's* place.

Called by *Jehovah* in the bloom of youth,
  The hallowed standard of the Cross to raise;
Boldly he preached the Gospel's sacred truth,
  The joyful tidings of unbounded grace.

His bosom glowing with celestial love,
  He calmly suffered persecution's ire,
Repaid his enemies with prayer, and strove
  To pluck the brands from everlasting fire.

A true expounder of the sacred word,
  The weak He strengthened, and the careless warned,
Cut the heart, the trembling sinner heard,
  The awful judgment of that God he scorned.

A lively preacher more than forty years,
  He faithfully fulfilled his high behefts,
Reared by his pious ministerial cares,
  Lo! ransomed thousands rise to call him blessed.

Called by his Master to the painful test,
  He nobly bore the consecrated cross;
You who have known the virtues he possessed,
  Alone can fully estimate his loss.

Just granted here to hail Immanuel's birth
  Then summon'd to behold His face above,
To join in heaven the ransom'd sons of earth,
  And share the purchase of redeeming love.

Disrobed of all his terrors, death drew nigh,
  Behind a band of shining seraphs stood;
He pointed Hersey to the opening sky,
  And dipped his dart in the atoning blood.

The faithful christian felt the stingless wound,
  And to his God resigned his fleeting breath,
Behold heaven's portals thro' the gloom around,
  He shouted victory ! victory !! in the arms of death.

O blest conclusion of a glorious race,
  The goal attain'd the promised prize is given :
With holy joy, thy blissful soul we trace,
  Escaped from earth to happiness and heaven.

MISCELLANEOUS.

BEING A DIARY OF

FATHER HERSEY,

From April 18, 1853, ending November 29th, 1853.

ALSO

SERMONS AND ADDRESSES,

With Extracts from his Writing and Letters,
to his friends.

The author was desirous of procuring the entire diary of Father Hersey, so far as the same was kept by him, and to this end he has sought its procurement. Diligent inquiry has developed the fact that the writer is not the first person who has sought to place in tangible form the memento of the subject of this sketch. In the course of his researches, it was ascertained that from various persons who at one time were in possession of portions of the diary, detached parts had been obtained by those who purposed to put into memorial form, the object now sought, and were by them lost, suffice it to say, they never prosecuted their purpose to a consummation.

The diary (or so much as we have been able to get,) shows how a busy life was spent. Father Hersey was no laggard ; he worked as diligently in his ministerial calling, as the banker or merchant toiling after gain. During the time he was Baltimore City Missionary, he kept his office in the rear of the Fayette Street Methodist Church, and he was warmly sustained in his efforts by substantial aid rendered by Bros. E. C. Thomas and H. W. Drakely of the Fayette St. charge.

The sermons and the addresses are inserted as specimens of his style, while the letters speak the inward thought of the man ; they best illustrate the pure heavenly atmosphere in which he dwelt on earth, and are a legacy to his friends ; both rich and varied in religious experience. In modern days they may not be agreeable patterns of piety, because of their exactness ; but we opine that as the embodiment of that genuine christianity, which is needed to turn worldly things upside down, they contain the doctrinal elements needful for success.

Monday, April 18, 1853.—There have been very few calls at my office, and I have concluded to attend there in the morning hour only. Visited a few sick and afflicted souls— one man when I spoke to him on the subject of religion, turned over in his bed with apparent contempt from me I then spoke plain, strong, awful things to him ; he turned back and softened down, and said he was not an Infidel— wanted religion, &c. I fear his state is indeed, desperate. In the evening attended a meeting of the William Street Station and tendered them the new chapel, which was unanimously accepted—with only one dissenting voice.

Tuesday, 19th. This has been a wet day. Very few at the

office. I called to see a poor sister near her end; read and prayed with her; she appears happy and resigned; Lord comfort and take her home to heaven. Have made but few visits; should have gone to the Battery, but the distance and rain prevented. Will this excuse stand in the Judgment day? Lord save, or I perish.

Wednesday 20th.—This day I have given up our office; the proprietor wanted it for his own purpose. The poor sister whom I visited yesterday, has gone, I hope to Abraham's bosom; she died rejoicing in God, her Saviour. I have been very busy to day, doing as usual, almost nothing. Preached at William Street Church for Bro. Brown—a good congregation—a solemn, and I hope a profitable season—walked home and felt no fatigue.

Thursday 21st.—I have visited some heart-rending cases to-day—one poor heart-broken mother with five little children, eight months since her husband went out to collect some money, and has never since been heard of; she was confined two months after his disappearance, and had neither doctor, nor female friend with her; her poverty and suffering are indescribable. Bro. D. Ball gave me a dollar. I will endeavor to get her children into the asylum. Another poor afflicted daughter had been too unwell to visit the office, and had suffered; she is retiring and very grateful for favors. Baptized two interesting families of children. Heard Bro. Gear preach at Fayette Street Church to a small congregation.

Friday 22nd.—I have walked over most of our ground to-day. Had a considerable weakness in my back this morning; which however, subsided after considerable effort. Visited the Aged Women's Home; found a number of these afflicted both in mind and in body. Nothing can satisfy an unholy heart, and so few enjoy that blessing. That few indeed are contented and happy. Attended class; Bro Reese, led and made some very judicious remarks in reference to my own case.

Saturday 23rd—I have walked much and have done but little, either for God, or my fellow mortals, or myself. May I not say with Titus—"A day has been lost." Another week gone to return no more. Shall I meet the events of this week with joy, or shame and sorrow? Lord help me.

Sunday 24th—This has been a cold, wet, uncomfortable day, yet it is the Lord's holy day. I preached at the Seamen's Bethel, with some light and liberty. Took dinner with Bro. Brooks and attended his Sacramental meeting at 3 o'clock, after which they had an experience meeting. Those meetings I am compelled to leave to others, not being able to decide fully on their propriety. If I am called on by friend or foe, or on any suitable occasion, I feel bound to give a reason of the hope that is in me—but to call on the public frequently to hear me speak of my christian character and experience, is something of which I do not understand the principle. To me it savors not of that retiring delicacy; that deep humility of soul which should characterize God's children. Heard Bro. Reese preach a good sermon at Fayette at night. I closed with a few words of exhortation.

Monday 25th.—This has been a wet gloomy day. I have however, run about nearly all day. Have seen only a few sick, and prayed with them. Attended prayer meeting at Fayette St. Church. A good congregation for the night. A good feeling; yet my heart was like a stone—cold, dark, dead. Oh! for a revelation of burning light and power from heaven to infuse life into this dead soul.

Tuesday 26th.—This morning I took a long walk over into Old Town, to correct a falsehood told on Mrs. F—— by one of her unprincipled neighbors. Called to see Mrs. H——, a poor, afflicted woman, with five children; one I got into the Manual Labor School; the other two—a little boy and girl. I wished to place in the Orphan Asylum, but the poor heart broken mother with a deep sigh, said—Father gone, and that boy, oh I cannot, cannot part with him; I said it will be better to part with him, than hear him cry for bread, and you with none to give him. "Oh" said she, "I don't eat the bread, I give it to him." Called to see a poor sister, very near her latter end, but who was resigned and happy in view of death.

Wednesday 27th.—Collecting for the little chapel has caused me to walk much; did not therefore, make many mission visits. In the evening walked down and preached at night at High Street, for Bro. B. Brooks—plain and pointed—a good and very attentive congregation.

Thursday, 28th.—The duties of our chapel have kept me

employed; yet, doing almost nothing. I did however, make some interesting visits. Called at the Old Women's Home, and visited the sick there. Heard Bro. Reese preach to a small congregation, but better than usual, at Fayette Street Church.

Friday, 29*th.* We have given ourselves so little time to finish our chapel, that it will be with great difficulty that we shall be ready. I have been running myself all day, making arrangements for the dedication. Bro. R. Brown and myself administered the Sacrament to a poor sister about to leave our sin-polluted world. It will be a glorious exchange for her, if she is indeed, prepared to enter into the marriage supper of the Lamb. Led Bro. Drakely's class; a profitable season for my own soul.

Saturday, 30*th.*—Met the Building Committee and Bro. Younger. Settled all claims against our chapel, which is to be dedicated to-morrow, free of debt. Called to see R. G——, who has been confined to her bed for eight years, more or less; a patient sufferer. Poor H—— is in great distress; one son deeply afflicted for some months; another grown son has become deranged within a few days. The brethren have done the cause of God an injury, which cannot be measured, in calling the new chapel by my name; it has grieved me to the heart —they have done it ignorantly, and out of respect to me. But alas, in the estimation of the church, I am thereby made to refute all I have been contending for, for the last thirty years. I have been crying "how can ye believe who receive honor one of another;" and they will now think and say, "He is willing to swallow the poison himself." It is now too late to remedy the evil.

Sabbath, May 1*st.*—A dear, fine, precious day. Our little chapel has this day been dedicated to the worship of God. Bishop Waugh preached at 11 o'clock, to a good congregation, from John iii: 16, and offered up the chapel to God. I preached to a good congregation at 4 o'clock—a solemn profitable season. Text: "In all places where I record my name, I will come unto thee, and I will bless thee;" Exodus xx: 24. At 8 o'clock, I. P. Cook preached to a small, but attentive congregation, from Isaiah lvi: 7; "For my house shall be called a house of prayer for all people." May this house be accepted of God, and rendered useful to the people, for Christ's

sake. Amen. Rode nearly home with Bro. Perry, and retired to bed without weariness or fatigue. "Praise the Lord,
Oh my soul."

Monday, 2d.—Oh, that I had more wisdom, and more faith.
I know not how to act—Lord help me. What I know not,
teach thou me. Poor Mrs. H—— has sent her son to Mount
Hope; her second son is no better. How mysterious is the
providence of God! How deep the afflictions of the poor!
But God will remove the vail in due time; then shall we see
that all His dealings were marked with infinite wisdom and
mercy. We love and pant after good things. But will not
our eyes be opened, when we awake in hell, and hear Him
say to the rich man, "Son, remember that thou received thy
good things, &c."

Tuesday, 3d.—My soul has been grieved this day, to see
and hear the suffering of the poor. It appears to be impossible to better their condition, socially or spiritually. They
have sunk so low, that they seem to have lost all the energies
of their nature. And our standard of religion is so low, that
it makes little or no impression on them. Preached at our
new chapel at 8 o'clock, to a small congregation, with great
liberty, and comfort to my own soul. "Praise the Lord."

Wednesday, 4th.—Very little done this day for my Divine
Master, others or myself—an idle day, and an unprofitable
servant.

Thursday, 5th.—Have been visiting among the sick, the
poor—extremely poor, and among the rich. Bro. P——gave
me ten dollars—an article always in demand, and always dangerous in its tendencies. Attended a meeting of the male
members of Fayette Street Church, to promote church exten-
sion, and to build another church.

Friday, 6th.—This has been a dull, heavy day, both literally and spiritually. Have only been making some unprofitable visits. At class in making my humble confession before
God, I felt condemned, and yet I hope strengthened and en-
couraged to do better.

Saturday, 7th.—Have made a number of visits. Was
much distressed to see a poor heart broken mother with one
son, a young man, in bed, deeply afflicted; another deranged
and sent to the hospital, at an expense of five dollars per

week, whilst her sister had left on a drunken spree. Surely this is a dark and wicked world of sorrow and misery. Why, oh why, do we not seek rest and peace in the arms of Christ, bear His cross, and follow Him to heaven.?

Sabbath, 8th.—Bro. Reed, from Chillicothe, led B. Wilson's class this morning. I asked him about his soul—all is well, he replied, the Lord hath done great things for me. He hath cleansed my heart from all sin; I am now ready; the fire burns in my heart. He spoke with tears streaming from his eyes, and clasped me in his arms. Praise the Lord for such mercies. I preached at the Seamen's Bethel, with plainness and liberty. It rained hard until nearly night, yet I went down to the Mission Chapel, and spoke to a few, and the school. Returned home and heard Bro. R—— preach a good sermon at Fayette Street Church. It is not however, the kind of preaching that will reach the heart and save the perishing sinners.

Monday, 9th.—This has been another lost day. Oh Lord, when shall idleness and folly have an end? When shall I be diligent in every good word and work? This day another month ends. Our board met; a small attendance; they accepted my resignation and concluded to continue the mission, but did not choose a missionary.

Tuesday, 10th.—Have visited a number of families in the vicinity of our chapel, and a few sick in York street. Led Bro. Perry's class—a great want of faith on my part. When I hear God say, Ahab humbled himself, when he put on sack-cloth; when I know that Christ hates a proud look, and then hear our sisters, when dressed quite in the fashion, say that they hunger and thirst after righteousness, and that the spirit of God bears witness with their spirit, that they are the children of God—I am confounded.

Wednesday, 11th—Have visited only a few families. Distributed some tracts, and walked much. Preached at William street to a good congregation; with liberty and some effect. Retired at a late hour without fatigue. Oh for more grace, wisdom, humility and pure love.

Thursday, 12th—Arose half an hour after my usual time. Oh may I not be after the time, when the Master cometh. Had a good time in my morning devotions. Attended sister Mary Hewett's prayer meeting; there were a number of fine ladies present from our own and other churches. I read a chapter and made some plain remarks. I fear we are sinking in the arms of the world, and God will cast us off. Attended and heard Bro. Gear talk to a small congregation at Fayette Street Church.

Friday, 13th —I have fasted to-day as usual, but alas! how little do I think about it; oh how formal and offensive are all my attempts to worship God. Called with Bro. Calvert at Bro. Brooks' and spent some time. Lord help me to redeem time. Visited among the poor and afflicted. Took tea with Bro P—— and preached at Columbia street to a good congregation, with liberty and effect. Lord help and pardon all my follies.

Saturday, 14th.—Rode out this morning early, to the cemetery—a solemn place; but alas! it makes no impression on our minds. Custom blinds our eyes, and reconciles us to our doom. Felt quite unwell for a few hours—made some visits among the poor and others. Another week is gone, and with all its infinite realities and responsibilities, it has been permitted to pass like others, unheeded and unimproved. Is it possible? Can nothing but the thunders of the judgment day arouse us from our unholy slumbers?

Sabbath, 15th.—Rode out on horseback to the Grove, and preached with liberty to a good congregation. Returned, and walked down to the Mission Chapel, and preached to a good congregation, but not with much liberty. Returned and heard Dr. Roberts preach at Eutaw. His subject: Sanctification. If our efforts on this subject does not amount to more than words, we shall achieve no important results, notwithstanding all our light on the subject.

Monday, 16th.—The weather has become very warm. I promised to lead Bro. Stevenson's class; but having taken a counterfeit five dollar bill, in my anxiety to ascertain of whom I received it, I forgot my promise until it was too late, and reached the room when class was nearly over. Oh the danger of this entangling world. Happy are those who keep clear of its fatal allurements. Attended a missionary meeting at Dr. Fuller's Church, (Baptist.) My heart was pained, and my judgment disgusted at the perversion of christianity—all now is pomp and show. If we commit adultery with the world, we will in vain strive to blind the eyes of the people, by the cry of Catholocism or Protestantism. Let us not be deceived; God is not blind. We shall have our reward.

Tuesday, 17th.—A very warm day—have visited some sick and suffering families. One sensible man, Mr. B——, who is recovering, and discovered his true colors—*Universalism.* He could quote Scripture freely and correctly—oh the danger of the present day. False colors in the churches, and false doctrine out of them, and so we go. Promised to take supper with Bro. C——, and forgot it, and so *I* go.—oh, the danger of life—blessed are the dead who die in the Lord. Preached at the Home Missionary Chapel to a small congregation with liberty, as usual. Returned home fresh, and free from fatigue. Praise the Lord, Oh, my soul. Ever, forever.

Wednesday, 18th.—My time has been occupied running about doing nothing. I have bought and paid for a horse— Oh, Lord, let thy blessing rest upon this, as upon every act of my life. Thou, Oh God, knowest that I desire to do all I do, to please Thee; Oh forgive, and help me, and guide all my steps below, and grant me a lot among the holy in heaven.

Thursday, 19th.—A most windy, blustering day; the dust has been exceeding] annoying. Have made but few visits; yet, have been busy fixing my wagon, which I bought for twenty-five dollars. Attended Fayette Street Church. Heard Bro Reese preach—was sleepy—Lord, forgive me. I closed with some very plain remarks, but they avail nothing, nor will anything but the thunders of Jehovah's judgment arouse a slumbering church to a sense of her duty and her danger.

Friday, 20th.—Have attempted to fast as usual, but as usual, it has been in a formal and unprofitable manner. Visited a few families, and attended and led our class; very few out, as usual—a cold, dry time. Lord, help us.

Saturday, 21st.—Was sent for to see a very sick woman; when I reached her room, she had gone out, either on business, or to visit others. I found all she wanted, was some assistance; this it was easier to give than spiritual food.

Sabbath, 22d—I went to lead Bro. Younger's class, and behold, the family had removed. I had long been promising, and when I went, it was too late. Oh, the danger of procrastination. Lord, help me to act promptly. Preached to a good congregation at Whatcoat Street Church with liberty; again

at the Home Mission Chapel at 4 o'clock, to a good congregation, with much liberty, and comfort to my own soul. None
of the official brethren present. Took supper with Bro. Brooks
and preached at the Seamen's Bethel at night to a good congregation—two mourners. Walked home, and felt no perceptible fatigue, either of body or mind. Praise the Lord, Oh,
my soul. This is the Lord's doings, and it is wondrous in
our eyes.

Monday, 23rd—Thank the Lord for sleep and rest. Arose
at my usual hour ; had a comfortable time in waiting upon
the Lord, and quite a precious season in reading my morning
lesson, the first chapter of Revelation. Oh for a heart to
praise my God. I want nothing but God—but the living
God. I have been patching up my little wagon, and have done
very little to-day. Mercy, mercy, is all my plea. Jesus
died for me—for me the Saviour died.

Tuesday, 24th—This has been a wet day. I have visited
very little. Read and wrote some. Went down in the
evening to the Hill, to fill my appointment at the chapel ;
but the brethren thought it would be unnecessary to go out,
as there would be no one there, so I returned home.

Wednesday, 25th—Praise the Lord for health, and a
brightening prospect for a resting place in heaven. The Lord
will not be angry forever. His mercy endureth forever.
Praise the Lord. This has been quite a wet day. Have
made but few visits, and preached at William St. Church to a
small congregation, very little liberty. Stayed with Bro.
Armstrong on the Hill.

Thursday, 26th—Wrote in a huary, a part of an introduc-
tion to a little work on prayer. Ran about all day doing
very little. Heard Bro. Gear preach at night to a tolerable
congregation—all, all, dead, dead.

Friday, 27th—Have visited a number of friends among the
poor and others. Have as usual, fasted, and have felt no inconvenience therefrom. Yet is there a great want of spirituality in this privilege. Led Bro D——'s class with some
liberty ; said some plain things ; made some important declarations. Lord forgive, if I erred.

Saturday, 28th—Arose at my usual hour, a few minutes
before four o'clock. Had a comfortable hour in waiting on

the Lord in prayer. In reading my precious Saviour's sermon on the Mount, my soul was softened and comforted. Praise the Lord, oh my soul. I have been very busy—walked much; dined with sister Hiser. Took supper with Dr. Knight. Have sold five sets of Madame Guyon's life.

Sabbath, 29th—This has been a dark morning to my soul; have felt dull and stupid. Heard **** Wentworth preach a splendid sermon at Columbia street, with a considerable feeling. Attended a Sacramental occasion at the Seamen's Bethel at three o'clock, but there was too much hurry. I am always pained here to see the folly, and the gaudy dress of the females who commune. Preached to a small congregation at the Mission Chapel; there was a good feeling. Preached at eight in William street to a small congregation, with great plainness, but not much effect. Returned home, refreshed and without perceptible fatigue. Oh for a heart to praise my God.

Monday, 30th—This, like other days, has been passed unprofitably. Collected money and paid Bro. H——'s doctor bill. We should bear one another's burdens. Poor sister A. Robertson is sinking into eternity; I found her in a better frame than usual. Alas, my own cold heart. Lord, save me.

Tuesday, 31st—Have been very busy, walking and visiting. Preparing to leave Baltimore. Have walked over nearly all our territory in the city. Administered the Sacrament to sister O—— and the doctor. Preached at Eutaw, with very little light or liberty.

Wednesday, June 1st.—Left Baltimore. After running about most briskly, arranging my wagon and horse, with which I had much trouble, I left Baltimore at four o'clock; came to Elkridge without accident, or injury from cars, or my horse, for which I desire to be truly thankful. Stopped at Bro. Newton's house; he immediately ran out and gathered up a congregation, to whom I preached with great liberty; still, after the burden of the day, and after walking nearly a mile to preach and back; blessed be God, I felt no fatigue whatever. Oh my God, pardon my unbelief, and forgive my ingratitude.

Thursday 2nd.—After a pleasant ride for me, but a laborious one for my horse, I reached Georgetown about four o'clock; stopped with —— ——. Here I found pride and folly on the increase. Went to the church, and found no one there, except the sexton. After waiting a long time, the preachers came in; they invited me to preach. I had some liberty and preached with great plainness; brought their sins before their eyes; but I fear it will be labor lost. The church is fully set to go with the world and draw down ruin on ourselves and also on the wicked world. I found they were all preparing for a frolic down the river. They were to take the Sabbath School children along for a cloak for their own naked hearts. But God is not deceived, nor will He be mocked. He will tear the veil away, and fully expose their nakedness.

Friday, 3d.—Have, as usual, attempted to fast; yet, formality nullifies this, and most other efforts I make to serve the Lord. Visited some of my old friends in Washington. I greatly fear the god of this world will deceive and ruin my old friend, M. W. L.

Saturday, 4th—Have visited some of my friends in Georgetown; but, alas! time has left but few of the old standards, and soon we will all be called to appear before the Judge of all the earth. Oh, may we be prepared.

Sunday, 5th—Led Bro. Brown's class. Have found a few of the old members, and only a very few were present; was very pointed with those present. Preached in Bro. Landstreet's place, at eleven o'clock; the Sacrament was administered; Bro. Slicer consecrated the elements: but, alas! I fear the shadow only remains here also. Preached again in the Market House to a good congregation, at 3 o'clock, with some liberty and I hope good effect. Preached again at 8 o'clock for Bro. Cox, in the M. P. Church, with but little liberty. Walked home with my nephew, and blessed be God, felt no perceptible fatigue. Surely this is the Lord's doings, and it is marvellous in our eyes.

Monday, 6th—Went this morning to Alexandria. Had to run to reach the boat in time. Dined and supped with Bro. B. Waters. Preached at night to quite a large and most attentive congregation. Stayed all night with Bro. Davey.

Tuesday, 7th—I was beset and pained by a wicked dream. Surely the heart is not here—nay I know it is not, or those dreams would not exist. Arose at 3 o'clock, and after spending more than an hour and a half in my morning devotions, I preached to a good congregation at 5 o'clock with liberty and comfort. Came away in the boat at seven o'clock in company with Dr. Legenball; walked from the boat to Georgetown, which is called three miles. Left Georgetown after dinner and came to Bro. J. S. Hennings', at Rockville, when I was very kindly received by the family, and preached at eight o'clock to a good congregation, with liberty and apparent effect. Praise the Lord, I still feel no fatigue of body, or mind. Oh for more gratitude and humility.

Wednesday, 8th—Came to Clarksburg, but did not find Bro. Cullom at home. Put up however, for the night, and preached at eight o'clock in the school house, to a little flock of rather insensible hearers. My voice was much restricted and all was cold and dark. Well, I have tried, but alas! how very unimportant is the arm of flesh. All our help must come from God. Lord help me.

Thursday, 9th—Clouds and darkness still cover my sky. Oh for a clear morning of salvation, a heart burning with love for God and all mankind. I rode up to Fredericktown on horseback, but found not Bro. Miller, nor Bro. Tippett. Stopped with Andrew Boyd. Very unexpectedly met with sister Pendleton, at Bro. Miller's house—a poor, friendless, disconsolate sister. Preached at eight o'clock to a good and very attentive congregation, with liberty, and I hope good effect.

Friday, 10th—Spent most of the day in Frederick City doing nothing. Returned to Clarksburg in the evening; met with Bros. Cullom and Brown.

Saturday, 11th—Have felt dark and gloomy for some time. This morning more light dawned upon my soul, and I enjoyed more comfort in waiting on the Lord than usual. Rode to school house and preached to a little handful of dull hearers. Rode home with E. Beale and took dinner; returned and preached at the school house to one dozen hearers; Bro. Cullom very much discouraged. Rode one mile or more to rest for the night with Bro. Lewis.

Sabbath, 12th—Held a love-feast at 9 o'clock; all kinds of people present, almost—at least from the careless and gay, to the plain and thoughtful. I preached at eleven o'clock in the open air, to a large and attentive congregation, with much plainness and I hope some effect, After an intermission of an hour, more or less, Bro. Crawford preached quite a good sermon, and at night Bro. Cullom preached a very long, plain sermon, and closed quietly and without much effect Another precious Sabbath day, We stayed with Bro. White.

Monday, 13th—Returned to Clarksburg and spent the day with Bro. Cullom.

Tuesday 14th.—The weather very warm. We rode out and paid several visits. Preached at Bethesda, at night, to a good congregation, with some liberty and effect. Passed the night with Bro. Walker.

Wednesday, 15th—Returned to Clarksburg, and felt much disappointed in not hearing from Bro. Armstrong. Spent an unprofitable day; the weather very warm. Rode up to Hyattstown and preached with liberty to a good congregation. Stopped with Bro. I. Umsted.

Thursday, 16th—Slept tolerably well. Left after early breakfast, and drove my wagon up to Frederick City. Met Bro. Miller at Bro. Tippett's. They all wished me to preach at night, to which I consented. Rode out to Bro. Boyd's; my horse behaved pretty well. Thank the Lord for His mercy. Preached with some liberty, but very little effect. Rested for the night with Bro. Tippett.

Friday, 17th—This has been a very warm day. I have as usual, attempted to fast, but alas, how formal are all my efforts to worship God. Have been in suspense about my book, but patience must have her perfect work. Walked out and stayed with the Elder, Bro. Boyd.

Saturday, 18th—I have been much perplexed about my book ; no letter, but a package of books that I did not need, and no word about the book on prayer. I wrote a letter of very plain import, which may offend Bro. Armstrong. Perhaps I am wrong in my object, and had better left the books and gone unincumbered. Well, if so, I will give them up ; yet like poor Balaam, perhaps my heart is in the money. Oh Lord, search me, and try me, and purge every stain of earthly love out of my soul. Save, oh save, that I perish not.

Sabbath, 19th—Have felt very dull and dark this day ; my sky is much beclouded. "Lord, what wilt Thou have me

do ? Heard Bro. Miller preach to the colored people, at ten
o'clock, and at three preached to them myself, but without
life or liberty. Preached to the whites at night, very little
liberty, yet the Lord enabled me to say plain and pointed
things, and the congregation were considerably affected.
Lord help me and forgive my follies. Returned and stayed
with old Bro. Boyd.

Monday, 20*th*—Attempted to visit with Bro. Miller, but
failed ; Bro. M—— feels very much discouraged. Two
years ago, there were more taken into the church in a revival
than the entire number on record. Our modern revivals are
measurably delusions. The devil is busy ; his servants have
opened their synagogues—the theatre, and the multitude press
into it and pay their money to be ruined I preached at
night to a good and attentive congregation ; it was a solemn
and impressive sermon.

Tuesday, 21*st*—Left old Bro. Boyd's after early breakfast.
Spent some time in town, then rode in my heavy wagon over
a most hilly road, to Barnesville, where I fed and took dinner
with Bro. Nichols. Came on to Poolesville and stopped with
Bro. Sissel, one mile from town. Spoke with some liberty ;
one poor mourner at the altar. Returned to Bro. Sissel's,
and after riding twenty-three miles, more or less, over a most
hilly road, and walking in the broiling sun up nearly all the
hills, I felt no perceptible fatigue. Praise the Lord, oh my
soul. My refractory horse has behaved well to-day ; this I
impute to the goodness of God in answer to prayer.

Wednesday, 22*nd*—Have spent the day in visiting with
Bro Cullom. We spent a few hours in the evening with a
Presbyterian family, but most unprofitably. I felt very vacant
and gloomy, had scarce a word to say, and at night attempted
to preach, but had neither light or liberty, nor divine unction;
it was a dark time ; after which the meeting closed and we
went to Bro. Sissel's to stay all night.

Thursday, 23*rd*—Left Bro. Sissel's after breakfast ; my
horse behaved well, until I came to the canal. The culvert
was low and dark and rough and watery. I was almost deterred from attempting to pass it ; the horse was very unwilling to go through. I however, got an old woman to lead
him through ; the top rubbed nearly all the way. Surely it
was grub and go. Praise the Lord, he brought me through

and over the river in safety. Reached Leesburg before ten.
Supped with Bro. Rogers, and concluded to remain all night.
Put up with Bro. Smith, and called to see a number of old
friends. Preached at night to a good congregation, with
liberty and effect. Rain caused the congregation to be
smaller than it would have been.

Friday, 24*th*—Preached at five o'clock to a good congregation with some liberty. Left for Middleburg, where I was
kindly received by Bro. Hurst. Preached at night to a large
congregation with some effect. Stayed with Bro. Brown.

Saturday, 25*th*—Preached at five o'clock to a good congregation. Sold several books in Bro. Brown's store. Then
rode up to Upperville and left my wagon at Bro. Calvert's
and rode on horseback to Cool Spring, where I met Bro.
Hurst. Stopped with sister Kitty Shackett.

Sabbath, 26*th*—Preached at Cool Spring to a good congregation with great plainness; there was deep interest felt.
Rode to Salem, and preached at four o'clock with much
liberty and physical strength. Stopped with Bro. Allen.
Bro. Hurst preached at night to a good congregation.

Monday, 27*th*—Called to see an amiable family. The
girls are members, their brothers are kind sinners. Preached at a school-house at eleven o'clock to a good congregation;
very little liberty Took dinner at Bro. Harrison's. Rode
up to Rectortown ; stopped with Bro. Sampson ; preached at
night ; congregation not large, and very late assembling.
Here a scene of discord and confusion has prevailed, which
delights the devil, and grieves God's spirit.

Tuesday, 28*th*—Rode out and spent a short time with a
family. Bro. Hunt's family came through a hot sun to Upperville. Felt very much exhausted with the heat. At half
past four o'clock lectured on the Apocalyptic Witnesses ; and
at eight o'clock preached to a small congregation with some
liberty.

Wednesday, 29*th*—My horse has been stolen, or has left
the pasture. This is a hard trial, but blessed be God. I can
give him up most freely, though the best horse I ever owned.
I have spent a very tedious day ; it has been very warm, and
have felt very weak. Visited and took tea with Dr. Brown.
Heard a Baptist, Bro. Dodge, preach at a late hour ; closed

after him, and thus closed an unprofitable day. Lord forgive and help me for Jesus' sake.

Thursday, 30th. This has been another warm day. My time has been spent very unprofitably. My horse was brought to me by a neighbor to-day. Thank the Lord for his mercies, either prosperous, or adverse, shall be alike acceptable to me.

Friday, July 1st—Arose very early and started before sunrise in my wagon; but, alas, how uncertain are all human efforts and calculations. I had progressed only a few miles, when I met a wagon loaded with machinery, in a very narrow part of the road. My horse became frightened, nor could I manage him; the driver refused to stop; my horse turned short round, how, I know not; yet through mercy there was nothing broke, nor any injury sustained, other than the fright to the horse. Oh may my heart ever be in heaven. Finding my system very much exhausted, I took dinner with a plain pious family, in Perryville, consisting of a brother and two sisters, by the name of Noble. Bro. Eggleston dined with me. After much labor for my horse, in the heat and upon the tough road, I reached Charlestown early in the evening, having traveled about thirty-two miles. Met Bro. Eggleston. I put up with sister Tomlinson. Her husband from home.

Saturday, 2nd—This has been an idle day. The most oppressive of all other labors; wrote a few letters, and read a few papers and slept again.

Sabbath, 3rd—The weather still sultry and warm. Preached to a small congregation for Bro. Eggleston; no light life, light, or liberty. Rode out to a school-house and preached to a good congregation of sinners. Rode home with sister Yates, James Walker's daughter; very kind, rich people, A fine rain. Sister Yates called to see her husband's sister who has just had her leg broken. Oh uncertain, delusive world. Save me, oh my God, from its smiles and also from the fear of its power.

Monday, 4th—This has been a dreary day; the church and the children away in the woods, frolicking. I, however, spent the day at Bro. Brown's. Had sent an appointment to Harper's Ferry; it was not delivered. A large number of harvest hands, white and colored, were present at night, and I gave them an exhortation, before and after prayer.

Tuesday, 5th—Came up to town and spent rather an idle day again. Met Bro. Eggleston's class at three o'clock. The most fashionable and gay dressed individual in the class was a Methodist preacher's daughter. No marvel now. Preached to a good congregation, on temperance, at night, with some liberty and I hope good effect. Bro. W. G. Eggleston gave a most pointed and severe exhortation.

Wednesday 6th —Have not as usual heard from my books, which should have reached town yesterday. I left on horseback with some books, and left my wagon to be sent on to me on Saturday. Dined at Smithfield, and stopped for the night, with Bro. J. Payne.

Thursday, 7th—Rode into Winchester. Stopped with Bro. Nulton, a kind man; he immediately published an appointment for me to preach at night. There was a good congregation: they were attentive and I preached with some comfort.

Friday, 8th—Preached this morning at five o'clock. Only a few out. Surely the Lord Jesus must spue us out of his mouth. Left after breakfast and rode to Newtown; stopped with Bro. Alemony; he appears to be a zealous and kind man, but there is something which I cannot understand. Eternity will unfold all secret things. Then shall we return and discern between him that serveth God, and him that serveth Him not. An appointment was agreed upon to preach, but the Lutheran brethren were about holding a Sacramental meeting, I was requested to preach in their church. There was a tolerable congregation, but dull, and all seemed to be dark amidst a profusion of light.

Saturday, 9th—Left Newtown. Stopped in Winchester. Sold an old blind man, named Sterritt, some books at half price to sell again; he is supporting himself in this honorable way. Rode to John Payne's and preached to a good congregation at five o'clock. So ends another week.

Sabbath 10th.—Rode five miles to Smithfield, met Bro. Eggleston, and preached to a good congregation at eleven o'clock, with much liberty, closeness and effect. Praise the Lord. Rode up with Bro. Harley in his buggy to Lee Town and preached to a handful of hearers; the rain having kept the congregation from assembling. Returned and spent the night with Bro. Harley.

Monday, 11th—A leisure day; what a shame. Took dinner with James G——, a rich 'man; had very little comfort or benefit: all belongs to the world, children and all. Called to see his brother, William G——; he is more pious, but all is not right here. Oh, this delusive world; a bankrupt, and yet his daughter dresses extravagantly, and is just from a Baltimore boarding-school. Preached on temperance in Smithfield at night to a good congregation; plain but too rough. Lord in mercy forgive me.

Tuesday, 12th—Left Smithfield after breakfast; horse behaved only tolerably well. Came to Mr. Ruckle's and found an appointment made to preach at night; had a small congregation of still hearers; preached plainly, but with little liberty and effect.

Wednesday, 13th—This morning sold out all my encumbrances to Bro. Ruckle, horse, wagon, harness, saddle, &c., for one hundred and forty-five dollars. I am now foot loose and alone in the world. Lord, in mercy direct my way. Came to Shepherdstown; stopped with Bro. Thos. Hersey, a plain, kind, good family. Preached at eight o'clock to a good congregation, with plainness and some effect.

Thursday, 14th—Preached this morning to a very small flock at five o'clock. Sold some books. Walked over to Sharpsburg, where I met Bro. Monroe and others from Boonsboro. Heard Bro. M—— preach a funeral sermon. Came in the stage to Boonsboro, and stopped with Bro. Kendle, a printer. He was rather too late to make an appointment to preach.

Friday, 15th—Left B—— in the stage; had to ride on the top; a very unpleasant seat. Stopped at Middletown with Bro. Haugby, who is getting rich. Called to see some of the friends. Made an appointment and preached at night to a few. None of Bro. Haugby's family were out. Oh the danger and deceitfulness of riches. Who can resist their fatal influences?

Saturday, 16th—Was disappointed in getting a passage to Frederick City. Left Middletown with Bro. Dill and visited doctor Marlow, where we spent the night. Oh the influences of this wicked world. Lord save us.

Sunday, 17th—Called to see a very deeply afflicted sister. Preached at Jefferson to a good congregation with some liberty, but too long. Took dinner with Bro. Sparrow. Preached to a good congregation, at three, in Z——s house. Stopped all night with old Bro. Z———, who has no family, but some colored people. A very poorly regulated family. Oh my God, how little is Thy name respected, or known.

Monday, 18th—Praise the Lord, I enjoyed a most comfortable night's sleep. Came into Frederick City. Bro. Miller absent. Remained until three o'clock, and took the cars for Baltimore; arrived there about seven o'clock without injury or accident. Found Bro. W——'s family all well. Praise the Lord for all his mercies.

Tuesday, 19th—Called to see some of my old friends. Wrote some letters, and heard Bro. Morgan, Presiding Elder, preach at Eutaw to a small congregation; a good sermon.

Wednesday, 20th—Left Baltimore at eleven o'clock, in the cars, came in safety to Elkton. Praise the Lord for His protection. Bro. Way not at home. Took his horse and carriage and rode to Bro. Smith's house, where I met my sister in good health. A kind man; spent the night comfortably.

Thursday, 21st—A rainy morning. Remained until after dinner, then rode over to old Bro. Beatty's, who is now like myself, an old man; remained here for the night. Oh, how much is wanting, even among us old professors of the spirit of Christ. Humble love, holy zeal and deep devotion.

Friday, 22nd—Rode up to B. Shakespear's, and spent some time there. My health not good. I took dinner. Thus we glide away, and easily make a compromise with the flesh and the world. After dinner rode to William Shakespear's house, but as himself and wife were from home, I returned to Elkton. Took tea with sister Torbert, and preached to a good congregation at night, but with little liberty. Put up with Bro. Kennard; though out of the church, he appears to be a pious, good man.

Saturday, 23rd—Spent the day in Elkton; made some visits; called to see a very pious, sensible young sister, who professes to enjoy the blessing of sanctification. Oh, that she may be faithful until death.

Sabbath, 24th—My health is better this morning. Preached at ten and a half o'clock in Elkton, with some liberty and effect. Bro. Way administered the Sacrament. The members were dressed shamefully. Lord save the church. Rode to Glasgow with Bro. Way to hear Bro. Sampson preach, but he was sick and did not attend. I preached with much liberty and some effect. Returned and preached at night in Elkton. I mistook my text and preached for some time on another subject, than the one I read for my text; however, the Lord helped me and I got back without much difficulty, though it embarrassed me considerably. Lord help me and forgive all my follies, Through mercy I feel no fatigue of body or mind. Praise the Lord.

Monday, 25th—Rode down to the camp this morning; found very few on the ground. The preacher in charge was called away to see his sister die. The junior preacher was also absent. I preached in the evening to a very, very few; cold and indifferent, no one to sing, no prayer. The prospect gloomy in the extreme.

Tuesday, 26th—This has been a most gloomy day. It has rained nearly all night and all day, all wet and gloomy. Bro. Atwood came in the course of the day. Preaching in the tent; very few, very cold.

Wednesday, 27th.—Still gloomy; I preached this morning to a few careless hearers. Bro. —— preached at three o'clock, a sermon without unction. Preaching again at six o'clock; preachers coming in abundantly. The weather has cleared off and prospects are brightening, although there is little prospect of good being done. I had a very plain conversation with the Presiding Elder, Bro Atwood, but in good feeling.

Thursday, 28th.—The weather fine. A good congregation. Bro. Way preached a good sermon, though he reached rather too high, and was not as pointed and practical as he should have been. After the sermon a collection was taken up, to the great annoyance of Bro. Way's feelings. At three o'clock Bro. Miller preached At six, Bro. Humphries preached, but without much feeling or effect. Little doing. In the night a poor drunken soul came into the camp, and caused much disturbance ; but he soon went to sleep.

Friday, 29th.—I have sold very few books, but all is right. Bro. —— preached this morning without much feeling, or effect, and after the congregation had become confused and were going away, the dinner bells having wrung, Bro. Storks asked me to exhort ; I had much liberty, arrested the current and spoke plainly, and then left the ground. Rode with Bro. Cantwell to Elk; where I took the cars and came to Baltimore. In the cars, met with Bro. McCoy, who had seen me at his mother's house many years ago, but still recollected me. He lives in Mobile ; appears to be a fine man ; wished me very much to visit the South.

Saturday, 30th.—I have made but few visits to-day. Have packed up my books and walked considerably. The weather very warm. Called to see Bro. Wilson's family, who are deeply afflicted ; their little son, some seven years old, the last time I was there, had lost the use of his lower extremities, both feet and legs. The doctor said he never would recover. I prayed with the family and for him ; he arose and threw away his crutches and walked as usual. The doctor said it was an effort of nature. Oh, infidelity, thou enemy of God, when wilt thou cease thy folly?

Sabbath 31st.—Walked down to William street and had my appointments changed for this day. - Walked back to Eutaw, to let Bro. McM—— know; then returned to William street and preached to a tolerable good congregation, with some liberty and I hope effect. Attended Bro. Brooks' Sacramental meeting at the Seamen's Bethel ; then walked home and at night preached to a small congregation in Eutaw Street Church, with liberty and some effect ; and after those labors, I feel no effect of body or mind. Again I say, praise the Lord, oh my soul.

Monday, August 1st.—Last night I had a precious night's rest. Was much comforted and blessed in my soul. Praise the Lord. Left Baltimore at four o'clock, in the mammoth steamboat for Tangier : we had a number of passengers. Two young females who wished to pass for ladies, continued to play back-gammon, though I admonished them most pointedly. Bros Poisal, Register and Brooks.—Methodist preachers, and Bro. Williams—a Baptist preacher, were on board. After supper, I preached a plain, pointed sermon ; -

all were respectful and attentive. Our Baptist Bro. appeared much pleased and gave an appropriate exhortation. Spent a good night amidst all possible disadvantages. Praise the Lord.

Tue.day, 2*nd*—To-day I am *sixty-seven years old.* Surely I may say with Jacob, "Few and evil have been the days of my earthly pilgrimage." The Lord has indeed dealt bountifully with his unprofitable servant. My health is good and I am able to do as much labor now, as I could thirty years ago; seldom if ever feel any physical fatigue, even after toiling all day, and after preaching three times a day. This is the Lord's doings, and it is marvellous in our eyes. Landed at Pongateague at about eight o'clock. A stranger took my box of books to Onancock, whilst another took me in his carriage, where I met a warm reception from kind hearted sister Hill. In the evening I took Bro. Hill's carriage and rode down to Bro. Garrettson, where our brethren were and took some books for them to sell at their camp meeting. We had, I hope, a profitable season in this kind family.

Wednesday, 3*rd*—After breakfast rode back to Bro. Hill's, when I called to see a few friends, and in the evening rode down with Bro. Dobson to Bro. Ed. Poulson's, where we remained all night. Mosquitos rather troublesome.

Thursday, 4*th*—This morning all is bustle; the boat is going over to the island for camp meeting. I had a uncomfortable night; the cramp annoyed me some, but it is all right. Praise the Lord, oh my soul. We were much lumbered up in the boat; the wind was ahead, blowing fresh, which prevented us from reaching the island until about one or two o'clock. Found it a desolate looking place, a sandy beach. All was bustle; could not get ready for preaching, so the day and night passed without any religious services. Mosquitos not bad.

Friday, 5*th*—Had a tolerable good night's rest. Fasted only from my breakfast; took dinner and preached with liberty and effect at three o'clock; several mourners have come forward and appearances are favorable. Bro. —— preached at night, a very inefficient sermon, yet there was quite a stir and a number of mourners.

Saturday, 6*th*—My health not good. A good prayer

meeting at eight. I preached at ten, from "Casting four anchor and wishing for day," without much effect, yet there were a number of mourners. At three Bro. Brindle preached a good sermon with good effect. Bro. Leatherbury preached at night very inefficiently, yet a good work went on.

Sabbath, 7th—Two boats arrived from Baltimore, with five, or six hundred human beings; no advantage to the meeting and no credit to themselves. Dr. Williams preached at ten a good sermon, but not the doctrine of the text. Bro. Gray preached at half past two o'clock a long, long, uninteresting talk; many went to sleep, others walked away; but Bro. Evans rallied the people mightily, and there was a good time. I preached at night with much liberty and physical energy—a powerful time.

Monday, 8th—I expected to leave for Baltimore after breakfast, but did not get off till after morning preaching. Bro. Brindle preached and exhorted, after which we embarked on board the schooner *Jasper*, Capt. Gaskins, for Baltimore. Got becalmed; however, the wind soon sprung up and we had a fine run. The weather very hot and the cabin very dirty; a most gloomy place.

Tuesday, 9th—Last night I sat up and slept in my chair. The wind left us in the night and about eleven o'clock I had the mortification to see the steamboat pass within a few miles but could not reach her, so I am doomed to this place another night. It was right hard to say fully, "Thy will be done;" yet I thank the Lord for disappointment. Passed a lonely, barren day in heat.

Wednesday, 10th—This morning reached Baltimore early, but too late to go on to the camp meeting in the Philadelphia boat. Fixed up some books and prepared for an early start. My room is a most uncomfortable place, very, very hot. I could with difficulty sleep.

Thursday, 11th—Left Baltimore at half past six in the steamboat for the Red Lion camp meeting; had an interesting conversation on board the boat. Reached the camp ground about twelve o'clock. An immense crowd of people here. There had been, so I was told, sixty preachers there. I met with some old acquaintances. Spent the time not very profitably. It was with some difficulty I got a place to sleep.

Friday 12*th.*—Through mercy I had a good night's rest, and preached to a very large congregation at five o'clock; most solemn and attentive. Mentioned my book and sold nearly all of them before night. I say nothing about the preaching; my views are not in accordance with the views of the present day. At a late hour left the camp, reached Elkton about midnight; stayed with Bro. Bradbury.

Saturday, 13*th*—Had a few hours of comfortable sleep, and took the cars at half past ten and reached Baltimore, about one o'clock. Arranged my book and left for Shrewsbury camp at five o'clock; reached the camp ground about dark. A large encampment. Found a comfortable berth in the preachers' tent and slept well. A goodly number of preachers.

Sunday, 14*th*—Bro. Busey preached at eight o'clock. I exhorted after him, with liberty and feeling. Bro. Morgan preached at ten o'clock, a good sermon, but too long, not much excitement. At three o'clock Bro. Collins preached a long, dry sermon, and at night Bro. Brown preached very pointed, some mourners and some feeling.

Monday, 15th—I preached at five o'clock to a good congregation, which was late in meeting, not much liberty or feeling; mentioned my books and sold nearly all I had, in little more than an hour. Took the cars and came again to Baltimore about one o'clock. Still very warm.

Tuesday, 16*th*—A warm night—slept but little; left Baltimore in steamboat at 7 o'clock: because they had an open bar in the boat, I would not take dinner, although it was included in the passage asked; I had paid the full charge. Quite a number of Methodists on board going to the camp: reached Princess Anne between four and five o'clock. Stopped with Bro. Humphries and found Bro. Sedler waiting for me. I rode with him and stayed all night at his home in Potatoe Neck.

Wednesday, 17*th*—Rode out with Bro. Sedler and his son, to the camp. Met with many of my old friends; Bro. R. Waters was quite grieved and offended, because I did not know him, whom I had not seen for fifteen years, more, or less. Lord help and forgive my sins. Preached to a large congregation at three o'clock, with some liberty and effect. Bro. Hill preached at night. There came up a storm; I had to leave my berth and lay on the ground with a few clothes under me, and my saddle bag for a pillow. Yet praise the Lord, I felt no harm.

Thursday, 18th—I read and exhorted at eight o'clock; said some very plain things. Bro. Daily preached at ten. It rained, but the people were quiet and attentive. At three Bro. Quigg preached: and at night, although the ground was still wet and raining, I preached; the congregation was very large; part of it very attentive in the rain, but part were very unsettled and refractory; there were several converts. Had a good night's rest.

Friday, 19th—After breakfast I left the camp, rode to Bro. Williams', near Newtown, where we were kindly treated Took dinner with Bro. W——, who is now eighty-eight years old, and quite active—hears well. Came on to Snow Hill and stopped with Bro. A. W. Williams.

Saturday, 20th—Called to see several families and walked out to the camp. Found the best accomodations for the colored people that I have found. Preached at three to a small congregation with liberty and effect. Bro. Dobson preached at night; not much feeling.

Sabbath 21st.—The colored people kept up their meeting, without let, or hindrance through the night. Bro. Daily preached a very short sermon at half past ten o'clock. No feeling, or interest. I preached at three to a large congregation; although quite sick, I had strength and liberty, and quite an excitement followed. Bro. Sommers preached at night, very dry, no light, no life, no liberty, So ended the day, with but little visible good effected.

Monday, 22nd—Very little devotional feeling on the ground. Bro. ——, from Berlin, preached an unprofitable sermon from an important text. I mentioned my books deliberately, and scarcely sold any of them; where I expected to do much, I did scarcely nothing. I did feel disappointed, but that is good and profitable for the soul. Bro. Hazard, a local preacher, preached at three; made a wonderful effort, felt, or feigned much; but little effect. Bro. Magee preached at night, with much zeal.

Tuesday, 23rd—I preached at half past ten with some liberty. There was much feeling in the congregation, and a number of mourners.   Left the ground immediately and came to Snow Hill, where Bro. J. P. Robins met and took me on to Princess Anne, where I preached to a good congregation, with more ease and liberty than usual, and felt no perceptible fatigue.   Oh for a heart to praise my Lord.   God is good, and that my soul knoweth right well.

Wednesday, *24th*—Left Princess Anne this morning in company with Bro. J. P. Robins, for Baltimore.   Again I choose not to eat on board the boat where they keep a public bar.   After dinner, the passengers assembled on the upper deck, and I preached to them; felt however, but little liberty; yet will not all the seed fall to the ground.   Reached Baltimore about sunset.   Heard that Tarring was buried this evening.   Oh death, how wide thy conquests, and how felt thy power.

Thursday, *25th*—Have called to see a few of my friends. I am not clear on the subject of the mission here ; they are however desirous that I should take it.   Have written some letters.   Declined attending church, because I did not wish my friends, especially the poor, to think I was in the city, and did not call on them.   Perhaps this is wrong, as error marks nearly all I do.   Lord help me.

Friday, *26th*—Last night my sleep was disturbed by alarming and impressive dreams.   I greatly fear that not only the church, but the ministers generally, are under bondage to the world ; I am myself bound by that unholy bondage.   I fear we are courting the smiles of the world, whilst we should alarm their guilty consciences, by plain gospel truths.   Last night Bro. ——'s daughter came in at the time that the young men came from the store ; she and Laura behaved very bad ; sung and laughed and trifled very much with sacred things, and refused to come in to prayer.   She is a popular preacher's daughter.   If the blind lead the blind, both must fall into the ditch.   My mind has been seriously exercised about changing my boarding house ; this step will be painful to my own feelings and also to sister W——, yet it may be prudent and necessary.   Lord in mercy direct my steps wisely.   At half past three o'clock, I had arranged to leave in the cars for Georgetown, but my trunk was not sent down, until the cars started.   Thus will mercy come, after the door of heaven is closed, and we have no apology to offer.   Lord help me to watch and pray, that I may be ready and account-ted worthy to enter into the marriage supper of the Lamb. I met with Bro. Brooks, took supper with him at Bro. Young's. Preached for him to a good congregation in the Bethel. Stayed all night with Bro. Kramer.

Saturday, 27th—Left Baltimore at nine o'clock in the cars. Reached Georgetown after eleven o'clock. Was very kindly received in the street by Bro. Edes and others. Spent the night with my nephew, A. E. *Eliason*; his youngest son very sick.

Sabbath, 28th—A pleasing change in the weather. Opened Bro. Edes Sunday School at nine o'clock; after an exhortation, I read the Sunday School teacher's dream, which made a deep impression upon the children, as well as the teachers. Preached at eleven o'clock to a large congregation in the M. E. Church; there was profound attention; I had liberty and hope the seed will not all be lost. Took dinner with Bro. Edes and at three o'clock preached for the colored friends with liberty and some effect. Called out with Bro. Edes to see the poor man Mr.—— condemned to be hung, but there were with him three ministers and two lawyers, so that I did not go in. Returned to Georgetown and preached for the Methodist Protestants, at 8 o'clock, to a good congregation with comfort to my own soul and feeling to the congregation. Thus ends another precious Sabbath day. Lord, in mercy forgive the wrong this day and help me to be better, and do better Amen.

Monday, 29th—It was not convenient to get a passage to the camp and I remained in Georgetown. Called to see —— the man to be hung on Friday; he was perfectly reckless; knew as much as any man could teach him; was unwilling that I should pray with him. Poor mortal, the way of the transgressor is hard. Took dinner with Bro. T. Brown; not much satisfaction. Paid a few vists. Took tea with S. Rand.

Tuesday, 30th—Left Georgetown in a hack with Bros. Brown and Brison for the camp. Reached the ground about eleven o'clock. Heard Edwards preach. Bro. Young preached in the afternoon, a very long sermon, and Bro. G—— gave a long exhortation. At night I preached with liberty and considerable effect; there were a number of mourners came forward. There are a great many preachers. Too many.

Wednesday, 31*st.*—Bro. Thomas Sewell preached at eleven a fine sermon; no effect, all dull. At three o'clock, Bro. Brison preached; he was too rough; it had very little effect. At night Bro. Prettyman preached, but with little feeling and effect. Some mourners went forward and quite a work ensued.

Thursday, September 1*st.*—I slept tolerably well last night, and have attended my morning hour of prayer before the other brethren were up Bro. James Henning preached this morning at eleven o'clock, a popular, zealous sermon; much feeling, yet, but few mourners came forward. Bro. Samuel Smith preached at three o'clock, a long, long sermon to the young, without much feeling, or effect. Bro. Trone preached at night, a very plain talk, and when he spoke of tobacco and other idols, Bro. Wilson, Presiding Elder, arose and left the stand; no feeling, no excitement, yet were there some mourners.

Friday, 2*nd.*—I took no breakfast. Bro. Ball preached at eleven o'clock, a good sermon for these days. A collection was then taken, after which the Sacrament was administered. It was not a profitable season. At three it rained and there was no preaching. At night Bro. Wilson preached and Bro. Jas. Henning gave a powerful exhortation; there were quite a number of mourners, and the meeting was kept up during the night. There was great disorder towards day, the rowdies having taken the ground; it was agreed that I should preach to them, which I attempted with some liberty; the outlaws quieted down and generally came into the congregation, and we had a peaceable, and I hope, profitable time.

Saturday, 3*rd.*—After preaching at five o'clock, the camp came to a close. There was received about thirty-three names, who professed to have been converted. I came with William Dulin to his father's and sent my trunk to Georgetown. Alas, the ravages of time, the vanity of all earthly things. *Here under this roof* I spent *many* of my early *sinful days,* but *now how changed* Bro. Dulin, an old infirm man, his son whom I used to nurse on my knee, is now an old man, his mother is gone, and his aunt, an *excellent* young woman, to whom I was much *attached* in *early life,* gone also and the entire picture is changed into a withered, gloomy scene, which will very soon be erased from memory's book. Lord, save me from this general wreck, and make me, one of

Thy servants—though least of all—so pure, that he may live forever, and behold Thy glory in, an unchanging and undying world.

Sabbath, 4th.—A very wet morning. I rode up with William Dulin to the Court House and preached with liberty and much plainness to a large congregation. Bro. W. W. Welsh, the preacher who was to take me to his afternoon appointment, excused himself and sent a youth with me. His apology was, that he had to preach at night. I greatly fear that the glory has departed from our Israel. I rode about seven miles to Anandale and preached to a tolerable congregation, with much plainness and some liberty, but the meat was too strong, they could not, as usual, shout under it. Bro. Cox then took me in his wagon, over a very tough, hilly, muddy road, nine or ten miles, to Georgetown. We reached the top of the hill after sunset. I walked over into town, carrying my saddle bags, over-coat and umbrella about a mile. Reached Bro. Edes a few minutes before the preaching hour, in a complete perspiration; yet blessed be God, not weary, or fatigued. I preached in Georgetown to a large congregation, with much liberty and as much physical energy, as usual at any time. There was a solemn feeling, and seven mourners came forward. Thus ends the labors of another Sabbath day, more, much more than usual, and yet through the extraordinary goodness of God, I feel little, or no physical fatigue. Praise the Lord, oh my soul. Long as I live, will I praise the Lord.

Monday, 5th.—Retired last night about eleven o'clock and was much annoyed with the cramps; had to rise and walk the room four times, yet I arose at four o'clock and was more animated in attending my reading lessons than usual. Surely God is good and that my soul knoweth right well. Preached at ten o'clock in the M. E. Church to a small congregation, with liberty and profit, I hope. It was a searching time. Took dinner with Bro. Brison, and preached at night to a tolerably good congregation. A number of mourners, four of whom professed conversion. Stayed all night with Bro. Ryan.

Tuesday, 6th.—Paid some visits among the poor and preached at half past ten to a very small congregation, with liberty and plainness, but little effect. Took dinner with Asbury Eliason. Paid some visits and preached at night to a good congregation, with liberty and some effect; there were present six, or seven mourners. Stayed all night with Bro. Dickson; had a comfortable night's sleep; very little cramp.

Wednesday, 7th—Took an early breakfast. Left George-town in an omnibus at seven o'clock and Washington at eight in the cars, reaching Baltimore twenty minutes before ten o'clock. Oh, how rapidly we whirl through this evil world, urging and hastening our way down to destruction. Found things in the city much as they have been; all, all pressing onward to death and ruin. Oh how little they think of God, His presence, His purity, His power.

Thursday, 8th—Called to see some of my old friends and at night went to hear Professor Wentworth preach at Columbia Street Church, where there is a great excitement; the altar is crowded with mourners. The sermon was below his ordinary standard.

Friday, 9th—Have been busy writing and delivering notices to the managers for a Board meeting on Monday night. Have not felt so well since my return. It has been a very wet day. I walked through the rain down to Federal Hill and preached to a small congregation in William Street Church; one professed to receive pardon Stayed all night at Bro. Armstrong's house.

Saturday 10th.—Finished giving notices, or nearly so. Bro. E. C. Thomas gave me five dollars for the poor. I paid off all the arrearages for bread in my absence, and am now prepared to enter anew on the work of mercy. Visited Bro. Wilson's afflicted family; found them as usual, cheerful, grateful and happy. The little boy whom God healed of his lameness is still well and cheerful. Oh, for more faith and humility. Lord forgive and help me.

Sabbath, 11th.—Preached this morning at William Street Church to a large congregation, on the subject of "Faith," with some liberty. Dined with Bro. Bell. Heard Bro. W. Haven preach at the Sailors' Bethel at three o'clock. I preached at Eutaw Street Church at night with some liberty, much plainness and some effect. One fine young man came up as a mourner. Thus another precious Sabbath has gone, and has been very poorly improved.

Monday, 12th.—I had this morning a slight attack of the cholera morbus.

Tuesday, 13th.—Beginning of Board month. Called to see some of my old friends. One, a member of our church, who has been confined to her bed more than three months, during that time her *leader* has not been to see her. She has three little children to support, and is indeed a woman of sorrow; yet her house wears the appearance of industry: it is neat and clean. Preached at Columbia Street Church at night, quite a crowd of people, and the altar filled with seekers. The Board met and elected me for the ensuing year, at the same compensation given last year. Lord, in mercy grant me wisdom and grace, to do much better than the past year.

Wednesday, 14th—Have called to see some sick and destitute people. They naturally look for pecuniary aid. It is not easy to abolish established laws or customs. Having an appointment to preach at the Seamen's Bethel, I went in a storm of rain, and got pretty wet; preached to a little flock, and stayed with Bro. G. Brooks.

Thursday, 15th—This has been a day of very little effort. I have felt rather dull and unbelieving. Have visited several families of diversified character. Preached to a large congregation at William Street Church, with some liberty and feeling, yet were there but few mourners. Returned home in a perspiration. Air quite cool.

Friday, 16th.—I have felt less inconvenience from fasting to-day than usual; yet there is so much formality in its observance, that the benefit is paralysed. Lord, help me to be more spiritual. Made some interesting visits to my old friends, who were very glad to see me. Attended the preachers' meeting. The difference between Justification and Sanctification was discussed. The sentiments on that subject, which I expressed a few years ago, were condemned by the Church as dangerous and heretical; now they are avowed and defended by a large majority of the preachers, and one Presiding Elder. We had a profitable class-meeting, though but few present.

Saturday, 17th.—Was considerably annoyed last night; caused me to loose much sleep. My soul was greatly refreshed and my eyes melted into tears, in my devotional exercises this morning, particularly in reading the inimitable account of Joseph's discovery by his brethren. Have visited several sick families ; was compelled to relieve their wants. Have been taking thought for a coming day, by searching for a place to deposit wood for the Winter ; yet no anxious thought. All shall be well, if my heart is pure, and I do my duty faithfully.

Sabbath, 18*th*.—Opened Wesley Chapel Sunday School, with exhortation. Preached at the Causeway Mission Chapel for Bro. Day. Walked down and held a prayer meeting at the Mission Chapel on Light street extended ; three mourners came forward. Rode up with Bro. Alwine and preached at Emory at night, with some liberty, to a small congregation. Lord, in mercy, pardon the errors of this day and enter not into judgment with Thy servant.

Monday, 19*th*.—This day I have visited some of my old friends ; some sick, others poor. None striving for the kingdom of Heaven, with all their powers.

Tuesday, 20*th*.—Embarked at seven o'clock, on board the steamboat for Cambridge, to buy or get some wood for the poor. Very few passengers ; so that my pride, or indifference for the cause, prevented me from preaching to the passengers. Reached Cambridge at half past twelve ; stopped with Bro. Straughan. The place is well nigh dead, spiritually. Attended a funeral at three o'clock ; very, very few present. Neither preacher, nor people, nor relations appeared to feel any interest on the occasion. An appointment for me to preach at night, but rain prevented. The house was not opened. If the people can reach heaven in a clear sunshine, and ride in a comfortable carriage, some of them would condescend to enter in ; yet, there appears to be a few, a very few even in Sardis, who have not deeply defiled their garments.

Wednesday, 21*st*.—Had an interview with Dr. Thompson, about some wood ; I found however, that his circumstances would not justify him in giving the wood, and the terms he offered were not important, so that I declined buying any ; wood is generally scarce and high. Rode down with the junior preacher to Bro. Connor's, and preached to a good congregation at Beckwith's meeting house ; had some liberty and was very plain—the meat was for their delicate appetites ;

rather too strong. Gave a rum selling friend a very strong *pill.'* I hope it will operate well.

" *Thursday, 22nd*—Having failed in my effort to get wood, I concluded to return in the steamboat Cecil; found a crowd on board : the captain a warm-hearted Methodist. I was however, annoyed with one or two men, who knew me. they being half drunk. I however, preached with some liberty and I hope effect. The company were very attentive and respectful, with the exception of one of my drinking friends. Strange that they will keep rum to poison their passengers. Reached Baltimore at half past seven o'clock. Thank the Lord for his kind protection. Oh, may I be better and do better, than I have ever yet been, or done.

Friday, 23rd.—Attended the preachers' meeting this morning. The subject of "The difference between justification and sanctification" was continued, but without any prospect of reconciliation of views. When doctors disagree, what will become of the patients? A poor woman whom we have been assisting for sometime, said, if she had all her children together, she would take them into the woods and kill them and herself. Our class was still and solemn, but I hope profitable.

Saturday, 24th.—Praise the Lord, oh my soul.

Sabbath, 25th—Another blessed Sabbath morning. Precious emblem of that rest which God has provided for his people. Praise ye the Lord. I opened Sabbath School at Fayette Street Church with prayer and exhortation. Preached at Whatcoat with some liberty. Assisted Bro. Brooks in the administration of the Sacrament, then preached at Montgomery Street Hall to a small congregation. Baptised a child and gave an exhortation, or explanation of the ordinances. Preached at night to a large congregation in William Street Church with some liberty, but not much effect. There was however, an altar nearly filled with mourners. Walked home and retired to bed feeling no more fatigue, than if I had been setting in an arm-chair all day. Oh, to grace how great a debtor, daily, hourly and momentarily I am constrained to be

Monday, 26th.—Have applied this day to visiting. In one poor family, the husband has been sick nearly a year. The eldest son came home a few weeks since, quite sick. They .

are now in great distress. The father is a Catholic, but not prejudiced; was glad to hear a prayer; has two Bibles. They are connected with some of the most respectable members of our church, but, alas how slow to extend the hand of mercy in time of need. Another interesting, but very poor family I visited; they are acquainted with some of the most respectable people in Essex County, Va. They have sold almost every article out of their house, rather than let their wants be known. Sickness has brought them down. They have five children, who are very, very bare of clothes; unable to attend school, or church. They must be cared for. Preached at night for Bro. Brooks, in the Bethel with some liberty and effect.

Tuesday, 27*th*—Have collected some money this morning for a few cases of destitution, which have been relieved. My old disease has returned again, viz: Anxiety, mental intemperance, hurry and bustle, when all should be calm tranquility; and whilst a holy zeal should cover my soul, as with a garment. Attended preaching at Columbia Street Church—the work still goes on there.

Wednesday, 28*th*—I borrowed a horse, and rode out fourteen miles to see Bro. ——, who has been very sick, but he is now recovering. The horse was rough, and riding fourteen miles without alighting, benumbed my poor limbs very much, but in a few minutes all was right again.

Thursday, 29*th*—Had a more comfortable season in my morning devotions than usual; rode back to Baltimore, and felt very little fatigue—visited a few families—one deeply afflicted—two children very low—the husband has been afflicted for nearly two years. Surely, some appear to have a larger portion of sorrow than others; 'yet, the Judge of all the earth will do right. Preached at Columbia Street Church—the revival still continues.

Friday, 30*th*—Oh, how hard to shake off old habits. My fasting is so formal, it loses all its efficacy; shall I therefore, give it up—not so. Lord, in mercy, spiritualize my devotion. Visited a few sick and poor; the poor are more anxious to have their temporal wants relieved, than to have their spiritual maladies healed. Attended the preachers' meeting; Bro. Register read a very good essay on the subject of *Sanctification.* The advocates of the old-side could not argue, but

plead only for the old land-marks, and cried, WESLEY! WES-
LEY! whilst the other side proved their views fully, from Mr.
Wesley's own words. Their views must and will obtain, because they are in accordance with reason, and scripture and
righteousness. Preached at William Street Church to a good
congregation, who were solemn and affected ; yet, were there
no mourners.

Saturday, *October* 1*st*—Enjoyed a softening and comforting
influence in my hour of prayer this morning. One smile
from Jesus is worth more than all worlds could be to my poor
helpless soul. This has been a wet day, I have however, visited and relieved several poor afflicted families.

Sabbath, 2*nd*—Have spent the morning in reading, meditation and prayer. Heard Dr. Roberts preach at Strawbridge,
receiving and assisting in the administration of the Holy Sacrament. Preached at Eutaw, to a small congregation, at
3 o'clock. I had some liberty, and all was not spoken in
vain. Preached again at Whatcoat, to a good congregation,
with liberty and effect. One came to the altar. Returned
home. If I had more pure and undefiled religion, I should
be perfectly contented and happy.

Monday, 3*d*—In visiting, I met an old acquaintance with
little twins in her arms. She was very poor, but cheerful,
with those twins, and two other children. She sews and has
scuffled through the summer, but said she would need help
in winter. She has no stove. She said "all is peace now,
though the children cry, yet I have peace." Meaning I have
no drunken husband to come home and abuse me. Another
squalidly poor Irish family was recommended to me by a brother, though he had given them nothing. All their furniture
was one small dirty stool, their bed, a pillow and quilt. An
enemy hath done this. Rum has been here.

Tuesday, 4*th* Though my rest was disturbed by unpleasant
dreams, yet was I permitted to get a little nigher the fountain of all good in my devotions, this morning. One precious
smile from Jesus is far more desirable than all earth and
heaven besides. I have walked nearly all day, visiting some
poor families. Preached at the Widows' Home, and visited
the Orphan's Asylum. Exhorted and prayed in one room,
and visited their sick and prayed in two other rooms there.

Preached at William Street Church at night. A good

congregation, and a good time. Solemn feeling, and a number of mourners. Returned home quite refreshed.

Wednesday, 5th—Rode out with Bro. Richard Brown twelve miles, to see Bro —— in regard to a lot in Biddle Alley, to erect a school house upon for colored children. He was three or four miles farther off than we expected. Bro. Brown was compelled to return to Baltimore, and had no time to go with me, so I walked to William Fite's, but Bro. —— had rode out, and I was compelled to stay all night. I could not however, succeed in getting the lot. Poor, dear old man, though rich—rich, and eighty nine years old—said he was not able to *give* the lot, but referred me to his Agent in Baltimore, and promised to do something. Oh, the dangers of riches! Alas! the love of money is one of Satan's strongholds in the heart, and perhaps the last he will surrender.

Thursday, 6th.—Praise the Lord for his abundant mercies. I have enjoyed a greater nearness to God this morning than for a long, long season. The favor of God is more, —far more than life in its most elevated enjoyment ; indeed, all in heaven and on earth would be a perfect blank, without the smiles of Jesus. There being no convenient way to the cars or omnibus, I concluded to walk to the city, so that I had a very pleasant walk of fifteen miles, more or less, and reached home about one o'clock, feeling very little fatigued. Visited a few friends, and closed the day in peace.

Friday, 7th.—This has been rather a barren day with my poor soul. Visited a few friends and fasted, but in a very formal way. Oh when shall I escape from this enemy's leaden grasp—formality! Preached at Emory to a very small congregation, with considerable liberty.

Saturday, 8th.—Slept soundly, but did not awake in a spiritual frame of mind. Visited some families. Paid my weekly baker's and grocer's bill. Was pressingly requested to assist Bro. Hearn, at Warren factory, with his meeting tomorrow. Having no positive appointment of my own, I went with him, but found a very unpleasant state of feeling between him and his colleague, which made my visit unpleasant. Bro. Collins preached at night; several mourners.

Sabbath, 9th.—Passed a most unpleasant night, had to sleep on feathers, which caused a restless, sleepless state of feeling. Bro. H—— held a lovefeast and received nineteen members on probation. I preached at eleven, with great liberty and effect. Preached again at three, not so much liberty. Bro. Collins preached at night. A number of mourners came forward. I dined and stayed all night with a very kind intelligent Adventist.

Monday, 10*th*—Arose early, and spent an hour and a half comfortably and happily in reading the good word, and in prayer. Walked to Cockeysville, three miles, and took the cars some minutes after seven, and reached Baltimore a few minutes after eight. In a few hours I received subscriptions amounting to nearly five hundred dollars, to build a Sunday School house for the colored people, in Biddle Alley.

Tuesday, 11*th*—Month begins. After visiting a few families, I rode out with Bro. Hilt to Randallsville, and preached to a crowded house, in the new free church, built by a female of the Universalist persuasion. I had great liberty and used plain words, showing clearly the fallacy of that church.

Wednesday, 12*th*.—Enjoyed a comfortable season in prayer this morning, though it was cold and I had no fire. Bro. Hilt sent me to the turnpike ; I walked six miles and rode only two in the omnibus. Found some of my friends here sick and destitute of the necessaries of life. Oh, how gloomy the prospect for the poor ! The winter before them and no provision : a poor cripple, with four very interesting children —no wood, no food—nothing but want ; a decent man—children respectable,—but gloomy. Preached at William Street Church with physical strength, but no liberty. Two mourners.

Thursday, 13*th*.—I enjoyed a most comfortable night's rest, a desirable blessing. My hour of devotion appeared very, very short. Spent some time in procuring funds to build the school building for the colored children ; was not very successful. Made some very interesting visits ; had no appointments to preach—visited the Widow's Home. Heard of Bro. Brison's death—solemn thought—suddenly called away ; his death might have been more triumphant. It is a warning to me ; oh, may I profit by it.

Friday, 14*th*.—Have been visiting very busily. Many of the poor suffer much ; money is scarce, and provisions and

wood high—raining. Yet the Lord will provide! Attended
Bro. Brison's funeral at 2 o'clock. Called to see a sister, who
had a parcel of children around her, whilst she was sinking
into the grave, yet was she resigned and joyful.

Saturday. 15th—Visited a few afflicted and destitute families. Intended to pay my bills, but forgot one. Alas, will
there not be many things brought up in the judgment day
which I had forgotten? Lord, help me to watch and pray.

At eleven o'clock I took the cars for Philadelphia, and was
numbered among the transgressors. Took the poor man's
car, among the darkies and poor whites, but it did not soil
my soul, whilst I saved one dollar for the poor. Reached
Philadelphia in safety about four o'clock, and was warmly
received by my old friend, Andrew Manship.

Sabbath, 16th—Preached this morning to a congregation
of twelve hundred persons, in a house which was built out
and out in ten days. We had a precious time. but, alas, the
bane of vital godliness—money, spoiled all, and rooted up the
seed sown. Preached again at three o'clock. The house
and aisles were crowded full of human beings. I gave them
strong meat, and it was well received, but the money scraping
killed the whole. At night Bro. Manship preached. Only
two came forward, both of whom professed conversion. I
find my voice much affected. Have taken cold. I see not
how I am to labor again here, efficiently, but the Lord's will
be done.

Monday, 17th—Called to see a number of my friends, and
stopped a few minutes at the preachers' meeting. They were
discussing things of no interest to their own souls, nor calculated to promote the salvation of the people. Oh, may God
sound an alarm in Zion, and awake the watchmen to a sense
of their danger and their duty. Preached at the new Tabernacle to a large congregation with liberty, and more
physical power than I could have anticipated from my previous
feelings. There were two who professed to experience a
change of heart.

Tuesday. 18th—Finished this morning, reading through
the New Testament, whilst on my knees, this year, the fourth
time. My soul is much affected at the approaching doom of
the Church and the christian world as specified in the Apoc-
alypse; but, alas, the watchmen are all asleep, and that awful

day—the day of God's wrath, will come upon us all. Have visited a number of friends, who are very kind, but alas, I fear they respect the servant more than the Master. Have been pressed to preach in different places, but must remain with the poor, the short time I can stay here. Preached at night to a large congregation with liberty. There were quite . a number of mourners, and some converts.

Wednesday, 19*th*—It was my intention to close my labors · here this day. But the brethren plead so hard, and offered to make a collection for our mission in Baltimore, if I would stay one day longer, which I reluctantly consented. Bro. M. and myself have spent the day in visiting. Preached to a large congregation at night but had not much liberty. There were a number of mourners, and several converts.

Thursday 20*th*—Made a few visits with Bro. Manship. Preached at night with much liberty and effect to more than a thousand people, yet was the collection for the poor very small, only $9,18. Bro. M— said if I had allowed him to make it for himself, it would have been large, but they have poor themselves in abundance, and do not feel it to be their duty to give to those of other cities.

Friday 21*st*—Last night after preaching, I rode to the depot, took the cars and reached Baltimore about four o'clock, having slept very little. Although it has been wet, I have visited nearly all day, and have felt no drowsiness. Visited the Widow's Home, and comforted and prayed with the afflicted. Attended class, and closed the day in peace.

Saturday 22*nd*—I have met with a number of needy people to-day. Some deeply afflicted. They anticipate a hard winter. Almost every article is very dear. I have given sparingly out of my own scanty means. Have paid all my bakers and grocers bills, and in regard to this world, I stand where every individual should stand, free from debt.

Sabbath, 23*d*—Opened the Sabbath-school at Strawbridge. Preached at Wolf's church for our Presbyterian brethren at eleven o'clock, to a good congregation, with much liberty. I fear, however that the meat was too strong for my hearers. Heard Bro. Reese preach at 3 o'clock at Fayette St. Church, and preached there myself at night, to a good congregation, but had no liberty—all was dark and gloomy. Lord Jesus, shine, oh shine away those clouds, and let me behold Thy glory.

Monday, 24th—This has been a stormy day—snow and rain. I only visited one afflicted family in the morning, and a few in the evening. Must I say, a day lost—nearly so. Who can tell the value of a day?

Tuesday, 25th—Have visited some deeply afflicted families; some of them were professors—very few were prepared to die. Visited and preached at the Widows' Home—dead place; not much religion here. Preached to a few at the Mission Chapel out Light street, and walked home quite refreshed; feeling no kind of fatigue.

Wednesday, 26th—Have been very busy to-day, doing nothing but visiting a few sick folks; administered the Sacrament to Bro. S. Henderson. Preached to a small congregation at William St. Church. Walked home and felt much refreshed.

Thursday, 27th—This has been a damp and unpleasant day. I have taken cold; yet, I have visited all day. If my patients were more spiritual, it would be more encouraging. Attended the funeral of a poor unfortunate man of dissipated habits. He had but a short notice, and was not in his right mind from the first of his illness. The sober thought, of an immortal soul lost forever, should arouse all my dormant powers to save others from that awful doom. But alas! how indifferent is my poor soul, and how insensible. Have mercy on me, oh, my God.

Friday, 28th—My soul has been more comfortable to-day than usual. Have visited many poor distressed families, and given them a little food for the soul as well as the body. One poor unbeliever has gone to eternity. It is possible that I was too negligent with him. Should it be that his soul is lost through my carelessness, how awful the thought. Attended class. Bro. R—, who led, thought I was too rigid with myself and others, but a still greater degree of scrutiny in worldly matters would be called prudence.

Sabbath, 30th—The weather has been very uncomfortable to-day. I have done very little for God, or the people. Preached at 11 o'clock, at the Seamen's Bethel, and attended there in the afternoon, a Sacramental meeting, but took no part in their experience meeting, because I do not understand them. Heard Bro. Register preach at Spring Garden Chapel. Returned home and closed the day. Oh Lord, enter not into judgment with thy servant.

Monday, 21st—I have nearly finished my collection for the School House for colored children. Though it has not given me much trouble, yet, does it detract from the dignity and glory of the gospel, to beg so much money ; it gives riches and rich people an importance unknown to the gospel.

Thursday, Nov.1st—My soul cannot shake off all the clogs of unbelief and shame Oh, when shall I the victory gain? Have visited a number of distressed and afflicted cases to-day. How thick, dark and cold the gloom that hangs over the destiny of the poor in the world, but there is a better day approaching. Lord hasten it. Have baptized three households to-day.

Wednesday, 2nd—This day I have done what I never did before, I voted at a public, popular election, to put down drunkenness in our State, and have I think, done so in the fear of God. Have visited and partially relieved quite a number of poor suffering mortals. How little do the rich know or care for the sufferings of the poor, This account will have to be settled at another tribunal, where at last Christ's word will be fully realized. Woe unto you that are rich, for ye have received your reward.

Friday, 4th—I have been striving to live for a better world. Praise the Lord for the prospect. Have furnished two poor families with stoves, aided by Bro. Thomas' advice and money. It is more blessed to give than receive. Preached at Wesley Chapel with much liberty and comfort to my own soul, and with some effect.

Saturday, 5th—I have felt quite discouraged this day. The poor and distressed seem to increase, nor can they be relieved except in a very small degree. Some are maimed, some sick some blind, and all in want of both food and raiment. It is not pleasant to visit the poor without means to relieve in part their pressing wants.

Sabbath, 6th—Opened the Wesley Chapel Sabbath School with a long lecture. Preached at William Street Church, with much liberty. Quite a solemn season. Visited the wharves and vessels, also the tippling shops which were open, distributing tracts, and lecturing the idle sinners. I think the election has already intimidated the licentious rum seller.

Praise the Lord for this also. Walked over to Bro. Reed's in Old Town, to preach for him, but he had gone to the country. Returned and heard Bro. Farrow preach at Strawbridge, and thus ended another Sabbath.

Monday, 7th.—My attention has been divided among the sick and poor in different parts ; a fact which entangles my mind and weakens my usefulness. I had made an engagement to meet a poor woman at the Asylum, to get her children a home and forgot it ; Lord, in boundless mercy again forgive me.

Tuesday, 8th.—Last night I had a most alarming and admonitory dream, and it should arouse me. Have walked nearly all day. Visited and relieved some afflicted, worthy widows. Attended a prayer meeting, at Exeter Street Church, with Bro. Reed. Cold, cold. Walked home and feltqu ite refreshed.

Wednesday, 9th.—This has been a very inclement day. Very rainy ; but I felt so much mortified about the poor woman, whose case I forget to attend toat the Asylum on Monday that I have to-day procured annual subscribers to the amount of nearly sixty dollars, which will entitle the children to a place in that institution. Thank the Lord and thank my kind friends for their liberality. Bro. Perry took two, and Bro. E. C. Thomas took two for himself, and two for sister Thomas, and Bro. Drakely took six ; may they have a letter of admission into everlasting habitations, for Christ's sake. Preached at William Street Church to a small but deeply interested congregation.

Thursday, 10th.—Visited a few families and attended the collection for the children and the colored school. Handling money, to the christian, is as dangerous as edged tools to children. I am afraid of it. Yet it smiles and allures and chases fear away. Attended a social meeting at Bro. Perry's. There were but few present, yet enough to claim the promise.

Friday, 11th—I have walked more this day than any before since I have been in Baltimore. A drunken woman asked me for money, which I refused. How she did pour out her anathemas upon the old hypocritical Quakers. What a terrible sight, a fallen, depraved drunken woman presents to the eye.

We had a better class than usual, I had liberty and comfort in leading it.

Saturday, 12th—This is my pay day. I have visited some

who have to wade through the deep cold waters of poverty and sorrow. Called to see what we poor mortals call a respectable family. The mother said I called to see her mother when she herself was a child, and she had never forgotten the circumstance; it made a lasting impression upon her mind, and she had ever since been desirous of seeing me. I gave her and the family a plain lesson which they will not forget. At 4 o'clock left in the cars for Bro. Samuel Kramer's. Arrived about dark.

Sunday, 13th—A very wet, inclement day. No congregation in the morning. A very small one at three, whom I preached to in Bro. Kramer's own chapel, built on his own farm by himself. Rode three miles to Stabler's meeting house, and at night preached to a large congregation, with much liberty. Two professed to embrace religion.

Monday, 14th—Returned to Baltimore in the cars. Got home after nine. Visited some distressed families, and baptised several children. I have received for benevolent purposes in the last two months about one hundred and seventy dollars, and have paid out about two hundred. The times wear a dark aspect in view of the high prices of provisions, and the meagre pay given for common sewing.

Tuesday, 15th—There is so much sameness in my operations, that it is well calculated to induce formality in worship which must ever be offensive to God.

Wednesday, 16th.—Have been engaged in visiting the sick and closing some unsettled accounts, which the trustees of the Light St. Chapel had assumed, but neglected to close. Neglect in business leads to carelessness in religious duties; and carelessness in our devotions, leads to deception and final ruin. Rode in the evening to Parkton and preached at Stabler's Meeting House, to a small congregation; the rain prevented the people from coming out.

Thursday, 17th.—Reached Baltimore about nine o'clock. Have visited some deeply distressed families. Have done very little, yet I have been going and busy all day. Heard Bro. Gear preach at night. A few mourners present at Franklin Street Church.

Friday, 18th.—Oh for a sensibility of sin, a pain to feel it near After visiting among the poor through the day, I attended class at night and saw and felt more than ever my delinquencies. So I think did the rest of the class. It was a profitable time.

Saturday, 19*th*.—Have visited several patients who are just on the confines of eternity. Alas, the responsibility! If I deal very plainly, it will grieve the living and the dying, and if I do not, their blood will be found upon my garments. Awful thought. Lord in mercy grant me grace and wisdom, that I may escape Thy just indignation and save others from the damnation of hell. I gave some loafers at the door of a rum shop, some tracts and some plain talk. They received both plainly.

Sabbath, 20*th*.—Walked the streets and wharves and distributed tracts. One old man who keeps his store open on Sundays, became very angry, called me very ugly names and denounced the hypocritical Methodists to perdition, without mercy, or reservation. On the wharf, a hearty, strong man, had his wares spread out largely; he too fought for his master, the devil, valiantly; a decent looking man joined him, and some one joined with me. A large crowd collected, and I spoke many things to them in an exhortation and distributed a number of tracts. Preached at the Seamen's Bethel. Preached again at three o'clock, at the Mission Chapel, on Light Street to a large congregation, with much comfort to my own soul. Preached to a large, attentive congregation, at Columbia Street Church, with liberty, and I think good effect. It was a profitable season. I was very close, but it was well received.

Monday, 21*st*.—Alas, what has sin done for our world? I have visited some cases of great suffering. A poor woman with a cancer in her breast and arm. She is a deep penitent, but cannot exercise saving faith in the atoning merits of Christ. I heard a very strange rumor in regard to myself. For a moment it gave me some uneasiness, but I was enabled in a few hours to feel no more than what it really was,—an empty puff of wind.

Tuesday, 22*nd*.—A wet, unhealthy day, yet I have walked and visited all day, and must say with the unsuccessful disciple's "Master, we have toiled all night and taken nothing."

Wednesday, 23*rd*.—Have visited some of my most afflicted patients. The poor woman deeply afflicted with the cancer, seems to be much comforted and feels an humble assur-

ance, that God, for Christ's sake, has pardoned her sins.
Preached at three o'clock to the children at the asylum; about
one hundred present and only one moved from the seat, and
one slept.   A more attentive and respectful congregation, I
have perhaps, never preached to.   I feel honored and humbled and comforted in their presence.   Collected from a few
friends, twenty-five dollars to buy some shoes for the poor
families.   The Lord bless those kind friends.

Thursday, 24th.—I rejoice that our State authorities honored God, by appointing a day of thanksgiving.   Yet, do I
believe, there is more sin committed on this day, than there
would be in a week of working days.   Surely labor is a
blessing, for which we should be far more thankful than we
are.   Heard Dr. Roberts preach to a small congregation at
William Street, and took up a small, very small collection for
the poor.   Attended the Tract meeting in St. John's Church
at night.   Drs. Johns, Heiner, Plummer and Hamner spoke.
A good congregation, but the collection dragged exceedingly.   They are not as good beggars as the Methodists.

Friday, 25th—I have felt less inconvenience from fasting
to-day than usual.   After walking all day, having taken nothing for twenty-four hours, I feel no weakness, no more need
of food, than if I had taken my regular meals.   A friend on
the wharf, Levin Jones, gave me a cord of wood, for which I
thank the Lord for this, also.   Led the class for Bro. D—.
Few out.   It was a cold, unprofitable season.

Saturday, 26th—I have visited nearly all of my sick patients
this morning.   Some of them are very great sufferers.   Oh,
that I could feel as much for them as I should.   I procured
for the sister with the cancer, a bed comfort, and although
she was too diffident to say that she needed it yet she was very
grateful for it, which gave me a double reward.   At half
past three, left in the cars with Bro. Kramer, and rode up to
his farm.

Sabbath, 27th—Last night it was cold, and I could not sleep;
my mind being deeply affected in reflecting on those friends
suffering with most painful cancers, and one of them without
bed-clothes to keep her warm.   Preached to a small congre-
gration at half past ten o'clock, with some liberty, and to a
large one at three; when I was very plain and close.   The
seed will not all be lost.

Monday, 28*th*—Reached home at nine. Visited and comforted, warmed and clothed some poor hungry, striving souls. Oh, that I could feel more deeply for the afflictions of my fellow mortals, whom I must love as myself, if they are moral, correct people, or never see their Father in Heaven, in peace. Oh for a pure heart, and a self-denying spirit. Attended Love Feast. I think it was a dull season, yet some thought otherwise, and praised it. So will the merchant praise all, yes, *all* his goods.

Tuesday, 29*th*.—I was again admonished, by a solemn and an alarming dream of my duty and of my danger, and yet, alas, I will still plod along in the old tracks. Lord help me from this moment to do better, and God alone can make this heart better. Have visited and relieved a few poor distressed mortals, and collected some money for the African school.

CHRISTIAN WARFARE.

SERMON BY JOHN HERSEY.

"For the weapons of our warfare are not carnal, but mighty through God, to the pulling down of strongholds."—2 *Cor.*, x, 4.

We find ourselves placed in a world of conflict and danger, surrounded by a mighty host of enemies, good and evil, virtue and vice, are irreconcilable enemies. If we secure any earthly good, we have to fight for it. It requires labor and care and diligence to gain the necessary comforts of food and raiment; to insure success, we have to wage war with animate and inanimate nature; after we have toiled to prepare the ground and have deposited the seed therein, both wild and domestic animals will array themselves in hostility against the labor of our hands; hence we have to close the ground, to guard against their incursions; the birds of the air, the crawling reptiles of the earth, will endeavor to destroy the good seed. Thus every article of real value, which grows out of the earth, is surrounded by enemies, while the weeds and briars grow spontaneously without care or culture! Not only has the earth been cursed on account of man's sin, but the

atmosphere is full of deadly poison. The human heart in a
very especial manner, is exposed to the assaults of deadly foes.
The devil goes about, like a roaring lion, seeking whom he
may devour ; he also assumes the form of a serpent and transforms himself into the appearance of an angel of light, the
more effectually to destroy poor, frail mortals ; and further,
to increase our dangers and call forth our energies in life's
conflict ; we have to meet and conquor enemies in our own
bosom, our degenerate heart ; our passions and our appetites,
are our deadly foes. Indulge children in all their desires
and they will be invariably and inevitably ruined ; men are
but children of a larger growth ; thus in our present fallen
condition, we must fight, or fall, conquer or be ruined forever.
There can be no neutrals in this war ; therefore in the improvement of our present subject, we will

1st.—Advert to the character of our inveterate enemy,
(the devil,) and expose to view a few of his "strongholds."

1.   His character : He is an active, restless foe, he goeth
about like a roaring lion, a malicious enemy ; hence he is
called Satan.   An artful, deceptious foe ; his strength now
lieth in his cunning, his artifice, his deception. Paul says,
we are not ignorant of his devices. It will, therefore, be
necessary that we have not only the wisdom that cometh from
above, but divine power also, to enable us to meet and conquer this artful, insidious enemy.

2d.   His Strongholds—As the devil has been foiled and
conquered by the Lord Jesus Christ, his hope of success now
depends not only on his devices, but he erects entrenchments
and fortifications to aid him in his work of destruction.   On
the present occasion we will only notice three of his strongholds ; Infidelity, Pride, Love of the world.

First stronghold—Infidelity—The devil can now gain very
little by an avowal of open infidelity. Learned and pious
men of God, by writing and preaching, have well nigh demol-
ished this stronghold of Satan; there are now very few open
and avowed infidels, their theory will not bear the light. This
artful seducer however, has covertly gathered up the fragments of this favorite fortification, and while by his crafty
devices, he denounces infidelity, and even his open friends are
unwilling to appear entrenched within its tottering walls, he
changes the name, and enters the church, where he carries on

his work of ruin and infidelity under cover of Christianity.

Hence upon a close examination, it will be found that many professors of religion, both in the ministry and membership, are only specious infidels. Alas, what a multitude of professing christians are living at ease in Zion; are slumbering in a lukewarm state; nor do they believe Christ's solemn declarations when he says: "He will spue them out of his mouth, all those who are living carelessly, viz; without fasting and diligent, persevering prayer, that they may be purified and made holy now, not to-morrow, that do not believe that sin is hateful to God, and must exclude us from Heaven. Again there are many professors, who do not really believe in the existence of the attributes of God. First, his omnipresence; "Do not I fill heaven and earth," saith the Lord Almighty. But who really believes it? No man that says or does any thing which he would not say or do, if the Lord Jesus were personally present. But, who, may we not ask, uniformly observes this rule?

2nd. *God's Omniscience*—Who really and consistently believes in the existence of this attribute? No man wishes to conceal from man, his actions, thoughts, motives and desires; surely if he is ashamed of those secret things before men, he should feel infinitely more ashamed to disclose them to the view of a pure and holy God. May we not find infidels? viz. unbelievers, in the bosom of the church. Again, there are many who would feel insulted, were you to call them infidels, or unbelievers and yet they do not believe God's holy word: if there is one declaration in the Holy Bible, which I do not believe, I may as well disbelieve every word written therein. The word of God says, "This night thy soul shall be required of thee," and "without holiness no man can see the Lord." If I am not therefore, in possession of that pearl of great price, or striving with all my ransomed powers to secure it, I either do not believe God's word, or place a very low estimate upon the value of my soul. In God's word it is written—"But the day of the Lord will come as a thief in the night; in the which the heavens will pass away with great noise and the elements shall melt with fervent heat, the earth also and the works that are therein, shall be burned up."—2 Peter, iii, 10. That awful day will come as a thief in the night, in an unexpected hour. Do we believe this solemn declaration? All of us who are living, unprepared to die, viz.; in an un-

holy and unsanctified state, without making every exertion in
our power to realize a pure heart, do not believe it; to prove
this fact, let us suppose a case—a stranger informs us that an
incendiary will burn down our house one night next week, he
heard the plan arranged for doing this dreadful deed; would
we during that week retire to bed, without making a judicious preparation to guard against the impending calamity?
We feel conscious that we would not; and yet, when Almighty God speaks and unequivocally declares that He may
burn up the world this night and under those solemn circumstances, we retire to our slumbering bed with an entire indifference, conscious that we are not prepared to meet our God.
Now if we regard the word of man, more than the word of God,
can we meet the Judge of all the earth with joy? We believe
our neighbor and we promptly acted. God speaks and we
disregard His word. Are we not therefore virtually unbelievers, infidels? This specie of infidelity forms a favored position, or stronghold for the devil.

3d.   *Pride*—The pride of the heart forms a most pleasing
lurking place for Satan. God hates a proud look, and "he that
exalteth himself shall be abased." In the arms of our infidelity, Satan feels himself secure, for God has said, "he that
believeth not shall be damned." The devil revels and takes
peculiar delight in the heart where pride is countenanced.

A proud beggar would be truly a contemptible character,
the devil however knows that we are beggars, dependent on
God for every drop of water, and every crumb of bread. A
poor culprit condemned to be executed to-morrow, and infla-
ted with pride, would present a most despicable sight in the
eyes of reflecting men. All mankind are condemned to die,
and may meet their solemn doom the next moment. As pride
in its nature is unnatural, unreasonable, hateful to God, and
destructive to human happiness, it behooves us to examine
our hearts with great care and candor, lest a particle of this
soul-degrading, God-dishonoring principle, in which Satan delights, should be found to exist within. A desire to be seen
and admired of men, is unequivocal proof of the existence of
this evil in the heart. Can anything but pride influence a
dying condemned mortal to wear fine and costly apparel, or
build elegant and expensive houses, and furnish them with
costly furniture only to be seen and admired? It is however
frequently asserted that we may be as proud when dressed in

Osnaburgs as in broadcloth. While the possibility of this supposition is admitted, the subject involved in the case, is of too much importance (even the loss of the soul) to pass over the argument carelessly. We must appeal to higher authority than poor erring men; we must hear what Almighty God says in regard to this important subject. When Ahab laid aside his royal robes and put on sack-cloth, (a coarse hairy garment) and fasted, the Lord beheld it and said to Elijah, "Seest thou how Ahab humbleth himself before Me, I will not bring this evil in his days." Our Saviour's words are in perfect accordance with the above declaration, "Wo unto thee Chorazin! woe unto thee Bethsaida! for if the mighty works which were done in you, had been done in Tyre and Sidon, they would have repented long ago in sack-cloth and ashes."— Matth. xi, 21.

When Almighty God expressly declared that sack-cloth, a coarse hairy garment, worn by a man, was a mark of humility, will mortal man say, that to wear gay and costly apparel is no evidence of pride in the heart? Let God be true, though every mortal man be found guilty of falsehood.

Therefore, prudence and common sense dictate to us, that we should imitate the conduct of Ahab and also of the Ninevite, by laying aside every mark of wealth and show in our houses, our furniture and our apparel, especially as our blessed Redeemer laid aside His exalted glory and bore the cross and despised the shame, being born in a stable and having marked the pathway to heaven, in and through the deep valley of humility and self-denial! O let us imitate the example of our Lord Jesus Christ in this great conflict. May we like our Lord and Master be clothed with the beautiful garments of genuine humility, and thus drive Satan from his favorite haunt of pride in our heart.

3rd. *Love of the world*—Where the devil has been driven from his haunt of infidelity and pride, he retires, as his last subterfuge, into the stronghold of the love of the world. Here he generally makes his most powerful and successful attacks upon the heart of man; Satan well-knows that the love of the world is the darkest crime a human being can be guilty of; the most malignant and fatal disease to which he is exposed in this unhealthy clime. It was the only disease, the Great Physician failed to cure, when he was on earth; when the rich young man was directed by the Lord Jesus, to sell all his posessions and give the proceeds to the poor, he went away sorrowful, for he had great possessions. O how powerfully and successfully did the devil fight for this impregnable fortress erected in this amiable young man's heart. And to the present day, this stronghold is Satan's favorite rendezvous.

Let us, therefore, examine this point with care and candor. Were we called on to sell all our earthly possessions and give the proceds to the poor, could we promptly and cheerfully comply with the requisition? or would we rather not go, like the rich young man, from Christ, with a sorrowful heart; if so, would it not afford proof positive that we love the world and thereby afford the devil a most desirable stronghold in our heart. Again, were we only tried as was the old patriarch, who lived in a very dark age of the world, could we meet the trials and triumphs as did Job? When all his large possessions were swept away, he bowed in submission, and praised the Lord. Satan well knows that if we love the world its money, its property, its honors, its gratifications more or less, we cannot love God, and must be banished from his presence, and the glory of his power. There are many who deceive their own souls by saying, "I love God better than I love the world." Were the wife to use this specious argument, and comfort her husband by assuring him that she loves him better than the other favorites, it would be mockery, and yet many who pass for good christians, will cast this dark reproach upon the Saviour, and wipe their loins and say, "I have done no wrong."

Others console their own hearts by saying, "It is true, I am not yet sanctified wholly, I still feel the remains of the carnal mind, but I intend and expect to secure the wedding garments, viz., pure love, before I die." Was the wife to adopt this language and comfort her husband by assuring him that it was her sincere desire and intention to love him perfectly before she died; when she became old and wrinkled, it would be an insult which human language cannot describe, and yet, professing christians will carelessly assume this ruinous position in regard to the Holy One of Israel and sit down contentedly, and smoke and laugh and jest and murder their precious moments, which should be spent in fasting and prayer. Hence, the love of the world may be considered Satan's most favorite lurking place, his principal stronghold, the last from which he will be driven. Having briefly and imperfectly examined some of the devil's strongholds, proceed we,

Secondly—To notice the nature of the conflict and the means through which we may gain a triumphant victory.

1st. *The nature of the conflict.*—It is a spiritual warfare ; hence the weapons of our warefare are not carnal, &c. It is a good cause ; "Fight the good fight of faith." It is an incessant conflict; if we are only one minute off our guard, the insidious enemy will take advantage of that careless moment to inflict a deadly wound. It is an important battle ; if we are conquered, eternal ruin must ensue, including shame and ceaseless misery. "These shall go away into everlasting destruction from the presence of the Lord and from the glory of His power."—MATTH. xxv., 46.; 2 THESS. i, 9. If we are courageous and gain the victory, eternal life shall be our great reward, including an inheritance—incorruptible and undefiled, that fadeth not away. A home—a house not made with hands eternal in the heavens; and to crown the victor's head, a glorious crown of life shall be given. It is enough, it is an important conflict in which we are engaged.

2d. *The preparation for battle*—The christian armor; "The weapons of our warfare." The ancients used both offensive and defensive armor, and as our foes are numerous, insidious and malignant and we shall have to fight at every step through life, for liberty and all our gospel privileges, it will be important and necessary, that we put on the whole armor of God, as cowardice invariably marks the soldier's character with shame and disgrace ; all slavish fear must be laid aside.

The Apostle to the Gentiles, has given us a full description of the christian soldier's armor, Ephv. i, 13–18. (1) "Stand therefore, having your loins girt about with the truth." God's word is truth. The girdle for our loins must be composed of scripture doctrines; if our doctrine is defective or not true when the discovery is made, it will weaken our loins and cause our knees to smite together; it behooves us, therefore, to receive and preach that doctrine which will stand on the judgment day, viz: the proper divinity of Jesus Christ, that by his death, he made atonement for us, that by repentance and faith, only, we may receive pardon, regeneration, and sanctification, and that through faith in Jesus Christ, we may live holy, righteous and godly lives on earth, and enjoy eternal life in heaven. "He that believeth shall be saved, and he that believeth not shall be damned."

2nd.—The breastplate of righteousness.—Nothing but this breastplate can protect our vital parts from the assaults of our enemies. Our hearts must be made perfect, and right and pure and good by the mighty power of that God who has done all things well, whose signature is purity and perfection. We must keep this important piece of armor bright by faith and prayer. May our righteousness never become dim or rusty.

3d.—Your feet shod with the preparation of the Gospel of Peace.—We must expect to meet with briars and thorns in our pathway to heaven. We shall be assailed frequently by persecution and sore temptation, piercing our feet most painfully; our feet must therefore, be shod with peace; a pure spirit of peace and love in connection with a pure heart will enable us to trample all the briars and thorns beneath our feet, not only those which proceed from the mouth of bitter and enraged men, but also devils; God will shortly bruise Satan under your feet. Let us therefore put on the gospel shoes of peace,—peace and love.

4th.—The shield of faith.—A defensive piece of armor used by the ancients; sometime made of metal, but more frequently of tanned hides, that were anointed with oil, in order to render them smooth, compact and firm. Faith is the christian soldier's shield, which if dexterously managed, will successfully ward off all the fiery darts of the wicked one.

Infidelity. Unbelief, constitutes Satan's most successful stronghold; but faith, strong faith, demolishes that fortification at a blow and leaves the enemy exposed to the triumphant assaults of humble, fervent prayer. All things are possible to him that believeth; we should, therefore, always keep the shield of faith in active exercise. The christian is never safe, no, not for one moment, without the shield of faith. Paul says, "For we walk by faith, not by sight." So that every step through life should be regulated by the rule of faith, "Whatever is not faith, is sin;" so that whatever we do or say, should be done and said to the glory of God.

5. *The helmet of salvation.*—"God is my salvation, therefore, I will not fear what man can do unto me." The saving power and the grace of our Lord Jesus Christ should always rest upon the christian soldier's head; add to this, "The sword of the spirit," which is the word of God. This is our two edged sword; its promises foil our enemies and crowns us with peace and safety; its commands, denunciations and

inflexible justice conquers and slays every assailant. O let us wield this sharp sword dexterously and wisely, and certain victory will ensue; we must not fail, however, to accompany all our efforts with prayer, humble fervent prayer ; it is not the soldier, but the Captain who gains the victory in all our battles ; hence, we must implore and secure the presence and aid of the Lord Jesus Christ in every conflict; in our prayers we must be careful to avoid formality, they must be accompanied with and enforced by supplication in the spirit; we must strive, fight, press our cause upon our knees; we must "pray without ceasing;" and yet, further, we must watch as well as pray, or watching thereunto with all perserverance. We must watch every motion of the enemy, either from without, or from within, watch diligently every thought, every word, every desire, every motive and action. By a judicious application of the christian armor, we shall learn that the weapons of our warfare are not carnal, but mighty through God, to the pulling down of all Satan's strongholds. Thus through the grace of our Lord Jesus Christ, we may gain and secure a glorious, a triumphant victory over all our enemies, and enter through the gates triumphantly into the New Jerusalem, the Holy City of God, to go no more out forever, where we shall lay the weapons of our warfare by, where eternal peace shall be proclaimed to all Christ's faithful, valiant soldiers— Amen.

There having been some doubts expressed about his views on the Methodist doctrine of Sanctification, we here insert a short address on that important subject taken from his writings.

PART II. ·

Address to our Christian Friends who do not believe that God's children can be perfect in this evil world.

INTRODUCTORY REMARKS.

"See that ye fall not out by the way."—*Gen.*, xlv: 24.— This salutary counsel is as applicable to Christians in this nineteenth century, as it was to Joseph's brethren. We are

all strangers in a strange land; all travelers, and all children
of the same merciful Father; therefore, we should all strive
together for the faith of the gospel in a spirit of meekness and
affection. The plan of salvation revealed in the gospel of our
Lord Jesus Christ, presents a fountain of unmingled mercy
poured forth upon a guilty world, not with the voice of thunder and a stormy tempest bursting from the summit of a
smoking Sinai, but in noiseless, boundless streams issuing
from the throne of God and of the Lamb, in floods of infinite
and eternal compassion and love. When their mighty maker,
the eternal God became man, the angels left their high abode
and flew with joyful haste to bear the news to our world; to
the humble watchful shepherds they disclosed the secret of
redeeming love, "Fear not, there is no cause for trembling
now, no sound of terror comes from heaven to-day: we bring
glad tidings of great joy to all your fallen race; pardon and
peace and holiness and heaven, are all in Jesus' name, unto
you a child is born, unto you a son is given; and the government shall be upon his shoulder, and his name shall be called
Wonderful, Counsellor, the mighty God, the everlasting Father
the Prince of Peace."—*Isaiah* ix, 6. The gospel of the Son
of God is a system of rich and abundant privileges which all
may freely claim and richly enjoy. All the guilty sons of
Adam may look and live, for our God is no respecter of persons. Although the rich men of the earth are almost exclu-
ded from the Kingdom, yet even they need not despond, for
the Lord Jesus declares that with God, even their salvation
is possible. Why should we therefore contend and fall out by
the way, seeing we are all equally guilty, yes, verily, guilty
of our brother's blood ; yet through His atoning merits, we
all have an equal claim on mercy's boundless store. Our
Brother is not only Governor of Egypt, but he is the rightful
sovereign of heaven and earth. His promises are not only
great, but they are very precious. "If ye abide in me, and
my words abide in you, ye shall ask what ye will, and it shall
be done unto you."—*John*, xv, 7.

In view of such abundant blessings and privileges, shall
we be more stupid and unwise, than the blind sons of Belial ?
Respecting earthly things, they claim and eagerly contend
for every cent to which they are entitled by law ; should a
friend bequeath to any one of them, a legacy of a few thousand dollars, he would urge his claim to the last cent, even
through the iron door of a legal process.

Shall our Heavenly Father bequeath to us the rich legacy of a *pure heart, perfect love,* a spotless, glorious wedding garment, which cost the precious blood of the Son of God, and shall we refuse to receive the unspeakable gift at his hand? Surely such conduct argues folly in the extreme. Rather let us claim all the rich privileges of the gospel, firmly and promptly, knowing that He who spared not His own Son, but delivered Him up for us all, will, with Him, freely give us all things—this in particular—a new, pure, clean heart, yes,

> A heart in every thought renewed,
> And full of love divine,
> Perfect and right and pure and good,
> A copy, Lord of Thine.

JOHN HERSEY'S VIEWS ON

LEARNING AND LEARNED INSTITUTIONS.

I now approach a subject of vital importance to the Church; and I am fully aware that in the expression of my sentiment in regard to it, I shall stand far—very far in the minority.

Few, very few, particularly in the ministry, will consider my sentiments either orthodox or reasonable. If, however, I can have God's word and reason's voice with me, I shall have nothing to fear. Noah stood almost alone in his day, Lot found very few who were willing to go with him when he fled from a devoted city, the Lord Jesus and his little band of followers, were very far in the minority, but they were not cast down. I will therefore, take courage, put my trust alone in Israel's God, and venture to show my opinion also.

My remarks in this place, will be confined to the subject of 'learning and learned institutions' in connection with the Church. I do not intend to undervalue knowledge, or human learning. I do not believe the unsound and enthusiastic doctrine, that "Ignorance is the mother of devotion." It will, however, be admitted by every unprejudiced mind, either in or out of the Church, that good things, nay, the best things on earth, may be abused and misplaced, and thus become curses rather than blessings; even literary institutions, when they

arc found out of their legitimate place, may produce discord
rather than harmony.   I assume the position, that colleges and
literary institutions belong to the world's' department and
not the Church.

The Lord Jesus says of his followers who constitute the
Church : "Ye are not of the world, I have chosen you out of
the world, marvel not therefore, that the world hates you."

Money has been called the mammon of unrighteousness;
the God of this world.   One reason why it is so called, is on
account of the power it possesses, and the homage generally
paid to those who have it in their possession.   Learning, (by
which I mean a finished collegiate education,) has still greater
power.

The rich man may oppress the poor, and cause his power to
be felt in divers ways; yet were he an ignorant man, he would
be looked on by men of refinement with pity and contempt;
but an accomplished education will procure for its possessors
an honorable reception in Kings' courts, and secure to him
(if he is an upright man,) the friendship and admiration of
the distinguished men of the world.   In ordinary cases neither
the rich, nor the learned and wise men, will willingly bow to
the cross of Jesus Christ, or treat those who consistently bear
it with common respect.   Should they be members or ministers of the church, when they speak on the subject of the
Cross, they confine all the pain, and shame and reproach connected therewith to Jesus Christ exclusively.   Nor will they
touch it with one of their fingers.   Paul glorieth in the cross
of Christ, not only in theory or imagination, but in reality, by
it he was crucified unto the world, viz, he was exposed to
nakedness and buffeting and persecution, and was counted as
the filth and off-scouring of all things.   In these he gloried,
but generally, our learned and wise men will beg to be excused
from such exaltation.

I know there are and have been, in every age of the world,
honorable exceptions to this general rule, when the circumstances of the Church require the aid of human learning.
God can call a Moses from the King's court and Saul of Tar-
sus from the feet of Gamaliel, and when they are powerfully
convicted, or converted to God, they will choose rather to
suffer affliction with the people of God, than to enjoy the
pleasures of sin for a season, they will esteem the reproaches

of Christ greater riches, than the treasures of Egypt; their language will be, "Yea, doubtless and I count all things but loss for the excellency of the knowledge of Christ Jesus, my Lord, for whom I have suffered the loss of all things and do count them but dung, that I may win Christ and be found in Him, not having on my own righteousness which is of the law, &c.;" in modern times, there have been many burning and shining lights in the Church, who were men of extensive learning, as they were also of deep piety; the Wesleys and Fletcher and others connected with them, shone as flaming heralds of the Cross and were abundantly successful under the influence of divine grace, in reforming and purifying the Church and also a wicked world; it was not, however, necessary, nor agreeable, to the order of the divine economy, that all who preached the gospel should be learned men in that day; the greater part of the labor, even of preaching, was performed by unlearned men; especially was the implantation and triumphant progress of Methodism, or pure and undefiled religion, in these United States, effected principally by unlearned men; and at the commencement of the gospel of Jesus Christ on earth, the principal part of the labor and efficient work, was performed by ignorant and unlearned men. Now, is it reasonable to suppose that the Lord Jesus when He laid the corner-stone of His church on earth, could make a mistake, or set an example which His followers in all after ages, could not pursue with safety and success? Jesus Christ could have called in to his aid, the learned and wise men of his day, but he chose in his wisdom, to act otherwise. He called His disciples, generally, from the lower walks of life, from the fishing net, &c. If there ever was a time, or circumstance, that called for human learning, it was at the commencement of the gospel dispensation; when an error in doctrine, or in experience, or in practice would have been attended with the most pernicious, if not ruinous consequences. It may be said that the apostles acted under the immediate influence and inspiration of the Holy Ghost.

True, and who can prove by the word of God, that the influence of the Holy Spirit has ever been (by divine appointment) withdrawn from Christ's Church and his ministering servants? If (as it is believed by many) the gospel and the grace of God shines brighter when it emanates from men of learning, than when it is preached by unlearned men, why did not Christ select all his apostles from the learned circles?

Surely wisdom and prudence would unequivocally dictate the course, as the best which could be, which was considered greatly preferable at a later period in the history of the Church.

If therefore the Church of Christ was originally built up principally by unlearned men, and when God greatly revived the cause of pure religion in the earth, and visited his people in great power in the eighteenth century through the instrumentality of J. Wesley and others, the work was effected principally by unlearned men, is it reasonable to suppose that it must now be perpetuated and secured from error only by human learning? Learning has not a tendency to harmonize and unite the Church of Christ, or to dissipate the clouds and difficulties which seem to rest on many parts of God's written word; on the contrary, extensive and ruinous discord has been introduced into the bosom of the Church, by learned and pious men. The doctrine of *Election* and *Reprobation* which has filled the Protestant churches with bitterness and discord, and still continues to becloud the glory of the Son of Righteousness, in many parts of the Lord's vineyard. Even this unreasonable theory emanated from a man of talent and learning, who is also represented to have sustained a good and pious character. Although this extraordinary system of divinity has been ably and I think conclusively refuted by many pious and learned authors; and never was it made to feel its own weakness and deformity, as sensibly as it was under the ministry of the early, but unlearned Methodist preachers, who assailed it with the powerful weapons of truth and reason, under the omnipotent influence of the Holy Ghost sent down from Heaven, yet it is still believed and advocated by many learned and wise and professedly pious ministers of the Lord Jesus Christ. Many of the advocates of the numerous and conflicting creeds which abound in the present day, are learned and wise and good men, yet they inflexibly adhere to the doctrine which has been instilled into their mind, by the force of education; and their prejudices are generally if not uniformly strengthened and confirmed by the power of their superior learning, which enables them to fortify and defend their errors by learned and specious arguments.

It may, therefore, be said without fear of successful contradiction, that learning does not particularly qualify ministers to enforce the plain, simple, experimental and practical truths of the gospel, as efficiently, as it does to defend their own peculiar views and tenets, and to explore what they esteem the errors of others ; hence a perpetual war is kept up by learned divines, not so much in support of truth and righteousness, as to establish and confirm their own peculiar sentiments. When young men are educated with a view to the ministry, they naturally conclude that as they know more than others, they must be better ; consequently they frequently and almost uniformly assume an air of importance, altogether incompatible with the holy religion of their meek and lowly Redeemer. Nor does this unholy leaven exist in a latent state ; they soon begin to think that their talents and intellectual advantages, entitle them to a higher seat in the synagogue, than their unlearned, but pious brother. Hence a train of evils are engendered in their own bosom, which soon diffuses its influence among others and contaminates the house of God with pride and dissension, where nothing but humility should exist. Our learned young men soon become critics and esteem a grammatical error made by a preacher, a sufficient crime to expel the ignoramus from the ministry. Many old veterans of the Cross, who have born the burden and heat of the day, and into whose labors those young students have entered, are afraid to speak in their presence, lest they should make a mistake and thereby become the objects of ridicule. This is a grievous evil, which many worthy servants of the Lord Jesus have been doomed to writhe under in silent anguish for years. As extensive learning is not an essential qualification for a gospel ministry, their divine Master has promised to give them a mouth and wisdom which all their adversaries shall not be able to gainsay nor resist. They speak by the authority of God, accompanied with the sacred influence of the Holy Ghost, and their word reaches the sinner's hearts, and becomes the power of God unto salvation, it is not reasonable to suppose that God calls foolish and improper characters to the work of the ministry ; and though they may not have the wisdom or the learning of the world to lean upon, yet have they the more important wisdom which cometh from above, and fully qualifies them to preach the gospel in its purity with power and efficiency. They are taught of the Holy Spirit of God ; hence they do not strive about words to no profit, but to the subverting of the heavens ; they study to show themselves approved unto God, workmen who need not be ashamed, rightly dividing

the word of truth, it is worthy of notice, that the gospel
shines brighter, and God is more glorified, by the ministry
of unlearned than of learned men. When Paul (who was
known to be a learned man,) reasoned powerfully before Fes-
tus, he cried out, " Paul thou art beside thyself, *much learning* doth make thee mad; " thus giving the praise and glory
to *learning;* but when Peter and John healed the lame man,
and preached Christ powerfully to the audience, they gave
the glory to God. "Now when they saw the boldness of
Peter and John, and perceived that they were *unlearned* and
ignorant men, they marvelled; and took knowledge of them,
that they had been with Jesus." If extensive learning is an
essential qualification for a minister of Jesus Christ, and will
indeed (as many believe,) qualify its possessor to enjoy a
higher degree of happiness in heaven, than an ignorant and
unlearned man, Christ certainly erred when he delivered the
following benediction, accompanied with a most solemn mal-
ediction: Blessed be ye poor, for yours is the kingdom of
God, but woe unto you that are rich, for ye have received
your consolation." There are very few of the poor of this
world, who are, or can ever hope to be men of learning, unless it is through the charity of those who are wealthy;
while the rich men of this world, are about uniformly favored with learning; yet hath God chosen the poor of this world,
rich in faith, and heirs of the kingdom which he hath promised to them that love him.

I shall now appeal to the law and to the testimony, by the
authority of God's holy word, and that rigidly and faithfully
applied, must we all stand or fall. There is not, I apprehend one plain text in the New Testament, which proves that
earthly learning or wisdom is necessary to qualify a minister
of Jesus Christ, for his holy duty. Christ says, "I thank
thee, O, Father, Lord of heaven and earth, because thou
hast hid these things from the wise and prudent and hast revealed them unto babes, even so Father, for it seemed good
in thy sight." Matt. xi, 25, 26. May it not be, that in accordance with this divine declaration, the purity, simplicity,
and harmony of the gospel has been "hid" from our D.D.'s,
therefore, division and discord has fallen on the M. E.
Church ? When John sent his disciples to Jesus to inquire
whether He was the Christ or not, the Lord Jesus said, in
reply to those messengers, " Go and shew John again these

things which ye do hear and see; the blind receive their sight, and the deaf hear, the dead one raised up, and the poor have the gospel preached unto them. Matt. xi, 4, 5. The poor are not often found among the wise and learned of this world; neither does it require extensive learning to qualify a man to preach the gospel to them. It may be said, "If we are qualified to preach the gospel correctly and learnedly to the rich, the poor may receive it also." Not so; the poor cannot comprehend or understand the import of many words and phrases in common use among the learned; but on the contrary, if we speak the plain unadorned language of propriety, simplicity and the holy scriptures, the rich and learned can fully comprehend the bearing and import of every word and sentiment expressed. Thus the wise and learned individual cannot but with the utmost difficulty obey the command of Jesus Christ—Go and preach the gospel to every creature, for they have received a language in the college which renders them partially barbarians to the ignorant and unlearned, it will, I apprehend, be generally, if not universally conceded, that the real design of extensive learning is not to qualify us to preach the gospel to the poor and illiterate, but to the rich and the learned. Were the point conceded (which is not the case,) that extensive learning is a necessary appendage to qualify us to preach the gospel to the learned and the rich, would it be wise or prudent to qualify every minister, (that, too, at a considerable expense of money and time,) to preach to a portion of the community who are seldom called; and so slender is their hope of salvation, that our Master says, that it is easier for a camel to pass through the eye of a needle, than for a rich man to enter into the kingdom of heaven. The anathema of our divine Redeemer rests on them—"Woe unto you that are rich;" and as it regards this subject, Paul makes the following strong remarks, "For ye see your calling, brethren, how that not many wise men after the flesh, not many *mighty*, not many noble are *called;* but God hath chosen the foolish things of this world to confound the *wise;* and God hath chosen the weak things of this world to confound the things which are mighty; and the base things of this world, and the things which are despised, hath God chosen, yea, and things which are not, to bring to naught things that are." I Cor. 1, 26, 28. I cannot conceive how it is possible for any individual possessed of common understanding to misunderstand the Apostles argument in the above passage, which will certainly prove anything else, rather than that the learning and wisdom of this world is necessary to qualify a minister of Christ to preach the gospel. The same apostle expressly declares that the wisdom of this world is foolishness with God. Again he says, " For Christ sent me not to baptize, but to preach the gospel; not with wisdom of words, lest the Cross of Christ should be made of none effect."

I might [transcribe nearly every paragraph in the first, second and third chapters of Paul's first letter to the Corinthian Church, with many other passages interspersed, throughout the New Testament to prove that extensive learning is not necessary to the success of the gospel preacher, but frequently a direct hindrance. I will only advert to the following quotation to which I must beg the readers most serious attention. "And I brethren, when I come to you, come not with excellency of speech, or of wisdom, declaring unto you the testimony of God, for I determined not to know anything among you save Jesus Christ, and him crucified. And I was with you in weakness, and in fear, and in much trembling; and my speech and my preaching, was not with enticing words of man's wisdom, but in demonstration of the spirit, and in power, that your faith should not stand in the wisdom of man, but in the power of God. Howbeit we speak wisdom among them that are perfect, yet not the wisdom of this world, nor of the princes of this world, that cometh to naught, but we speak the wisdom of God in a mystery, even the hidden wisdom which God ordained before the world, to our glory."

Paul was evidently himself, a learned man; but he laid even his learning down a willing sacrifice at the shrine of his divine Master's cross, together with his other numerous earthly distinctions, and went out in obedience to the call and command of the Lord Jesus Christ, into the streets and lanes of the City, and into the world preaching the gospel to the poor and the maimed, and the halt and the blind, ·nor did he fail to warn the rich and the wise of their imminent danger, whilst he invited them to forsake those vanities, and seek mercy and eternal life, through our Lord Jesus Christ. Paul was intimately acquainted with human nature, and also the power and efficacy of divine grace, when he said, "Knowledge puffeth up, but charity edifieth." As God hates a proud look, should we not feel somewhat afraid of that which has a tendency to swell a haughty worm, and thereby render us offensive in the sight of God? We should dread more than death any circumstance, or creature, or thing, which may by any means turn us from the unfrequented, but honorable path of deep and genuine humility, which always bears the impress of the meek and lowly Saviour's foot-steps. The Lord Jesus asks the important question, "How can ye *believe* which receive honor one from another, and seek not the honor that cometh from God only?" In open view of that dangerous error, he carefully guards us against giving or receiving titles of distinction. He says: "The scribes and Pharisees love greeting in the market, and to be called of men, Rabbi, Rabbi, but ye are not called Rabbi, for one is your Master, even Christ; and ye are brethren; but he that is greatest among you, shall be your servant. And whosoever shall exalt himself, shall be abased." Now are not our colleges openly and palpably arrayed against the sentiments and the positive commands of our Lord Jesus Christ?

Those institutions of learning deal out carelessly titles of honorable distinction, and many of our leading men in Israel receive them without one objection. O, God! the God of our fathers, arouse the Church, and may her strong men of Israel leave the lap of Delilah, and escape from the arms of the god of this world, before the Philistines put out both our eyes.

From the weight of testimony found in the New Testament against extensive learning as a qualification for the ministry, and the little that is said in favor of it, should we not pause and reflect, and fast and pray for pure light from heaven on this momentous subject? Is it not possible that we may be found on the side of the world, fighting against God, and the cross of our Lord Jesus Christ? As the gospel breathes a constant stream of mercy to the poor, and denounces the rich; if we must interfere in the subject of education, should we not rather recommend and encourage schools for the benefit of the poor? Something similar to the district schools, now established in most of our States and counties. Very few except the rich are benefitted by our colleges. A poor man cannot pay the board and incidental expenses connected with any of our colleges, were he to receive the tuition gratis. Nor is it reasonable or right in the sight of God, to receive money from the poor to educate rich

men's children.   Let the wealthy part of the community and
of the Church manage their own concerns, while we turn
with the blessings of the gospel to the poor; and if their
education devolves on the Church even in part, let us recommend all our members to give their children a good English
education—nay, let us see that it is done; and then teach
them (by example and precept) to save the money now wasted for fine clothes, and houses and furniture, and rich food,
and live like our Divine Master, a self-denying life in all
things; and teach them further, to apply the money thus
saved to the purchase of good religious books, including an-
cient and modern history, and then let all the time now
wasted in visiting and idle conversation, be occupied in reading, meditation and prayer.   An individual with a good
plain English education, and a mind well stored with scripture and historical knowledge, is better prepared to make a
good and useful citizen, than that man who has been polished for years within the walls of a college, and far better prepared to make a good and successful minister of Jesus Christ,
when God converts his soul, and fills it with holy zeal and
burning love for God and all mankind.   Can our wise and
learned men account for the simple, but astounding fact, that
in the early days of Methodism, though she was frowned on
and despised by the wise and great men of this world, and
her preachers were generally unlearned men, yet she fought
her way triumphantly through every opposing difficulty to a
high and holy eminence in piety, in numbers and in influence;
and now in these last days, we have raised up colleges and
seminaries of learning in abundance, and our learned men,
our D.D.'s abound everywhere, while our beautiful fabric,
raised up by the zeal and piety and faith of our unlearned
fathers, totters, and God's house is divided in twain, which
portends, by divine authority, speedy ruin; even now discord abounds through our ranks generally North and South;
confidence is fearfully shaken, and the prospect before us, to
every pious, rational mind, is anything but prosperous!   May
all not lean on the world for support, either its money, its
popularity, or its polished learning, but return to the feet of
Jesus, and there learn to do our first works over again, that
we may live and not die!

FATHER HERSEY'S PUBLICATIONS.

Father Hersey was an author of some pretentions, and his books had a ready sale in his day. His works may not belong to that class which will be acknowledged in the list of publications in the future, but they possess no mean merit. Whatever was the subject of their treatise, was carefully digested, the thoughts were practicable, plain and homely, inculcating the truths that were the embodiment of his inner and outward life. They are fit companion pieces of his uttered sentences; in letters, sermons and addresses every line possesses wholesome admonition, and are logically expressed in language well chosen and forcible. Whatever topic he discusses, is so carefully handled as to indicate maturity of thought before written expression. Apparently, he wrote as though the eye of God was peering over his shoulders, tracing every word his pen was inditing. He had a belief that for the truth and error of his printed pages he must answer in the last great day.

Below is appended a list of his publications, embracing all his larger and important books:

An appeal to Christians on the subject of Slavery. Published by Armstrong & Plasket, Baltimore, in 1833.

Importance of Small Things. By the same publishers and in the same year.

Inquiry into the Character and Condition of our Children, with Some Remarks on Baptism.

Advice to Christian Parents.

Life of M. De Renty.

These three volumes were originally published separately. They were, however, embraced in one volume and thus published by Armstrong & Berry, Baltimore, in 1839.

Practical Thoughts Selected from the Works of John Wesley, A. M. Published by Armstrong & Berry during the year 1836.

The Privilege of Those who are Born of God; or, a Plain Rational View of the Nature and Extent of Sanctification. Published by Armstrong & Berry, in the year 1841.

Prayer. Its Duties and Privileges. By the same publishers, during the year 1853. So great was the demand for
this work, that the first edition was exhausted soon after
publication, and a second edition followed in 1854.

The Design, Importance and Validity of Infant Baptism.
Also, a few thoughts on the mode of administering that
ordinance. By the same publishers in 1855.

The Identity of the two Apocalyptic Witnesses. Their Character, Death and Resurrection as Connected with the In-
troduction of the Millenium. Same publishers, in 1857.

Satan Unmasked, the Human Heart Unveiled, and the Mysteries of Revelation Made Plain. Same publishers, in
1862.

LETTERS.

*The following extracts are arranged according to the dates
of the letters from which they are taken.*

To REV. T. M. C.

June 6th, 1856.

Your esteemed favor in reply to mine of a former date has
been duly received. * * * After I left Harford, I visited
Baltimore and Philadelphia, and then proceeded on a tour to
the West. Spent some time in Cincinnati, and then visited
Indianapolis, the seat of the General Conference.

The city was very much crowded, and nothing of interest
before the Conference, so that I soon returned. Like poor
Balaam, my way seemed to be hedged up at almost every
step. I was afflicted for two months, almost incessantly with
a pain in my side, and became very hoarse, so I returned to
Baltimore, where I am better known than in the far West.

It was not my intention to have taken any regular work
during the present year, but the *finger* of Divine Providence,
I hope, directed my steps to a little Circuit, in the bounds of
the Philadelphia Conference. Since I reached this barren

field of labor, my health has very much improved. Sabbath, after preaching three times, leading two classes, and walking about ten miles, I found the pain in my side had left me, nor did I feel any perceptible fatigue either of body or mind.

Oh, to grace, how great a debtor, daily, hourly and momentarily I'm constrained to be. The hard end of the oar, is my appropriate place, and I have no doubt if our young ministers would labor more, it would be abundantly more beneficial to their own souls, and profitable to the Church, than the course which is too often pursued in modern times. It is not earthly wisdom and talent and eloquence we need; we want more deep piety, more grace, more wisdom from above, more genuine humility, more zeal, more faith, and abundantly more love for God, and all mankind. We want more of Christ, in our hearts, and less of self, more of Heaven and less of earth.

I have long seen and lamented, the barren, naked state of the Church, in contrast with what she should be, but I have never witnessed a more gloomy spectacle than this Circuit presents. Almost dead, twice dead and plucked up by the roots. One good house abandoned, and another about to be given up, because there are neither. members nor hearers.

In the immediate vicinity of one of these deserted churches, the members have built a new house in modern style, large and costly, and have incurred a large debt, which must weigh them down for years, if they are ever able to pay. There is however, one consoling circumstance in their favor, the preacher in charge is an humble unassuming, plain workingman, a man of good common sense. May he and his poor colleague be rendered a blessing to this people, and cause this barren spot to vegetate, and bring forth fruit to the glory of God.

Letter to Bro. R——.

November 21st, 1856.

* * * * * * * Strive to have things at the Quarterly Meeting straightened up in regard to the Church. Let nothing be deferred until to-morrow, that can be done to-day.

Carelessness is as nearly related to sin, as the shadow is to the substance. It stands both as cause and effect; hence I fear greatly for the religion of this day. I fear we are daubing with untempered mortar. We are at ease in Zion, and must meet the awful anathema of woe unto them that are at ease in

Zion. And if our beloved Saviour's words are true, we must be spued out of his mouth, for we are at best only lukewarm, when compared with the politician, the merchant, the farmer, the mechanic or even the gold-digger. Oh, that I could sound an alarm in Zion, which might reach to the deepest recess of my own heart, and awaken and alarm a slumbering, worldly minded, lukewarm Church.

N. B. Omit that dingy, dangerous, hateful title of "Rev." (?)

To the Same.

September 1st, 1857.

I am still striving to enter in at the straight gate which leads to that city where sin has never stained the soil, nor contaminated the pure air breathed by the inhabitants of that healthful region. I am fully aware that nothing impure or unholy can enter that blessed world of life and peace and joy, nor can the grave, nor old age, nor human merit efface or remove one stain, one spot or wrinkle. Nothing but the blood of Jesus applied by faith can purify our souls, and qualify us for a home in heaven; and if the next hour may close our earthly career and usher us into the unveiled presence of a pure and Holy God, it behooves us as wise and rational beings to be always ready, and well prepared to meet the bridegroom, who will come at an unexpected hour, and may come the next moment.

> "How careful then ought I to live, with what religious fear;
> Who such a strict account must give, for my behavior here."

I hope you and yours are living with a single eye—one object and one aim in all things, and that aim and object to please the Lord Jesus Christ. None but the pure in heart can see God, and if our motives in all things are not to please God, our hearts (the fountain of all our thoughts and natures,) cannot be pure, and if God was to admit into heaven, *one* impure thought or unholy word, it would operate like leaven and contaminate the whole heavenly world. Many professors of our day feel conscious that they are not now pure in heart—that they are living beneath their gospel privileges—but hope and intend (vain hope,) to secure the spotless wedding garment before they die. Yet they live carelessly, scarcely fasting one day in the week, and evidently living at ease in Zion, notwithstanding the *woe* of God which rests upon their heads. Were an adept at gambling to bet his opponent one million of dollars to one on a single game of chance, he would be esteemed a fool, and yet every one who lives carelessly one hour without a *pure*, a *holy* heart, is acting far more foolishly; he is risking on the chances of a moment, the loss of his soul, which is of infinitely more value than all the world, yet he risks another throw of life's dice in expectation that he will not die yet. In view of our folly and stupidity, our heavenly Father exclaims, "Oh, that my people were wise, that they understood this, that they would consider their latter end." While all heaven is interested for guilty, dying man, he is careless of his own salvation, and laughs and sports and slumbers on the crumbling verge of a burning hell. Oh, arm of the Lord awake—awake, thine own almighty strength put on, and snatch guilty, careless dying man from the gulf of eternal misery.

Letter to a Friend.

Baltimore, December 15th, 1857

Your esteemed favor of the 11th inst has been duly received. * * * * * * In regard to the request you make that I should mention the questions you will probably be called upon to answer in your examination for Deacon's orders, I presume they will be such as you have heard propounded to every candidate for such orders. A few questions of general import are always asked, such as " The fall of man," "Total Depravity," "The nature and extent of the Atonement," "Justification by Faith," and generally some of a more distinctive nature, respecting our own Church views of doctrine and discipline. Universal Redemption, Sanctification, The difference between Justification and Sanctification, Is Faith the gift of God, or the act of the creature ? Is Sanctification an instantaneous or gradual work? Or is it both the one and the other ? Upon all these topics I presume you are qualified and prepared to give prompt and satisfactory answers.

However, the nature and extent of the questions asked on such occasions depend very much upon the character and views of those who examine the candidate. Our Divine Master asks you and I an important question, addressed originally to Peter:

"Lovest thou me?" This I consider a fundamental point of inquiry, and if we can answer unwaveringly, unequivocally and understandingly, it will cover perfectly all the minor points, and secure for us all we can either ask or desire, viz: the immutable promise or assurance of our Lord Jesus, by his servant Paul, "All things shall work together for good to them that love God." This precious promise renders us independent, and places us above our most inveterate foes, so long as we continue to love God. And every man that has this hope in him, purifies himself even as he (God,) is pure." He purifies by asking himself honestly, Are my affections pure?

Do we not in part love the world, its money or pleasures, its smiles, the good opinion of men? and do we feel as willing to be poor as to be rich, as willing to be persecuted and despised as to be honored and applauded? Alas, how hard it is to have the gold made perfectly pure. It requires the furnace to be heated more than seven times hotter than was Nebuchadnezzar's.

Yet the gold is so precious, and the place where it is ultimately to circulate, so glorious, that no dross or alloy can be admitted into those pure regions, and into the presence of the King of Kings, and Lord of Lords. Oh, may we be well prepared to stand that last—that final examination, in the presence of the Righteous Judge of all the Earth.

Letter to the same.

Baltimore, May 18th, 1858.

I left Baltimore early in April, and visited New York, where I settled my first and last debt; one which has been standing more than forty years. My creditor has been dead many years. I found his son and widow, in very needy circumstances, which rendered the little act of justice in paying a few hundred dollars, a real pleasure. The young man thought it strange indeed that any one would hunt for a debt of more than forty years standing, and as he could find no record against me, he very willingly and thankfully gave me a receipt in full of all demands from his father's estate; so that I can now say what I could not say for the last forty years, viz: I owe no man anything, or rather no man can now say, that J. H. owes him anything but good will and love.

"Oh, to grace how great a debtor,
Daily I'm constrained to be."

Praise the Lord, oh, my soul. The day in which we live is one of very peculiar character. There is passing over our world, and especially over large and wicked cities, a wonderful cloud of mercy. Never before has there been such a religious influence. In that most wicked city, whose principal street bears a most appropriate name, Broadway, which indeed it seems to be, where thousands on thousands are pressing onward eager to secure eternal damnation; where every species of wickedness abounds and excels; there, religion occupies a most eminent position. Prayer meetings are being held daily from twelve to one o'clock in different churches, and other places, even in the theatre, where crowds assemble to pray, leaving their daily business; merchants, mechanics, laborers, lawyers and even learned Rabbis. They mingle together without respect to name or party, and appear to be in good earnest. In Philadelphia, the same scenes are daily exhibited. Jayne's Hall it is said, holds from three to four thousand people, which is crowded daily. Surely this means something. It is in my humble opinion, an unmistakeble evidence that the Master in coming, the bridegroom is at the very door. The important inquiry should be, Are we ready for the great event?

Letter to a Friend.

Mechanicsburg, Dec. 15th, 1858.

I left Baltimore yesterday (Tuesday) morning, or I would have called at your house again. The weather has been very wet and gloomy since I reached Mechanicsburg. From a remark you made the morning I called at your store, I feared you supposed that a part of my sermon at ——— Street Church was personal and intended particularly for yourself. I am seldom, if ever, personal in preaching; but to thrust wantonly a dagger at the kindest friend I have on earth, would be an act unworthy of a christian name, and to slight or garble God's sacred word and message to sinners, lest some friend's feelings should be thereby wounded, would disgrace my calling, dishonor my Master, and shut me out of heaven. In regard to my remarks on that occasion, I know there were some things that would be applicable to you, but if you had not been present, those remarks would have been more pointed than they were. For this deviation from the strictest rules of eternal justice, I humbly hope my merciful Master will pardon the smaller, as well as greater delinquency of his unprofitable servant.

The day in which we live calls for a faithful discharge of every duty. I was alarmed and pained at the Monday night services in ———. That an old Methodist preacher should leave the pure waters of eternal life, and the plain, wholesome doctrines of the M E. Church, and lecture on wild speculative subjects, and quickly receive unbounded applause openly and publicly given, while his Master impressively asks: "How can ye believe who receive honor, one of another?" How the preacher of righteousness should not only speculate but administer an unmixed cup of *National flattery* to his blind and wandering audience, I could not imagine. Take the speculation away and admit all his statements to be true, it was not calculated to effect any good result. Bro. —— says he is about to explode *infidelity*, but I fear he will make more skeptics, than real, genuine, holy christians. Perhaps, however, I am among—not only the old fogies—but the doubting Thomas'. Many will be induced to suspect that "the root of all evil" lies at the bottom of his lectures. Money, applause, &c. I hope this is not the fact, but though charity thinketh no evil, yet charity is not blind, and must see the mote in his neighbor's as well as the beam in his own eye. Perhaps I should be admonished by the Lord Jesus, when he said to Peter: "What is that to thee? Follow thou me." Amen. Lord help me so to do. I do greatly desire to follow my Divine Master *literally* when that can be done, and spiritually when that is practicable, and in good faith in all things, keeping at all times a conscience void of offense towards God, and also towards my fellow mortals. And if I cannot be an humble instrument in correcting and saving others, may I at least save my own soul, however difficult the task may be. Though the Apostle says: "If the righteous scarcely be saved, where shall the ungodly and the sinner appear?"

———

To Rev. T. M. C.

Staunton, July 26th, 1859.

Grace, mercy and peace from God, the Father, and from our Lord Jesus Christ be with you and yours evermore. The blessings of the gospel of the Son of God, how free, how full, whether they flow from the eternal—the infinite fountain—from the lips of Jesus, their author, or from the lips of His Holy Apostles. Enough for all—enough for each, enough for evermore. And yet, alas, how slow are we poor mortals to believe, and how careless to secure the crown—the kingdom—the momentous blessing of peace, and joy in the Holy Ghost The pleasing baits of sin—the snares of Satan—the world; its riches, its pleasures, its honors, its ease—how they *allure, deceive, entangle* and *destroy.* I have been for some time past in Virginia, where the Church is I fear, slumbering on a volcano, asleep in the arms of Satan. Should a spark fall into the magazine, there would be an awful explosion.

The Church and her ministers, have it is greatly to be feared bowed the knee to Baal. They fear the world, the opinion of dying men. They have closed their own mouths, and will have a fearful account to give in the great coming day. A large portion of the Baltimore Conference, situated among slaves, are in a most unenviable condition. Nor do I see any safety and final deliverance but in the favor of God, the strong arm of omnipotence, and I greatly fear that we cannot confidently claim God's grace and power to be displayed in our deliverance in the distressing hour. Oh Lord, in mercy hear prayer, and be merciful to our unrighteousness. The whole world is in commotion. The wicked, the unfortunate nations of Europe, are beginning to drink the cup of God's wrath that must be poured out on our guilty world, ere "Righteousness shall cover the earth, as the waters cover the great deep."

Well, the Kingdom belongs to Christ. He has the power and the glory shall be his. He that sitteth on the throne, ruleth all things well. The wrath of man shall praise thee, and the remainder of wrath thou shalt restrain. Amen,

Lord Jesus, take to thyself thy great powers, and reign in universal righteousness.

Letter to the same.

Alabama, Dec. 13th, 1859.

Strange and unexpected as it may appear, I am now in the far sunny South, in the center of Alabama. A wealthy man, Gen. C——, who spends his winters in this State, and his summers in Virginia, pressed me to accompany him to this

State, promising to pay my expenses here and back to Balti-more. *As I commenced my christian ministry* partly in this *State* and *county* nearly *forty years since*, and hoping that the kind finger of Providence prompted the movement, I con-sented to his proposition. His estate is near the village of Greensboro, in Green county, where wealth abounds as well as slavery in abundance. The slaves are, however, said to be treated well, and are happy and contented in their condi-tion. To give you some idea of the wealth of this county, I need only say that when the M. E. Church recently estab-lished a college here, in the town of Greensboro, two of our members gave each twenty-five thousand dollars, another twelve thousand. One family gave thirty-eight thousand dol-lars. You will at once see the difficulties which lie before me, and will, I hope, pray for me, that I may have grace and wisdom to declare the whole counsel of God, fearlessly and faithfully; giving to all their portion in due season. That I may not be turned away one hair's breadth from the truths of the gospel, by the smiles of wealth, nor deterred by the frowns of men and devils. I have not one doubt on my mind, but that wealth and literature are two of the greatest obstacles on earth to the spread of vital godliness in the world. It is not logical to reason from extreme cases, but I will notice the influence exerted principally by those powerful agents here. There are eight preachers attached to the Col-lege, and living in the village, yet the church is literally dead. Pride and indifference reign predominant. No preach-ing except on Sunday. I stopped with a friend where one of the principal professors, who is a Methodist preacher, boards. I asked the landlord, "What is your hour for evening pray-er?" He replied: "*We have no prayers here!*" And yet he was very willing and anxious to have prayers, and has be-come quite serious. I preached twice on Sunday to a large, cold, formal congregation of whites, and once to a colored congregation, where a little of the old Methodist fire was still burning. Many of the slaves will shine in heaven, while their masters will weep in hell. I am sure you will sympa-thise, and also rejoice with me in regard to my journey to this country. The family of one of the professors was placed in my charge, viz: the mother, and six children, one an in-fant, and a young girl, with eight large trunks to look after. The constant hurry and bustle—changing from train to train, and from train to boat, was anything but pleasant. However, through the goodness of God, we all arrived safe without loss or accident, for which I feel truly thankful, and glad that I am once more a free man.

———

To Bro. R——

Jackson, Tenn., Decr. 4th, 1860.

What are you and yours, and all my friends doing in these days of darkness, whilst the clouds are gathering and thickening over our heads, and the distant thunder of division and discord and restlessness loudly proclaim a coming storm of ruin for our sin-defiled world? Nothing but sin (that thing which alone God hates,) can give strength to *pain* and *fear* and *suffering*. If this be so, then are we the authors of our own maladies, and as wise men we know the remedies. The remedy is a proper application to the soul, of the balm of Gilead, the precious blood of Jesus. We should begin here at home, with our own hearts, and honestly inquire, Am I what I ought to be? Am I what God would have me to be? If not, let us not tarry; let us not confer with flesh and blood; let us make no compromise with an evil world, nor with our own wicked hearts. Was every one, minister and member, to begin with him or herself, and never rest until his or her heart was fully renewed in the image of God; cleansed and purified; the carnal mind destroyed, and the mind which was in Christ, fully imparted to us—as our Wesley finely expresses it:

A heart in every thought renewed, and full of love divine;
Perfect, and right, and pure and good, a copy, Lord, of thine.

how soon would our sin discordant world become a paradise, and God dwell in our midst? Then would idle men, and tempting devils plan their work of destruction and discord in vain.

If therefore, we know the cause of the disease, and the unfailing remedy, why do not men act like men, rationally, fearlessly, wisely, and have their own hearts thoroughly reformed.

I greatly fear that all our maladies, all the evils among men, and they are very great, immeasurably great, will be laid to the account of the *Church*. Christ says: "Ye are the light of the world, ye are the salt of the earth," and adds, "If the light that is in thee, be darkness, how great is that darkness, and if the salt has lost its savor, its saving influence, it is henceforth good for nothing but to be cast out, and trodden under foot of men." *Union is life, division is death.* This principle is applicable to Church and State. It is philosophically true, when the body is perfectly united, it is life, but death dissolves every adhering particle, producing only putrefaction and ruin The Church which should be the salt of the earth, and should save the world, is not prepared or qualified to stand like Abraham pleading for a devoted city. We can not consistently pray for the union and safety of our country, whilst we ourselves are in a state of discord., Sectarian prejudice rules most of us more rigidly than the authority of God. The death-like complexion, however, is not the worst symptom of our disease; pride, envy, sloth, ingratitude, selfishness and love of the world, its money, its pleasures, its honors spread their dark traits of misery and death all through our Ecclesiastical body. "The whole head is sick, and the whole heart is faint from the crown of the head to the sole of the foot, there is nothing but bruises and wounds and putrefying sores." This is a dark picture, yet it is painfully true.

O, when will the Church shake the world out of her lap, and assert her real dignity, and shine forth in the image of God, clothed with the garments of salvation, and richly covered with the robes of righteousness.

As it regards myself, I am still drifting about on the waves of uncertainty, a stranger in a strange land, who is still pointing others—poor sinners—to the Lamb of God, who taketh away the sins of the world. Yet, perhaps, while I mark out the straight and narrow pathway to heaven, I do not strictly and uniformly walk therein myself. Lord help me, all my help must come from thee. Oh, may I not foolishly throw stones at others, whilst there remains one blot, or wrinkle, or spot of sin or selfishness in my heart.

Letter to a Friend.

August 2nd, 1861.

Through the forbearing mercy and unbounded goodness of God, I have been preserved in safety and brought to see another anniversary of my life on earth. This day I am seventy-five years old. Few, very few, reach that advanced period of existence. I do not feel any, or if any, very few of the infirmities of old age, with the exception of my teeth. They are nearly all gone, yet I can labor as efficiently in my Lord's vineyard as I could forty years ago. Can preach three times

in the day and walk eight or ten miles and feel no perceptible fatigue, except yesterday and to-day, being extremely
warm, and the time of my weekly fast, and having walked
too much, I have felt weak, and unable to labor much. Some
months since, in-Tennessee, I preached seventeen sermons in
one week, including two Sabbaths, and felt no fatigue, but
went immediately to a protracted meeting at Holly Springs,
Miss., and labored there for sometime without any sense of
weakness. Oh, to grace how great a debtor ; daily, hourly
and momentarily I'm constrained to be. Surely I have been
more highly favored than any other person ever has been,
and I should be abundantly more humble and holy and grateful and faithful than I am or have been. I see, and to some
extent feel my nothingness and my unprofitable character before God. I cannot yet fully and reasonably and understandingly adopt the Apostle's sentiment, when he said : "Unto
me, who am less than the least of God's saints, is this grace
given." Nor even this, when he exclaims : "I am crucified
with Christ, nevertheless I live, yet not I, but Christ liveth
in me, and the life which I now live is by the faith of the
Son of God." I find that self is not yet dead: I am not as
willing to be hissed at and despised, as to be honored by men;
and yet I must die with Christ to all worldly and selfish objects, or I cannot rationally expect to live with a risen Saviour
in heaven. And yet I humbly hope that during the past
year I have grown in grace, at least measurably. Oh, that
hereafter, I may be willing to be led by the Spirit of God,
knowing that such only are the sons of God. I spent most
of the summer of 1860 in Missouri with my relatives, and
intended to spend the approaching winter in Alabama, the
climate being mild, and I had there been kindly treated and
apparently successful in my efforts to save souls. But the
Southern people had said if Abraham Lincoln was elected
President of the United States, they would secede from the
Union, in which case I would not go down there to spend
the winter. After preaching on Sunday, a sister came to me,
an old acquaintance from Virginia, and urged me to visit
their place in Jackson, Tenn., saying that they had not had
any revival or religious life for eight or ten years. I believed
it to be a providential call, and went. I remained there
about eighteen days and preached all the time, except one
sermon and a piece of one. In that time there were over 130
converts added to the church. I therefore desire to say in

future with the Psalmist: "Thou shalt guide me with thy counsel, and afterwards receive me to glory." Oh, may it be so. Amen.

A dark cloud now overshadows our Nation, and the desolatory scourge of civil war is sweeping over the whole land, with the besom of destruction, yet God will overrule all for good: "The wrath of man shall praise Thee, and the remainder of wrath Thou wilt restrain." The Church must drink a deep and bitter cup of God's wrath before sin shall be destroyed and righteousness established on earth. All our discordant opinions must and will be burned up before the will of God is done on earth, as it is in heaven. That day will come. Lord hasten the time when the kingdom of God shall be gloriously established on earth; when all shall be of one heart, and one mind. When the sword shall be beat into plow-shares, and the spears into pruning hooks, and all shall dwell together as one great family of God on earth. Come, Lord Jesus, and come quickly. Though all the wicked shall be destroyed, it must and will be so. Then shall the righteous shine forth as the sun in the kingdom of God, and peace and righteousness shall cover the earth as the waters the great deep. Oh, may I be ready. No mark of the beast in my heart or in my forehead, but the perfect image of God inscribed on my heart, and the Spirit of Christ richly implanted in my renewed and purified nature. Amen.

To the same.

January 1st, 1862.

Through the abounding and almost miraculous mercy and goodness of God, I have been brought to see and realize the commencement of another year of my pilgrimage on earth. Though now well advanced in my seventy-sixth year upon earth, the Lord enables me to preach and labor in his vineyard as efficiently as I could forty years ago. With the exception of a weakness in my back, I feel very little of the effect of old age. A few weeks since I preached on Sabbath three times, rode twelve or fifteen miles and administered the Sacrament alone, and felt no perceptible fatigue. The next Sunday I preached three times, and rode twelve or fifteen miles, and still felt no fatigue. On Monday morning at six o'clock I preached to a good congregation in Camden, Del., though it was raining quite fast. Having taken a cold, however, I have become quite hoarse, and preached in Dover with some difficulty to large congregations morning and evening. Last night, being still quite hoarse, I attended a watch night meeting at Kenton, with no ministerial help, and with but little from the laity. I preached a long sermon, and we lengthened out the services until the old year expired, and after renewing our covenant with God, by singing the Covenant Hymn, and by prayer, we welcomed in the new—the untried year—by singing, "Praise God from whom all blessings flow. Praise Him, all creatures here below, &c." I preached in Smyrna to a tolerable congregation upon the importance of redeeming time. Eph. v: 16. But, alas, here we are all guilty and condemned. We have trifled with God. We have murdered our time, impoverished our own souls, and grieved the Spirit of God. Oh, thou offended, but merciful Lord God of heaven, pardon for Christ's sake my stupidity, my folly and my unbelief. Oh, Lord, enable me by Grace Divine to redeem my few remaining moments of time wisely and diligently. Create in me, Oh, God, a clean heart, and renew within me a right spirit, even the Spirit of Christ, who, when he was reviled, taunted not again, and with his expiring breath prayed for his murderers. I ask not for earthly good, life or money, or fame or ease ; but the Spirit of my Lord and Master. That love that beareth all things, that endureth all, that believeth all things—all, yea, every word that is written in thy book. Oh, God, that I may be strong in faith, giving glory to God for all things, and under all circumstances. Knowing well that all things shall work together for good, if I do love the Lord, my Redeemer, the Holy One of Israel. Amen. Lord help me, for all, yes all my help must come from Thee. My cold and cough increased, so that I concluded to take the cars on Friday and spend a few days in Wilmington with my kind friends. Having promised, however, to preach at Raymond's on Thursday night, I concluded to do so, although it was very imprudent in my then state of health. However, after preaching, and particularly after a most unpleasant night, in which I got but little sleep, through mercy I felt much better of my cough, and at the pressing request of a brother I consented to remain in Smyrna over Sabbath. In the morning I preached too long, yet felt but little worse. At night I preached again with more than usual liberty and physical energy. The congregation was large and very attentive. After passing a restless night I awoke feeling much better of my cold, and came in the cars to Wilmington, where I was most warmly received by my very kind friend, J. S. K——. Here, I am too comfortable for a servant. Every convenience and comfort that this world can afford. Oh, may I not be lured away from the cross of Christ by the smiles of this alluring world and the kindness of friends.

To Rev. T. M. C.

Baltimore, June 20th, 1862.

I had hoped to hear before this time that our friends had buried the hatchet, and the log too, and all their unchristian feelings towards each other. But I have not heard from them since I gave them a plain talk on Sabbath morning, when I was poorly able to talk, much less preach.

It appears to me, that we live in the day John spoke of in the book—the mysterious book of Revelation, when he says, "Woe unto the inhabitants of the earth, and of the sea, for the devil has come down, having great rage, because he knoweth that his time is but short." May it soon end, and Satan and all his dark hosts shall be bound and cast into the prison prepared for the devil and his angels. Our Saviour also mentions a time which corresponds with the dark days in which we live, when he says : "Suppose ye, that I am come to send peace on earth ? I tell ye nay, but rather division. From henceforth there shall be five in one house divided; three against two, and two against three. The father shall be divided against the son and the son against the father; the mother against the daughter, and the daughter against the mother, the mother in-law against the daughter-in-law, and the daughter-in-law against the mother-in-law." Well it must be that offenses cometh, but woe to him by whom they come. But as Christ said to Peter, "What is that to thee ? Follow thou me." We cannot control or harmonize the Church or the World, but we can manage, and by the grace of the Lord Jesus Christ, we can and should manage our own heart. We can fear God, and keep his commandments always; even when he says, "When you are smote on one cheek, turn the other, and if any man sue the at law, and take away thy coat, let him have thy cloak also." Anything on earth, rather than contend with our brother, or with our neighbor, or any man on earth, even our worst enemy. When Christ commands us not to lay up treasures upon earth, we can avoid doing it. When he says : "When ye make a dinner or a supper, call not your friends or rich neighbors, but call the poor, and the maimed, and the halt and the blind." This also we can do.

But alas, who in this world regards the word of the Lord Jesus? It is to be feared they are few and far between. Lord what will become of our guilty world? The Lord Jesus says, that when he comes he will dispose of them as the Antediluvians were disposed of. Will all who are not Christ's be included in that number ? In all probability the number will not be few, if Paul's declaration be true when he says : If any man, rich or poor, bond or free, have not the spirit of Christ, he is none of his. When Christ was reviled, he reviled not again, but with his expiring breath, prayed for his murderers. If all who have not that spirit must fall, as did the Antediluvians, it will include a great multitude. Christ's spirit would prevent war, and abolish slavery, and every other evil on earth. Oh, why should not all secure that spirit, since God is more willing to give it to them, than a father is to give a good gift to his own children. Therefore, all should be righteous and holy.

As regards myself, my health is very poor. Some days I feel much better, again worse, so that it is pretty certain that my days on earth are fast drawing to a close ; nor have I any objection to leave· this sin disordered world, except that I have been such an unprofitable servant. I feel ashamed of myself—ashamed to meet my Divine Ruler, who, all through life, toiled and labored in tears and sweat and blood to redeem my soul from endless death.

There is another difficulty —the condition of the world and of the church and of our own once highly favored country. Yet my staying here would not better these evils. And·indeed as I am too old to learn, my longer stay on earth would not in all human probability better my country or the world, or the church, or my own soul. I desire, therefore, to say, with David, understandingly and honestly : "Thou, Oh, God, shalt guide me with thy counsel, and afterwards receive me into glory." Since the day I preached at Ebenezer and Friendship, I have not attempted again to preach. My energies of mind seem also dwarfed, and I have no resolution to read or write or talk. I recently went to hear one of our most popular preachers lecture on the Book of Revelation, and it was so wild and dark that I felt ashamed. It waked me up, and I sat down and wrote a short, plain explanatory epistle on that mysterious book, and I do wish you could see and read it. It surely presents views, new and old, and cuts the Church to the quick, and makes us far more clearly acquainted with the character and devices of Satan and the deformities of our own heart.

I may publish. It should be done. Yet I am too old to have it done. Well, we will leave all the future with God, just where it should be. Don't fail to write soon. Remember me affectionately to all christian friends.

The good Lord bless you all and give you all a home in heaven. Amen.

CONCLUSION.

The author has much to regret in the conclusion of his work. He deplores the scanty materials at his disposal out of which to write a correct and concise history. There are errors of arrangement apparent which he deplores and which under the press of circumstances he could not avoid. A few other errors of a typographical character have made their appearance, but despite the defects of his imperfect execution he has sought accuracy in every statement, and he sends forth this sketch of the life of Father Hersey, with the consciousness that what is recorded may be accepted as the truth. The reader will remember that more than ordinary difficulties have been encountered in collecting what appears in these pages. The subject of this sketch was not a member of any Annual Conference, he was simply a local preacher. His ministerial labor was self-imposed as a duty of obedience to the will of God. He was subject to no other command than the divine injunction, "Go ye into all the world and preach my gospel." He selected his own fields of service, and his own methods of operating them. He roamed over large sections of the country at his own will; he had no connected plan of visitation. Whenever a field opened before him there he would present himself; hence, there cannot be rendered a continuous history of his services, for no record of it is obtainable. Reference has heretofore been made in these pages to the disappearance of portions of his diary; it is also to be added, that the probability is that many of his letters and other papers were destroyed by the fire that devastated Henry G. Berry's book store several years since. Mr. Berry, it will be recollected, is the survivor of the old firm of Armstrong & Berry, who were the publishers of Father Hersey's books. Their store was a place where he frequently repaired. In a room up stairs he kept his papers in a pine box. He set much value upon them. He was systematic in filing them away. It is unknown, however, whether he kept a written account of his daily movements until an advanced stage in his life. But what will strike the reader as the most incomplete part of this "sketch" (sketch is all that is claimed for it,) is in relation to his earlier years, his co-adjutors of that period could not be found. Diligent and persistent inquiry has not enabled us to penetrate the secret of his earlier years, beyond what we have narrated, but they were not his eventful days.

They never are in any one's history, and while it would have been agreeable to have had a more complete chronicle of them, yet if any part of his biography must be meagre, it is preferable that it should exist at the start and not elsewhere. Since the day of his conversion, enough of him has been saved from the wreck of oblivion to transmit to those who are to be our successors, a tolerably clear idea of this extraordinary servant of God. And who will say, that he was not an extraordinary man; in every page of his life it is manifested. He was as unlike a pattern of your usual classes of men as could be developed. He was one who in his oneness stood conspicuous, not a conspicuosity that was painful to behold. It was not brazen, it was not effrontery, it was not an intended cultivated mannerism adopted as a mere eccentricity to distinguish him from others. No, there was a positive principle underlying the substratum of it all, and that was so apparent as to save him from that remorseless criticism that lays its violent hand upon your mere pretenders who artificially undertake to rear for themselves originality, when there can be none. You had but to look upon the features of Father Hersey's face to satisfy yourself that you were in the presence of a real man, who did not for a moment seem conscious that you were calculating the difference existing between himself and others in respect to general demeanor of manner and dress; and after all you were more favorably impressed than otherwise by his singularity. Probably, it never appeared to such advantage as when he heralded the tidings of salvation from the pulpit. There was an authority in his appeals that seemed imperative; the serious air and solemn admonitions earnestly and forcibly expressed, witnessed how deeply he was moved in the discharge of his ministerial functions. Nor was he without the gifts of oratory; and yet that rule of his life that dictated plainness in all things pertaining to himself, moved him to the use of plainness of speech whether in the pulpit or out of it. He was no star that sought to be conspicuous by startling brilliancy, but one giving a clear steady light and shining so distinctly as to attract, by mere reason of its clearness. The distinctive feature of his career, was the honest consistency that led him to model his life after patterns of the New Testament. He had drank of the bitter waters in earlier years ; the steel had entered his flesh ; his quivering heart had yielded to the voice of the heavenly call. He preached no formal doctrine to which he was a stranger; he was an example as well as a teacher. He dreaded the tendency towards innovations; the old standards he regarded as perfect; he was bewildered at all attempts at changing them. Possibly, he might not have held so tenaciously to his extremes had he not beheld so great a general departure from primitive methods. He sincerely believed destruction awaited the Church in consequence, and he warred and warned. He was a living admonition ; and the day may come when his example shall be recalled, and his life of exemplary self-sacrifice, shall be the instrumentality of rescuing our Zion from the jaws of that inertness that overpowers it. His ministerial qualifications were of a superior order. He possessed no negative qualities; he was pre-eminently fitted to preach the word. He was clerical in all his actions, sensitive to the uttermost, always on guard, lest by word, look or bearing, he should reflect upon himself and bring reproach upon the cause which he represented. Purity with him towered above all other considerations. His heart was the citadel of such religious faith that there was no room in it for any other armor than what was called for in the service of his Master. He was the embodiment of charity, and they who read these sketches will find that John Hersey did not neglect to look after the poor, and lend a hand for their relief; in doing of which, he was convinced that it was as much enjoined upon him as it was to preach. He performed it as one of the duties of his ministerial calling. Could the tears of the poor, their words of unutterable

warmth of gratitude expressed in "God bless you," and show-
ered upon John Hersey's head be fashioned into a monumental column, there would commemorate his memory no such
imposing monument on all this earth.

That his ministerial labors were successful, admits of no
controversy. They were constant; he was an untiring, indefatigable worker. He dwelt in continual communion with
God. He was His companion; he traveled with Him, and
would often turn from the road side and entering the woods
would bend the knee beneath the boughs of some spreading
tree and there commune with Him. No other person was at
all times so near Him, nor did he ever get so near to any one
else as to his Heavenly Father. No wonder, then, that he
preached seriously and powerfully. He had an analytical mind,
it may not have been of the highest order, yet it was more
than ordinary. He was fluent; his faith in the fulfilment
of all of God's promises to man was unbounded, and when
he preached he impressed, and conviction and conversion generally resulted. He was generous; his enlarged christian
heart throbbed lovingly towards his brethren of other denominations than his own. He took great pleasure in ministering in their pulpits, and visiting among their people. He was
never heard to speak disparagingly of them by way of com-
parison. In fact, he was so thoroughly without selfishness,
that it was not in him to disparage. He could no more do
so denominationally than individually, and he could do neither. He was not favorable to God's people contesting with
one another and wasting their resources so unnecessarily. He
was for warring against the evil things of the world held
under the dominion of sin, and in such a crusade he clasped
hands with men of other creeds than his, and worked with
them willingly and gladly.

Of course such a life could have but one conclusion; not
marred in any of its parts since the days of its consecration.
Death could not possibly disfigure it, it could only bring out
in greater prominence the glorious revelations that encircled
it. The test of a well lived life, is how the dying hour im-
presses the one who is passing away. Its seriousness cannot
be over estimated, nor can it be graphically depicted. O,
how precious are the dying triumphs of God's saints; how
their exclamations ring in unending tones in the very throes
of dissolution. The church treasures such legacies; they are
the grand coronation swellings of the redeemed soul's last

earthly song, sung for the encouragement of the pilgrims who tarry awhile longer in this vail of tears. We listen, and when breath and song are hushed, and the body is cold in the grave, we do not forget it. No, no: from the cold dust there speaks an inspiration. There is a hope and an encouragement that from no other source comes with such quickening emotion; it thrills all the cords of our being and makes us resolve "That we will die the death of the righteous, that our last days shall be like his."

All the churches have contributed from the lips of their departed worthies, contributions to last utterances of men whose deeds live after them. These utterances are beautiful and inspiring, but no church has furnished such examples of christian triumph and resignation in death, as have fallen from the lips of Methodists. Whether our emotional religion and emotional natures cause it, or whether there dwell more of the Holy Ghost among us, I shall not discuss, but that our people die well, and in their last moments shout victory over death, and with an unabated eagerness rush into the arms of the Saviour exultingly, has been too often attested not to be recorded as a fact. Our church literature is rich in this department, and many of the sententious utterances of our dying ministers, have been incomparably beautiful, and if collected, would make a volume of rare excellence. When John Hersey came to go, he departed gracefully and grandly; the winding up of his life's chapter is a glorious testimonial in behalf of the religion which he preached and practiced; there was no hesitation on his part to depart. How cheerful the christian patience with which he awaited the summons, "God will soon call me and I am ready to go," was a grand utterance, and when the night came and he stepped across the stream, he left behind him a dying testimonial that must have thrilled the angels and awakened echos of rejoicing in the sacred precincts of heaven, as his last utterance ' Salvation, salvation," echoed and reverberated throughout all its space.

Our task is done; there is recovered from forgetfulness, so much of our departed friend's history, as is embraced in these pages; but should they in time perish, in the great day when judgment is held, it will appear that there is one who will remember and award his servant, John Hersey, with a crown of glory and a seat at the right hand of the Father, where may we all appear washed in the blood of the Lamb.